Bittersweet

by Jennifer Labelle

Bittersweet

Limitless Publishing, LLC
Kailua, HI 96734
www.limitlesspublishing.com

Formatting: Limitless Publishing

ISBN-13: 978-1-68058-174-4
ISBN-10: 1-68058-174-0

Dedication

To my husband Martin for his patience and dedication. You kept the kids busy so I could finish this and encouraged me to pursue my dream.

Thanks for the support, babe. I love you!

**An accident on a rain-slicked highway
leaves *Jenna Baker* alone...**

Jenna is scarred, confused, and vulnerable after surviving an accident that took her husband's life. After a year of mourning Tyler and struggling to raise their son on her own, Jenna's best friend whisks her off to fulfill her lifelong dream of visiting Ireland. She never dreamed her trip would include a self-appointed tour guide in the form of a sexy Irishman with piercing blue eyes and a smile that promises to fill her empty heart.

**ced *Brady Connelly* is irresistibly drawn to
the lovely, broken Yank...**

As the weeks pass, Brady comforts and supports Jenna, convincing her to live and chase her dreams. His attraction to her grows and their chemistry ignites, but Jenna isn't sure she's truly ready to move on. How can he convince her to release the past and take a leap of faith...with him?

The impossible happens, and Jenna's world is thrown into chaos...Tyler is alive and reenters Jenna's life, burdened with guilty secrets. Jenna knows she has to try to make things work between them, if only for their son's sake, but she's blessed—or cursed— with vivid visions of Brady. The visions begin to consume her and leave her questioning her sanity and the bittersweet nature of her marriage.

Jenna's dreams of Brady become her lifeline as she questions the boundaries of fantasy and reality.

Is her one hope for happiness waiting for her across the sea?

Chapter One

Jenna

Jenna Baker had sat in the passenger side of the car for long enough. They were driving in the middle of a rainstorm. The Gravol she'd taken wasn't doing anything for her nausea, and the uneasy feeling in the pit of her stomach just wasn't going away.

"Oh, my God, pull over."

Tyler sighed. "Relax, Jenna. I was just about to." He put his hand on her thigh and gave it a little squeeze.

Tyler was right. She needed to rid herself of this frustration, but relaxing was easier said than done. Since waking up that morning, she just couldn't shake the feeling something bad was about to happen.

Her odd dreams weren't helping. Last night she'd been drowning, all alone and tangled in weeds, trying desperately to gasp for breath. Now rain was pouring down harder than she'd ever seen before, and it had her nerves on edge. Maybe the association with water was what had her so worked up. They couldn't even see two feet in front of them. Hell, maybe it was just anxiety because she missed her baby boy so much. Jayden had been visiting her parents in Cornwall for the last week on his annual summer visit, and Tyler had insisted they surprise them by picking him up a few days early.

"So how long do you think we'll have to wait this out?" she asked.

First they were stuck on the side of a road because of the rain, and then the stupid radio would only pick up static. Turning it off, she looked at him for an answer.

"Relax, Jenna," he repeated, and his mouth twitched as if to hold back a smile. "We'll get there soon enough. Honestly, sweetheart, I don't know how you made it through the entire week without him."

She knew he was treading carefully to avoid an argument and sighed, because he was right again. "I know, but I feel like a caged animal in here. And you know very well how I made it through the week." Thinking about Tyler and their fabulous week of busy hands, nude bodies, and spice made her hot all over, and she fanned her face. "Hmm," she mumbled, making him smile. "I made it through because I had you. This last week together has been pretty good, hasn't it?"

"It has." Tyler shut off the ignition and turned toward her. He reached across to caress the side of her face. "How did I get so lucky?"

"Lucky?" Jenna smiled and then licked her lips.

2

"Not lucky, babe, just unbelievably lov—"

His mouth crashed down on hers before she could finish her sentence, and her heart swelled with joy, replacing the bad feeling she'd had a few minutes before.

Tyler unbuckled her seat belt to pull her closer. She opened up for him immediately, and in no time at all, their kiss turned hungry and desperate. They were like two starving people who could only be filled by the taste of each other.

The rain still fell heavily outside, creating a soothing background noise, and everything around them disappeared in the moment. It was a hell of a way to spend their time while they waited for the storm to settle, and she felt as if they were back in high school again. They were making out in the car, and she couldn't remember the last time she'd done that. Tyler pulled back so they could catch their breath and nibbled on her lips. He pecked her once and then twice on the mouth before turning so he could kiss along her cheek, and then it all happened so fast it felt like a dream. A really horrible one.

Jenna felt his whole body tense. Before she could ask what was wrong, bright lights hit them. She turned her head quickly and saw the horrified expression on Tyler's face seconds before cool air replaced where his body had been. A loud bang accompanied a jolt that threw her forward, and then sudden blackness surrounded her.

***

She was floating, so light and carefree, and it

was dark at first wherever she was, so she kept moving forward through the haze. It was confusing but peaceful, if that even made sense, and she was soon met with something breathtaking. The dark faded away, and the most beautiful light she'd ever seen broke through it as if it were calling to her. It was bright white, and it cast glittery rainbow accents as she came closer to it. The magnetic pull kept her going farther in, and shapes started to form in front of her.

Memories filled her mind with an instant replay of her two favorite people, but she felt as though she was dreaming. Meeting Tyler her senior year in high school, the first time they'd made love in college, their marriage, and the birth of their first and only child were all coming back to her in flashes.

What the hell was going on?

She couldn't concentrate properly but still found comfort in her memories. Her thoughts drifted to Jayden, and she became a spectator in one of the most special moments of her life. It happened to be one of her son's favorite stories. Jenna must have told it to him a million times before and only hoped to tell it a million more.

"Tyler," she cried. Holy shit, is it supposed to feel this way? *"Tyler, ahh." She was in agony.*

"Jenna, what's wrong?"

"Isn't it obvious?" she snapped and muttered a curse under her breath. "We're stuck, and I'm about to push your big-headed child from inside me."

In the middle of January, they were stuck in the biggest snowstorm of the year. The piece of junk they liked to call their car was completely snowed in, and her water had just broken.

"You're doing great, Jenna," he encouraged, getting her back inside the house.

Her labor had started off as back pain, and her contractions had only begun about two hours before. They had plenty of time, right? Wrong.

Her husband dialed 9-1-1. "My wife's about to have a baby, what do I do, what do I do?" He yelled into the phone. "Where are they?"

"Relax, sir, I've got an ambulance on the way. Now I need you to remain calm. Can you see the head crowning?"

The nasal voice on the speakerphone seemed to annoy the hell out of him, judging by his expression. Jenna would have laughed if she hadn't been so uncomfortable. "Remain calm"? How the hell was that supposed to happen? Neither of them were doctors, and Tyler sure as hell wasn't supposed to be delivering their child. Also, Jenna felt awful. She was flushed, wet with perspiration, and between heavy breaths, she wanted to bite his head off. He was having it way too easy at the moment.

"Nothing yet, what's taking so long?"

"We're in the middle of a snowstorm, sir. They're on the way."

"Tyler," she moaned. "Argh, do something. This is your fault, you sorry sack of—"

"You're doing great, Jenna, that's it. Take deep, soothing breaths. How do you feel?"

Later, when she was back in a rational state of

mind, she might think he had been trying to give her encouraging words because he hadn't the slightest clue what he was doing. But at the time, it just wasn't the thing to say. Damn, that ambulance better get here pronto. I need it out. *Tyler definitely wasn't suited for this type of crisis. What if something went terribly wrong?*

"Don't tell me what to do," she snapped. "I'll soothe you one. How do I feel? I'll tell you how I feel. I feel like I'm being torn in two. Get. It. Out!"

He chuckled for the first time, despite the murderous glare she was giving him. But he abruptly stopped laughing as the last gush of fluid rushed toward him and the reality of the situation clearly struck home.

"Oh no," he breathed. His eyes bulged as he did a double take. "God help me, there's the head."

"I'm so tired," Jenna whispered. Now that it was time to push, she was exhausted.

"Hang in there. Push on the next contraction, Jenna, push. That's it, just a little more."

They'd tuned out the sirens in the distance. It was down to business now. "Please." She tried to catch her breath. Would this ever end? She felt as though she'd been at this forever, and if it took much longer, she was bound to pass out.

Luckily, she was soon rewarded with the most beautiful sound imaginable when her baby's first cry filled the living room.

"It's a boy." Tyler beamed, placing him in her arms.

The night's events must have overwhelmed Tyler, because he fainted as soon as the paramedics *arrived. Knowing he was being taken care of and having her perfect baby cradled in her arms, Jenna was finally able to laugh through her tears. Tyler never did enjoy the sight of blood, and it was a wonder he'd lasted as long as he had. In the meantime, she had the most precious little bundle imaginable.*

"Hi, Jayden." she whispered before kissing him for the first time. "Mommy loves you."

The moment the words were out of her mouth again, she was being sucked away. Her peace and the beauty of the pretty light surrounding her were replaced with so much pain. Her eyes fluttered open and closed a few times before she noticed all the machines and tubes sticking out of her. "Ugh," she groaned and tried to suppress a grimace. "What the hell happened to me?"

As she tried to clear her dry throat, the fog that seemed to envelope her mind disappeared. She was obviously in the hospital, but why?

"Tyler?"

"Jenna? Oh thank God."

"Mom?"

Her mother sat at her bedside and teared up while reaching for Jenna's hand. "Oh my God, you scared us, but you're going to be okay, honey."

"I don't feel okay," she whispered. "Where's Jayden? Is he okay? Please tell me he's okay. I can't remember."

The machine beside her bed started to beep loudly. "Try to relax, honey. Your heart rate is starting to pick up," her mother said. "Jayden's fine.

He's with Dad and can't wait to see you. I just didn't think it would be appropriate to bring him in until I knew you were okay."

Sighing with relief that her little boy was all right, Jenna had a sudden flashback. "There was a light coming toward us, and then everything went black. I remember a sparkling, beautiful bright light and I was at peace, then it disappeared. What happened?"

"There was an accident, and it was pretty bad from what they told us. It was raining hard, and you had pulled over to wait it out. A truck was coming the opposite way and swerved to keep from hitting an animal. The visibility was poor, and he didn't see you until it was too late."

A panic attack was threatening to surface, Her chest tightened, heart began to beat faster, and she felt short of breath. "Mom where's Tyler?" If she was this badly hurt, how was he? And where was he? "Mom, please…Where is Tyler? I want my husband. Please, just tell me where he is."

The commotion from her hospital machinery had drawn attention from the hospital staff. "Mrs. Baker, you need to calm down, or I'm going to have to give you a sedative and put you under again," a nurse said.

Nodding, she tried her best to even her breathing. The last thing she wanted was to get knocked out, but she couldn't control her emotions until she had answers. She needed Tyler, had to see him, and wanted to feel him. She had to know he was okay. "Mom, please, where is my husband?"

Her mother looked toward the nurse for approval

and sighed when she nodded. "Jenna, when they found you, you were hanging out of the windshield, honey. Neither of you had a seat belt on and..." She started to cry. "Tyler didn't make it, honey, I'm so sorry."

Chapter Two

"Mommy," Jayden yelled as soon as she got out of the car. He ran toward her and almost made her fall over when he threw himself into her arms.

Even though she'd only been in the hospital for two weeks, it felt like a lifetime since she'd last held him in her arms, and she broke down. Though filled with sadness and guilt over the loss they'd suffered, she was overjoyed to be with him again. He was Tyler in miniature.

"Why are you crying, Mommy?"

"Because I missed you," she held him closer to breathe in his scent.

"Where's Daddy?"

His question left her speechless and surprised that her parents hadn't already told him. She wasn't sure what to say, and thankfully her father came to the rescue. "Come with Poppa, Jayden," he offered the boy his hand. "We'll go out in the yard for a while and let your mom settle in first."

She looked to her mother for answers as they walked away. "What have you guys told him?"

"Jenna, I couldn't...I mean, we didn't know how. I should've told you sooner, I'm so sorry."

"Okay, I just need a little time to figure out how to break it to him."

She could feel another breakdown coming on and just couldn't fall apart in front of everyone. In the privacy of her old room, she let the stress consume her. Jayden was only four. How was she supposed to explain Tyler's death without traumatizing him? He and Tyler had been close.

She managed to pull herself together a few hours later to join them for dinner. Although not much eating was involved, thankfully Jayden didn't ask her too many questions, and Jenna knew then that she had to stop procrastinating.

"All right, Monkey, it's almost time to wash up and get ready for bed. Afterward, Mommy has something important to speak to you about." Her throat constricted, and her eyes watered just thinking about the horrible task ahead, and she turned her head to hide it from him.

"Aw, man," he whined. "Good night, Grandma. 'Night, Poppa." After he gave them his big, sloppy good-night kisses, he and Jenna headed upstairs for the night and into the privacy they both would need to grieve.

"Mommy, I can't wait to see Daddy. Poppa took me fishing, and next time—"

Her little boy ran into the room and jumped up and down on the bed with pure excitement, but he stopped suddenly when he realized she was crying.

Jenna still wasn't sure how to give him the news, but she knew she had to. "Jayden, did Grandma tell you why it took Mommy so long to come and get you?" she asked carefully to gauge how much he already knew.

"She said you got sick, but you're better now, so why are you so sad?" He placed his hand on her face and tried to wipe away the tears streaming down it.

"I'm sad because Daddy's gone, honey." Her words seemed to confuse him. "I was sick for a little while, and I was able to get better, but Daddy wasn't. They couldn't fix him, honey, and Daddy went to heaven. Do you understand?"

"Well, is he coming back?"

Jenna couldn't form the words to answer. She just shook her head and held him close, hoping he would understand while fearing at the same time that he would.

He cried just as much as she did, and they fell asleep in each other's arms.

***

Three days later, it was time to say their last good-bye. Tyler's funeral was long and exhausting but beautiful at the same time. If not for the support of her family and her friend Sam, Jenna couldn't have gotten through the day still standing. There were a few words said at the church in the small, intimate ceremony for close friends and family. She couldn't bear the thought of a burial, and instead she'd had him cremated so she could take him home with her.

Besides Tyler, Sam was her best friend. Just after

Jayden was born, Tyler had received a promotion and they were finally able to afford a bigger house. Sam was one of their neighbors, and she and Jenna had hit it off immediately. Sam was a professional photographer and got to travel the world, and Jenna envied her that.

Her last destination had been beautiful Ireland. Jenna admired the scenic photos she'd taken while Sam told her all about the amazing places she'd visited while there.

***

One Month Later

"It's not fair," Jayden screamed.

Tyler's parents had come for a visit, and at first her son didn't seem to want them there. He'd run upstairs and into her room to curl up on his father's side of the bed. Jenna had to take a deep breath before walking farther than the doorway. She hadn't slept in there since the last morning she'd woken with Tyler at her side. The room just wasn't the same without him.

"Jayden, are you okay?"

He turned around and shook his head, "I'm mad at Daddy, and I'm mad at Grandpa."

Through tears, she managed to whisper, "Why are you mad at Grandpa?"

"Because he looks like Daddy."

She laughed, startling even herself. "Yes, Grandpa looks like Daddy, Jayden, but so do you. You look just like Daddy, honey. That's why you're so handsome."

He hid his face again on top of Tyler's pillow and said, "But I'm still mad at Daddy. Why did he have to leave me? It's not fair. He's making me sad, and he's making you sad all the time too."

In that moment her heart shattered again. Life was a cold, cruel bitch at times, and this was one of them. "I'm sorry, honey, but it's not Daddy's fault. He didn't have a choice. I want you to know that he'd be here if he could. I need you to know that, Jayden, and it makes me sad to hear that you're angry with him, but I understand. He loves you just as much as I do and always will, even in heaven. Do you understand?"

"But it's still not fair," he whimpered. "I want him back."

"I know, Jayden. I do too, but it gets better with time. I promise." Those words were easier said than lived with. Jenna knew it would take a long time before the family survived Tyler's loss, but she looked forward to that day, anyway.

When he was ready to visit, Jayden went back downstairs, hugged his grandfather tightly, and apologized. "I'm not mad at you anymore, Grandpa. You don't look like Daddy; you look like me."

***

The months that passed hurt to live through, but Jenna's anger eventually faded, and life got a little easier with time. Jayden started to return to his normal self again, and he and Jenna developed a routine that got them through their rough patches.

Jenna was still numb, though; she felt empty and barely had an appetite. Regardless, the time flew by.

On the anniversary of his death, she and Jayden decided to spend the day by themselves, no matter how much Sam or her parents bothered her about not being alone.

"Do you know what today is?" she asked him that morning.

Jayden nodded and whispered, "The day Daddy left."

"It is, Jayden. So what would you like to do today?"

"Could we go to the park?" he asked, not making eye contact.

"The park sounds nice. Maybe we could stop and get some ice cream."

Jayden loved his ice cream, but the smile on his face was what she'd hoped for. Smiling back, she reached for his hand. "It's okay to be sad, Jayden, but it's also okay to feel angry or happy. It's okay to laugh or cry. I love you, honey, and I just want you to know that showing your emotions is okay if you need to, especially today."

"Can we bring Daddy with us?"

She nodded and went to get the urn. "Are you ready?" she asked, and didn't care how stupid it may have looked to others. Her number one priority was to do anything she could to make things easier on Jayden. They spent the day as a family, and her son got whatever he wanted and then some.

***

Jenna was finally able to have her meltdown after Jayden fell asleep. She'd gone upstairs to change into one of Tyler's shirts, but that night it just didn't feel the same. Anytime she'd put one on before, she could smell him, could almost feel his arms wrapped around her, as if he were still with her. But that night she felt nothing. He was gone, and she needed him back. She needed that feeling of security, but he'd left her, in body and now in spirit.

She ran to the closet and pulled out everything that belonged to him, but she still felt nothing. "No, Tyler, don't leave me," she cried, sitting in the middle of the heap of his clothes.

That's how Sam found her when she stopped by to check on her. "He's gone," Jenna sobbed.

Sam rushed to Jenna and hugged her tight. "He's been gone for a while, Jenna."

"No." Jenna shook her head, trying to explain. "I could still feel him, though. He was still with me. His scent still lingered, and I could sense him around me, and now I don't feel anything, Sam. Please, he can't leave me. Please, Sam, please, just make him come back to me."

"I'm so sorry, Jenna. I wish I could."

Hours later when she'd cried herself out, Jenna looked at her best friend through puffy, red eyes, and wiped at her runny nose. She whispered her thanks as Sam held her the entire time, to listen to and comfort her. Now, she just felt exhausted but was thankful to have let her feelings out.

"I know what you're going through, Jenna," Sam said. "I was married once. His name was Antonio, and I met him in Italy when I was first starting out.

We fell in love almost instantly. Ugh, that man drove me insane. I lived there for a year. Did I ever tell you that? We dated the whole time, but my visa expired. I tried to get it renewed, but of course I was denied. I was crushed. I loved him, and I had to leave him. Antonio got angry the night I'd told him I had to go, and we argued He stayed away for a few days, then showed up the night before I left. The expression on his face was priceless. He had this determination about him. I swear that night was the best sex I've ever had."

She laughed loudly, but Jenna knew the hard part was coming because Sam then started to cry.

"Anyway, I left, and he didn't follow. I waited as long as I could at the airport for him, but he didn't show up, and I cried the whole way home. About three weeks later I got a knock on my door. It was cold outside and really late. I lived in a really crappy one-bedroom apartment in a not-so-good neighborhood, and I was afraid to open the door at first. But the knocking wouldn't stop. I finally became annoyed enough to see who it was, and it was him."

She smiled. "The first thing we did was make love. Afterward, he proposed, and I couldn't have been happier. We had a simple ceremony and started our lives, together forever. On our third anniversary, we took a trip back to Italy. It was as beautiful as I remembered, but when we got back, Antonio became sick."

She turned her face away then and whispered the next part. "He died six months later." Don't you see, Jenna? I know exactly what you're going through, but I need you to know that although you'll never forget, it gets easier to cope with time."

Jenna looked at Sam and realized she'd gained a new type of respect for her that day. She was one of the strongest people she knew, and Jenna longed for the day where she could be that strong herself.

"Okay, enough of all of this," Sam announced, gesturing at Tyler's pile of clothes. "I'm going to help you find yourself again. I'm going back to Ireland. I know you've always wanted to go, so you're coming with me, and don't you dare say no."

Jenna had always imagined traveling with Sam but never thought it possible. But Sam wasn't taking no for an answer and cut through all of her objections. She had about a good six weeks before Jayden started school, and when she asked her parents if they could watch Jayden while she was away, they also thought it was a fabulous idea.

It was time she did something nice for herself, a time to try to move on, so with her parents' encouragement, Jenna accepted Sam's vacation proposal with mixed emotions.

Chapter Three

"Um, if I forget to say this later, thanks, Sam."

"You're thanking me in the airport," Sam said with a laugh. "That's very sweet, Jenna, but just wait until we get out there." She gestured at the beautiful scenery of Dublin visible through the doors. "I'm really hoping that you can have a good time. Start out fresh in new surroundings, have an adventure, live a little, let loose, and have fun. Now that's the vacation I'm hoping to have."

Sam put an arm around her, then stopped walking. "Speaking of beautiful scenery, what have we here?"

Jenna turned to see what she was talking about. Two men stood only a few feet away, staring at them. She felt an instant attraction when her eyes met the piercing blue ones of the sexy dark-haired man, and she panicked because it had been the first time any man had got a reaction out of her since Tyler's death.

"Sam, I don't think I'm ready for this," she whispered, wide-eyed.

"Relax, Jenna. It's okay if you're not ready today, but honestly, hun, how long has it been?"

Jenna was confused. "How long has what been?"

"My guess—in fact, I know—is that it's been over a year now."

She looked Sam straight in the eye and nodded because it was true. "But I'm just not ready to do that to Tyler yet, Sam."

Sam nodded while trying to hide her disappointment.

Jenna sighed in defeat and felt bad for her friend. Sam was obviously interested in the other man. The problem was, Jenna just wasn't sure where she stood with sex and men anymore, but she hoped to get there someday.

***

"Wow." Jenna sighed in delight. "This is place is amazing."

They had settled in at the Westbury, located right in the city's shopping district. After spending most of the first day looking for souvenirs, they dined in at Wilde, the restaurant located inside the five-star hotel. The next day Sam took Jenna on a tour of the National Photographic Archive. It had hundreds of thousands of beautiful photographs in there, but there wasn't enough time in the day to possibly go through them all. They strolled around Merrion Square looking at the sculptures and sat near some beautiful flowers while they had lunch. Finally, they went back to the hotel for some much-needed R&R before heading out that night.

"Well, how do I look?" Jenna bounced through Sam's room, actually excited to be going out. "I haven't had a girls' night out in God only knows how long."

Sam laughed, giving her a once-over. "You look great. Sexy but comfortable, I like it." Jenna wore a comfortable pair of skinny jeans and paired them with a slim-fitting shirt that draped off one shoulder.

Jenna laughed. "Thanks, but, um, where are we going?" She'd left the decision up to Sam because she'd been to Ireland before.

Sam shrugged. "Haven't figured it out yet, so I guess we'll have to wait and see."

***

Whelan's was just getting busy by the time they arrived.

"I think we need a few drinks," Sam announced, raising her voice to be heard above the band.

Jenna held on to her hand as they made their way to the bar to order. After getting their drinks, they found one of the only free tables and sat down to enjoy their surroundings and each other's company.

"I'm not sure I'd be able to drink this stuff too often, but it's not bad," Jenna said after finishing off her Guinness. The foamy, thick beer went down smooth. "Want another one?"

Just as Sam nodded, more arrived, brought to them by one of the waitresses working the floor.

"Wow, talk about service," she teased.

"They're from a couple of admirers." The older

woman gestured toward the bar. Jenna tensed as the woman left.

"Okay, Jenna, don't freak out," Sam warned.

"The same two guys? First the airport and now here? What are the odds? Did you know they were here the whole time?"

Sam nodded. "I noticed about an hour ago. Are you up to this? It'll be kind of rude if we just leave, don't you think? But we will if that's what you need."

Jenna shook her head and took a deep breath. "I'm fine, really. I mean, it's a free drink. Who could be upset with that?"

As a polite gesture, Jenna turned toward the bar, held up her drink, smiled at the same one who had caught her eye the day before, and took a sip. She told herself she was doing this for Sam since Jenna still felt bad about their earlier encounter.

"Wow, Jenna, I'm impressed, but now you've done it." She gestured toward the two men, who were now approaching them.

Jenna laughed. She was surprised at how comfortable she felt, as though her old self was resurfacing. Maybe it was because of the surroundings without the constant reminders of home anywhere near her, or, then again, maybe it was just the drinks. Either way, she'd felt better about herself in that moment than she had in a long time, and she enjoyed the change.

"Hi there," Sam purred, scooting her chair closer to Jenna so the men could sit with them. "My name is Samantha, and this is my lovely friend Jenna. It's a pleasure to meet you both."

Jenna gulped nervously as the one she was attracted to took her hand into his. He didn't take his eyes off her the entire time he spoke. "Lovely, Jenna, Samantha, the pleasure is definitely ours, I assure ye." He lifted her hand and kissed her palm before continuing, "I'm Brady, Brady Connelly, and this is my good friend, Caleb O'Donnell."

Is it just me or is it getting hot in here? Jenna pulled her hand away and blushed. *Good Lord, these men are beautiful.*

Brady Connelly knew how to make a woman's toes curl with just a look. Tall with thick, black hair, piercing blue eyes, and a smile that could make your heart skip a beat, he oozed sex appeal. He was the complete opposite of Tyler, who'd had blond hair and brown eyes, but the attraction was there nonetheless. She couldn't deny it, no matter how hard she tried.

His friend Caleb whisked Sam away with the excuse of getting refills at the bar.

"You guys are very good at what you do," Jenna teased. She was nervous and had to take some of the pressure away.

"What are we doin'?" Brady asked with mock innocence, and she could see he was trying to hold back a smile.

"Well," she said, smiling in return, "if you wanted some alone time, you could've just asked." Shrugging, she looked over at Caleb and Sam, who were sitting at the bar. Caleb was quite fetching as well, and Sam seemed to be enamored with him. He was tall, on the thin side of athletic, and exuberated confidence. He had dark eyes, dirty blond hair, and deep dimples on each cheek every time he smiled, and she could definitely see his appeal, but he didn't do it for her like the sexy Irishman in front of her did.

She sighed, he laughed, and she couldn't help but smile. "Next time, I'll keep that in mind."

"Hmm," she mumbled, "and you're confident too. I like that—next time?"

"Well, I was hopin' there would be a next time, if that's okay with ye?" he said, making her speechless as he reached across the table for her hand.

She felt as if a spark ignited within her at his touch, and she could feel butterflies in her stomach go haywire with the excitement. Her response both shocked and freaked her out a little.

Sam interrupted them. "Hey, Jenna, um, it's getting late. Are you ready?"

Jenna nodded. "It was nice to meet you, Brady," she said, stroking her thumb across his fingers before pulling away from his hold on her hand.

"Until next time?" he asked.

Unintentionally her smile grew wider. "Wow," she said when she meant to only think it, and he laughed. Shaking her head to clear her thoughts, she was distracted when Caleb wrapped his arms around Sam as they walked out. It was so like Sam to make friends easily, and they'd obviously hit it off.

"It's gettin' late. How 'bout a ride back to yer hotel?" Brady asked.

"A ride?" she repeated, making him laugh again.

"Aye, I just wanna make sure ye ladies get back

safely."

The ride back was pretty quiet. The only time anyone spoke was at the beginning, when Sam let Brady know where they were staying. Every once in a while, Jenna could feel him take his eyes off the road for a split second to look at her.

Feeling awkward with Sam's make-out session in the backseat, she began to laugh and fidget nervously. Hey, she'd been out of the game for a long time being married to Tyler and then grieving him; she just wasn't used to this kind of attention from a man anymore.

"What's so funny?" he asked, taking one hand off the wheel to brush his fingers against the side of her face.

"Nothing, really." She smiled up at him shyly. "Honestly, it's just been a while since I've been out. I'm not used to it." She shrugged, not knowing how else to explain things. "But it's nice to see that our friends are getting along." Chuckling, she gestured toward the back.

He nodded and looked at her quickly again. "So I'm curious," he said, "ye never did give me an answer. Can I take ye out sometime?"

"I was curious if you would ask again."

"Well, how 'bout it? I just wish ye'd say yes already."

"Yes already." She giggled.

He smiled as he glanced over at her again. "So is that yer answer?"

"Absolutely," she told him as the car came to a stop. "Well, now that you know where we're staying, I guess I'll see you around."

"Definitely." He nodded and then cleared his throat. His voice was huskier when he spoke next. "Jenna—" he slowly moved closer to her "—I enjoyed meetin' ye tonight." He moved one hand to the small of her back and adjusted her closer to him while he cupped the back of her head with the other. His lips were close to her ear, his breath so warm it made her nipples hard. "And I know we just met, but I have to kiss ye, darlin'."

She just went for it. His lips took hers in a hot, open mouthed kiss that left them both panting. She leaned back to look at him as she said good night and got out of the car. Sam waited for her by the hotel door. By the time they reached the elevator, Jenna was still flustered thinking about the kiss.

"See, it's not as hard as you thought, is it?" Sam asked as she pushed the Call button for the elevator.

"Sam," Jenna groaned, "please, don't rub it in. I'm enjoying the moment here. The last thing I want is to overthink it and begin to feel guilty. This is still new for me."

"Okay, okay." She laughed. "It's just nice to see you loosen up and have a good time."

"And have I said thank you yet today?" she teased. "Because I'm so glad that we're here." Thinking about it made her teary-eyed. "I'm sorry," she whispered. "They're happy tears, I swear."

"Aw, Jenna, just enjoy it, honey. I know I am. Hell, with those two tonight, it can only get better, considering we get to see them again." Jenna laughed as Sam wiggled her eyebrows suggestively.

"God help me, Sam, you are such a bad influence, but I love ya anyway. You're like family to me."

"Aw, Jenna, I love you too."

***

"Knock, knock," Sam announced her arrival to Jenna's room the next morning. "How'd you sleep?"

"Great. I'm showered, dressed, and ready for whatever's on the agenda today."

"I'm glad to hear you say that, because I've made plans with Caleb, and I believe Brady is coming to surprise you."

"Brady. Coming here? Today?" Jenna had to let that sink in. Yes, she'd agreed to see him again, but she didn't think it would be so soon. "Um, okay. I'll see you later, I guess. Just promise me that next time you do a deliberate setup like this, you'll give me a little more warning. Not last minute like you're doing now."

"You got it, toots. Have fun and don't do anything I wouldn't do." Sam wrapped her arms around Jenna. "On second thought," she whispered, "get wild."

Jenna shoved her aside with a chuckle. "Don't you have to go and get ready? Go on, get out of here."

Her date was certainly going to be a test. Had last night's courage come from the alcohol or was her confidence coming back?

Twenty minutes later someone knocked on the door again. "What now? Is there anything else you failed to mention?" Jenna asked. She'd barely finished applying her makeup.

"Did I come at a bad time?" Brady asked.

"Not at all." Heat flared to her face from embarrassment. "Sorry, please come in. I thought you were Sam. Just let me get my purse and I'll be ready to go."

He grabbed her hand and pulled her closer before leaning in for a kiss, but she was shyer today and only gave him a quick peck. "Brady," she whispered, leaning her head on his shoulder. "You seem like a good guy and I like you, but I need to go slow right now. I hope you understand."

His fingers traced slowly up and down her back in a comforting gesture. "It's okay, love, I won't bite unless ye ask."

She looked up and laughed at the mischievous smile on his face. "Thank you," she whispered. "I haven't genuinely laughed in so long."

***

"So where are you taking me?" she asked, admiring the scenery as they drove through Dublin.

"You'll see. Um, it's a good tourist spot."

Time seemed to pass quickly when she was in Brady's presence, and soon they were pulling up to a large open space with a helicopter. "Are ye ready for this?" he asked.

"Ready for what?"

He helped her from the car and led the way

"Um, what's that for?"

"It's our ride. Come on, Jenna, ye'll have to wait and see. Let me help ye up."

Bracing herself for anything, Jenna found the helicopter ride exhilarating and scary at the same time. Although the scenery was still breathtaking, it looked so different from being so high in the air. Everything was smaller, and you could see so much more all at once. It was breathtaking. He seemed pleased with Jenna's amazement and answered questions whenever she had them. She'd never been on a helicopter ride before, and who knew you could take a tour on one? Obviously Brady did.

As the helicopter descended, she began to panic slightly and clutched on to him for dear life until they were safely landed. Not that she minded. She liked the feel of his muscles under her fingers. Her nervousness faded, replaced by disappointment that the ride was over so quickly and she had to let him go. As he helped her out, her stomach embarrassed her by growling.

"Ye hungry, love?" he asked with a quirk of his lips.

"Starved."

"Good, I like a woman that likes to eat. I'm hungry too. Come on, I know a great spot."

They grabbed lunch on the go and took a leisurely stroll hand in hand. While walking down a trail, they engaged in small talk to get to know each other better.

"So tell me about yerself," he said.

"Hmm, let's see. I'm twenty-seven and an only child. Both my parents are still living and have been married the last thirty years. I currently live in Staten Island, New York, but I was born in Canada."

"What else?" he persisted.

"What else? What is it that you want to know?"

"Anything and everything ye'd like to share. How about ye tell me about the most exotic place ye've ever been to, where ye've traveled. Now that would be interestin'."

"Well, when it comes to traveling, it's simple because I've never traveled before this."

"Really?" He laughed.

Jenna played along. "Pathetic, huh? Honestly, Brady, with being a wife and a mother, I didn't have the time." The words slipped out before she could take them back. The laughter died quickly, and Brady's face fell.

"Ye'r married?" He was clearly not happy with the thought. "Ye'r here with me and ye'r married and have a child. Please, tell me this is some kinda joke. 'Cause if it is, it's not very funny."

Playtime was over. The atmosphere had become extremely serious, and Jenna began to cry. "No, it's not funny," she whispered, trying to hold back a sob. "The truth is I really am pathetic. I was married, Brady, *was* being the important word. My husband died a little over a year ago, and it was partly my fault. God, I still miss him, but I'm trying to move on. I need to for myself, and I want to for my son. It's been hard, but above all else, the most important thing in my life, my whole life, is my child."

She wasn't sure what to expect now that she'd told Brady about Jayden. She missed her son so much that thinking about him hurt.

"Shite, Jenna, I'm so sorry, darlin'." He wrapped

his arms around her and pulled her into the embrace. "But come on, love, ye'r far from pathetic, and it couldna been yer fault."

She cried on his shoulder, and being there felt so good. She couldn't remember the last time she'd had such strong arms around her, and God, he smelled amazing. "We didn't have seat belts on. We were stranded..." She sobbed. "There was a rainstorm and we couldn't see a thing, so Tyler pulled over. I was irritated, and I needed a distraction, so he kissed me. It's a bit of a blur and it all happened so fast. I saw the blinding bright lights of the truck in front of us. The driver lost control, and it nearly got the both of us killed. He's gone, and he shouldn't be, Brady. Why do bad things have to happen to good people?"

"It's not yer fault, Jenna. God, love, I'm so sorry, but thank ya for sharin'. Ye've helped me learn so much about ye. Now everythin' makes so much sense."

"What makes sense?" She sniffed and wiped her face.

"Well, when I seen ye at the airport, ye seemed like ye were interested, but then ye looked so panicked and left so quickly. Last night ye were different, easy to talk to, and I enjoyed yer flirting. Hell, ye even let me kiss ye." He gave her one of his killer smiles. "But today ye seemed so shy."

She smiled and then exhaled loudly. "I guess I'm not that hard to read. Thanks for listening." She felt both relieved and foolish at the same time. He probably thought she was a nut case. "You know, I'm still waiting."

"For what, love?"

"Well, I just figured that after hearing my story, any sane man would be running for the hills. I have baggage and a child, and you don't seem to mind at all."

He laughed louder than ever. "Yer baggage isn't all that scary, love, and I think kids are grand. But then again, maybe I'm just crazy."

He was so sweet and understanding he left her speechless. She barely knew the guy, and she'd already told him things that only the people closest to her knew about. Hanging on to her guilt was such a burden, and nobody knew she had blamed herself the whole time. Yet she'd told him, had bared her soul to a man she'd only officially met the night before. There was just something about him that made her feel so comfortable.

"Brady," she whispered breathlessly. "I'm going to have to kiss you."

A slow, naughty grin crossed his mouth, and there was no telling him twice. She stroked the side of his face and nipped his bottom lip before tracing her tongue over it to soothe the sting.

The moment their lips touched, a fire exploded within her. Sliding her tongue along his, she just barely resisted the urge to tear off his shirt.

Before things got out of hand, Brady pulled away. Acting like a smartass, he scooped her up, threw her over his shoulder, and began walking up the path again to continue their stroll. Jenna laughed the whole time.

"There, mission accomplished. Hearing laughter is so much better than watchin' someone cry."

"I agree. Not to mention, throwing me over your shoulder gives you a good view of my ass." She laughed and felt so much lighter after sharing her burdens with him. The fact that she could feel every defined and perfectly sculpted muscle on his chest and abs as he took his time putting her down was an added bonus she wouldn't mind repeating.

"Not really," he said, taking her hand to twirl her around. "I actually have a better view like this. It takes care of all angles that way."

She blushed and he laughed again. "Jenna, love, ye'r one of a kind."

Chapter Four

It was dark by the time Jenna got back to the hotel, but she was too full of adrenaline to go back to her room. The date had been amazing, and being with Brady seemed so much easier now that all her baggage was out in the open. Her shoulders felt a hundred times lighter, so she decided to go see Sam for some good old-fashioned girl talk.

"Sam," she announced as she barged in without knocking. "So let's hear it, how was your day? I had such a great time. I should have had a little more faith in you when you said—" The pure high of excitement she'd had when she'd walked in immediately evaporated. She gasped and was struck speechless.

"Uh, Jenna."

Sam was in bed, holding the sheet up to hide anything indecent while Caleb stood nude in the bathroom doorway with an unopened condom in his hand. Jenna felt her face heat with embarrassment the moment she noticed his lower-body salute, and she fumbled trying to get to the door.

34

"I'm so sorry." Stuttering and embarrassed, she was almost in tears by the time she got to the hallway. Caleb's laughter followed her halfway to her room. She'd brought all of this upon herself, though. Right then and there, she vowed never to walk in on anyone ever again, and she owed Sam and Caleb an apology.

***

"Jenna."

She could hear her name in the distance. She'd tossed and turned all night, thinking about her embarrassing encounter. *Stupid, stupid, stupid.* She'd even smacked herself for it. "Jenna?"

Wait, is that coffee?

She groaned. "Sam? What are you doing in my room?" But she was still half asleep and didn't care. Coffee waited for her, and that was all that mattered right that second.

Sam laughed. "Well, at least I knew you were solo, thanks to last night. I'm just here to bring you coffee and get some details about your date yesterday."

Jenna blushed.

"Come on, dish it. I wanna know how it went."

She needed to apologize before getting to the good stuff. "Sam, about last night—"

"Oh, hush. We really don't need to get into that part right now. All is forgiven. Now come on, what about Brady? Spill it."

"It was great." Jenna beamed and gave her every last detail.

"So you told him everything. Wow, that took guts. How do you feel about all of this?"

"I'm fine, really. But I've found that he can run hot and cold at times. He was genuinely sincere, comforting, and we had a good time, but I guess I'm disappointed that he didn't kiss me again after our one kiss on the trail." She shrugged. "I'm still confused. I didn't think I was ready to date, but he makes me feel so comfortable. There's just something about Brady. I can't explain it. So I guess maybe a holiday fling won't hurt. It has been a while."

Sam laughed and gave her a hug. "That a girl. Now, about last night? You obviously know that my date went very well"—She giggled.—"despite the minor interruption, so now there's just one more question to ask."

Jenna could feel the heat in her cheeks and could only imagine what shade of red they must have been. She cleared her throat and braced herself for Sam's question.

"I know you got a good look," Sam said and smiled wickedly. "Now, Caleb's gorgeous, but isn't he absolutely delicious without any clothes on?"

Jenna stared in disbelief, and her jaw dropped while Sam laughed.

"He is one fine man," Jenna agreed when she found her voice. "But he's no Brady." Then she laughed with her.

***

St. Stephen's Green was packed. It seemed to be

a popular spot as one of the many local bands played a catchy tune.

"Oh look, there's Caleb," Sam announced just as they got seated. She left Jenna and headed toward the tree-lined walkway to meet him.

"Oh, wonderful, all alone in unfamiliar territory." Still, she was probably better off standing at a distance. She wasn't sure she could look Caleb in the eye after seeing him naked.

"Don't look so glum, love."

She hadn't seen him approach but smiled when Brady sat down next to her.

"Much better." He smirked. "Listen, Sam wanted me to let ye know that somethin' came up and she'd meet ye later."

"What?" She sat there in disbelief; her friend had actually ditched her. That had to be a first. She was too angry to sit in one spot and abruptly stood.

"Hey, where ye goin'?"

"I can't believe she just left me like that. Something came up? I can just imagine what that something is. I mean, I'm glad that Sam and Caleb are hitting it off, but this is ridiculous."

He laughed.

"What?" she snapped, glaring at him.

"I've just never seen ye mad before. Yer cute when ye get angry."

She rolled her eyes and took a couple of deep breaths to calm herself. It was pointless to carry on. Sam was who she was angry with, not Brady, and the last thing she wanted was to make things awkward by acting like an idiot. Getting ditched wasn't the end of the world, but boy, Sam was going to get an earful when Jenna saw her again.

***

Brady

Brady wasn't sure what to do. It became clear that she didn't want to stay at St. Stephen's Green. She was upset—that much was obvious—and man, she was cute. He still wanted to laugh, but she was just calming down, and he didn't want her upset with him.

Christ, he wanted her.

"Would ya like me to take ye back?" he had to ask. Sam and Caleb leaving her had been at the spur of the moment, and he had to be at work soon.

"Do you have the number for a taxi? I'd hate to inconvenience you."

He laughed again. The only way this woman inconvenienced him was his inability to stop thinking about her. She was a gem, but she also drove him crazy with need. He was getting hard just standing close to her. Hell, he'd relieved himself in the shower that morning, picturing her breasts rubbing up against him the way they had when he'd lowered her to the ground the day before, only naked this time.

His mouth enclosed one of her nipples, teasing, licking, and suckling it. Her clit bloomed, and he'd smelled her arousal. Taking his time, he hadn't stopped until he'd tasted all of her. She'd moaned and trembled until she'd begged him for release, and then he'd given it to her fast and hard.

Just thinking of it again made his cock throb with anticipation, and he nearly groaned. He'd have to take a cold shower before heading to work now, but it served him right for getting himself worked up like that. Jenna was just too much temptation, and he knew she'd be dynamite. However, she was also special, and she'd been through a lot, so he had to be patient.

"Don't be silly, darlin'. There is no way I would send ye away in one of those when I have my car. Besides, I like spendin' time with ye, and I hope to take advantage of it as much as I can. If ye'll let me."

***

Jenna

She could sense him watching her, taking quick peeks while he was driving. "Do I have something on my face?"

"What?"

"Maybe a booger in my nose," she teased— praying that she didn't, of course.

She laughed but he was louder.

"What are ye talkin' about, Jenna?"

"Well, I've noticed that you look at me a lot, especially when we're in the car, and I was just wondering…" She took a deep breath, not sure if she wanted to know what he was thinking or how he was feeling. She lightened up and went with honesty. "Okay, maybe I was trying to be funny. I like it when you smile."

He smiled again but didn't answer, clearly lost in thought.

"You're awfully quiet. Are you going to give me an answer?"

"About what?"

"Do I have something on my face?" She liked playing with him a bit.

He stopped the car on the side of the road to give her his undivided attention and smiled again when he looked at her. "Well, let me see," he said, going along with it. He moved his face closer to check. "Nope, nothin'."

She turned breathless with his close proximity and had to resist fanning herself. The heat between them grew, and electricity intensified around them in anticipation.

"Jenna," he moaned, moving closer.

"Shut up and kiss me," she teased, loving that she affected him as much as he affected her.

She wrapped her fist in his shirt and yanked him closer so she could kiss him hard. It was so frickin' good she could kiss him for hours—among other things. Man, she hoped he had nowhere to be for a while, because her plans involved relieving almost fourteen months of sexual frustration. Damn, she'd forgotten how good being in such strong arms felt.

He broke the kiss first. "Jenna, we're still in the car, love. Let's not push it."

Her face heated again, and she started to shake with anxiety. He'd been right to stop. Thank God for that. With her track record, being in the car and getting all hot and heavy definitely wasn't the best idea.

"You're right, and thank you. I really don't know what I was thinking." *I am such an idiot.*

She covered her face and just wanted to crawl into a hole and hide. She was not only embarrassed but also in the process of trying to control an anxiety attack. Brady must have thought she was crazy for trying to start something in the car when in truth she hadn't been thinking at all. She'd been too absorbed with her desires. Thank God one of them still had a level head. "I'm so sorry."

"No worries, love." He reached across the seat to give her hand a little squeeze and pulled back out into traffic. "Really, Jenna, it's all right. Ye'll be out of the car soon enough. We've almost arrived."

By the time they reached the hotel she'd begun to calm but still didn't want their time to end. He left the car running, got out, and opened the passenger-side door.

"Would you like to come up?"

"Now that's a silly question. I'd love too." He kissed her again and groaned. "But I can't. Sorry, darlin', it pains me to say it, but I've got somewhere to be."

Okay, so maybe he wasn't as into her as she'd thought. *Or maybe you're just overreacting, Jenna.* Regardless, she was disappointed. She knew he had a life, obligations, and a job he had to go to, but the rejection kind of hurt. Opening up like this was hard for her. Tyler had been her life for so long, and she was finally willing to give herself to someone else. Yep, it totally sucked.

"Of course." She stepped away from his embrace and his car. It was stupid, childish, and deep down she knew she was taking things the wrong way, but all she wanted was to get away. "I'll, uh, see you later." Waving, she headed to the entrance.

"Jenna, wait." he called out and pulled her toward him again. "Shite, Jenna, I'll definitely take a rain check. I feel really bad for refusin', and if it hadn't been for that damn shipment I have to help unload at the boozer, I probably wouldn't bother goin' to work at all. Believe me, love, there is nothin' I'd rather be doin' than goin' up there with ye right now. I want ye bad." He sighed and pulled her up against the car to discretely place her hand on his crotch. "Feel how much."

He moaned when she stroked him. "Jenna," he said through clenched teeth. "Ye have to stop, or there'll be trouble."

"Is that a promise?"

He moaned again and took her hand off of him. "Ye can count on it. Look, love, I've gotta go before I change my mind and get in a heap a trouble. Ye don't want me to lose my job at the boozer, do ye? And ye can bet that I'll be seein' ye as soon as I can."

"Hmm," she mumbled. "Until next time, then."

***

"I can't believe you," Jenna snapped. "You ditched me when we had plans. What if Brady hadn't shown up, Sam? I've never been here before. You shouldn't have done that to me."

"Jenna, I'm sorry. I guess I'm just shocked that you're angry. I mean, I knew Brady was with you and knew he would bring you back. Honestly, you should be thanking me for giving you the opportunity to spend more time with him. I didn't think it was a big deal."

"Not a big deal? Are you kidding me? How would you feel if I took you to a place you weren't familiar with and left you with someone you barely knew? Brady is amazing, but the fact that I was with him is irrelevant. You could have had the decency to tell me yourself that you were leaving. Geez." Sam was about to speak again, but Jenna cut her off before she could. "Listen, I don't really want to fight with you right now, or ever for that matter. Just don't do it again and we'll be good." With that she left and slammed the door behind her. She just hoped she hadn't made things awkward. Caleb had been with Sam when Jenna went to give her a piece of her mind, and the last thing Jenna wanted was to cause problems between them.

Sam showed up an hour later to apologize again, and Jenna did the same.

***

She didn't see Brady as soon as she would have liked. The next day she and Sam were inseparable. They went out for lunch and took a walk to find somewhere to picnic. They talked, laughed, and cried.

They'd spent the whole day out in the open. Almost everywhere they looked they were surrounded by fields and fields of grass and beautiful landscape. It was peaceful, gorgeous, and serene—heaven on earth—and for the first time in a long time, Jenna's mind was free of worry, and damn, it felt good for once. That night she was able to sleep.

She dreamed of good things for a change, mainly Brady, but someone disturbed her slumber by pounding on the door.

"What the hell?"

Frustrated at being taken away from the really hot dream, she yanked open the door to find out who the hell it was. The light in the hallway was blinding and she had to squint to see. "Good Lord, get in here," she mumbled. "Who knew that light was so bright."

Brady laughed. "But now I can't see anything." She turned on the bedside lamp. "Much better. Now I can actually see ye."

"Brady, it's late. Is everything all right?"

"Yes," he whispered and sat on the bed. He pulled her over so that she stood in front of him. He moved his hands up her thighs, and she was so close to him that she could feel his breath hot on her stomach. His lips parted, and she began to breathe harder. God, if he kept it up, she wouldn't take long to reach her peak.

"Brady, you're driving me crazy." She was breathless, and damn, she wanted him to make her come, needed it. It had been way too long, and it just wasn't as good when she pleasured herself.

He chuckled and looked up. "I'm glad, love. I've wanted ye for a while. It's nice to know the feelin's mutual. Nice shirt by the way," he said and moved his hands up under the hem to get inside it. He stopped at the line of her underwear and stood with her so she was flush against him, his hard body to her soft curves. "I can't stop thinkin' about ye. I just can't stop thinkin' about the kisses we shared and the way ye smell. All flowery yet so unique. I bet ye taste just as sweet. I can't wait to taste ye, Jenna. Yer drivin' me crazy too, love."

He leaned in and took a deep breath against the column of her throat, and it made her shiver. It felt like a slow, torturous seduction, and she couldn't take much more. She took initiative and lifted the shirt above her head, then dropped it to the floor, leaving her in nothing but a pair of tiny panties. "Now it's your turn," she said and began to work on getting his pants undone.

He fisted his shirt above his head and took over getting naked to join her, then moved them back to the bed when he was done. Laying her down, he crouched above her and paid special attention to her breasts. He licked and suckled one while tweaking the other with his fingers, making her moan and arch for more of his touch. After paying equal attention to each, she began to squirm.

"Tell me what ye want me to do to ye, love. Let me hear what ye need."

"You, I need to have you inside of me." She was desperate and aching for him.

He smiled and eagerly rolled the condom on before he lifted her up to be on top. "Ye can control everythin' this way, and I still have easy access to all yer best parts." He cupped her breasts and watched as she slowly rose up and down to get used to him while he filled her. She wanted to take her time. It felt too good to rush, and he was big. Gradually she picked up her pace, and she was finally able to take him to the root. He moaned, looking strained, as though he was fighting hard to hold back. He let go of one breast and trailed his hand down her stomach to where they were joined. She was so hot and wet, and incredibly greedy for anything he was willing to share with her, so she leaned back a little to give him better access.

"Come for me, Jenna. I'm so close, darlin'. Come for me."

She hissed an appreciative sound and moaned as her orgasm built. Her body writhed, and she pounded down on him harder and harder, then it hit. She cried out and screamed his name as her pussy pulsed her incredible release around his cock. She milked him, and as his climax hit, he thrust up hard while holding her hips in place.

"Jenna," he moaned, and she could feel the heat of his seed as he filled the condom inside her.

Chapter Five

"Mornin'."

"Hmm, and what a good morning it is." She leaned over to give him a quick peck and snuggled closer. "So what's on the agenda for today?"

"I can certainly think of a few things." He chuckled and rolled her over so that she was underneath him. He began at her throat and trailed kisses downward, passing between her breasts as he tasted every bit of her with his tongue. She moaned and arched her hips, but he took his time. He sat up and lifted first one of her legs and then the other as he trailed more kisses from her ankle to her inner thigh, teasing her.

"Brady, please," she moaned and writhed in anticipation.

His chuckle was smug with male satisfaction, and he moved his tongue in slow, deliberate circles to prolong her pleasure while he continued to savor her taste.

Damn, she was so close. She stroked her hands through his soft hair, positioning him to where she needed that delicious, wet tongue. It was a silent demand for her satisfaction, and he gave it. She moaned over and over and got louder as the climax hit her hard.

They made love and cuddled most of the morning, but as much as she would have loved to continue, she knew Brady had made other plans for the two of them.

***

"No peekin', love."

Jenna couldn't remember the last time she'd been this giddy. Brady covered her eyes with his hands and led her through the lobby and outside.

"Are ye ready?"

"I think so."

"All right, darlin', here ye go." He slid his hands from her eyes and took a step back.

She had to blink a few times to take it all in and gasped. A horse and carriage stood waiting for them.

"I figured since ye had the tour in the air, it was time ye experienced one on the ground."

This had to have been not only one of the most romantic, but one of the sweetest things anyone had ever done for her. He took her hand to lead the way, and she began to tear up.

"Why ye cryin'?" he asked with wide eyes, clearly startled by her reaction.

She knew getting emotional was probably the last thing he'd expected her to do, and then she watched as his expression turned from concern to confusion when she smiled at him. "Because you're amazing, and this has to be the sweetest thing anyone has ever done for me. Thank you, Brady."

"It's no problem, love. Ye haven't really traveled before, and I didn't want ye to miss anythin' while ye were here. Ye had me worried that I screwed it up for a minute."

She smiled again and was left speechless that they were actually in front of a horse and carriage. The whole experience felt so surreal.

"Yer chariot awaits ye, my lady."

Brady pointed out different landmarks and sights, and they talked and laughed the whole way. She saw the view from the ground this time, and every detail stood out. They saw government buildings, Saint Patrick's Cathedral, Merrion Square, the Four Courts, the Mansion House, and plenty of churches. It was all so educational and so beautiful.

She'd been so wrapped up in him, she didn't realize the tour was over until Brady helped her down. "Where are we?"

They stood in front of a small bungalow in the outskirts of town.

"This is where I live. I'd really like to get to know ye, Jenna, and I'm hopin' ye'd like to get to know me better yerself, so I thought I'd show ye a few things."

"Absolutely." She was touched by his nervousness and completely flattered to be there.

The house was a great setup for a bachelor. The cozy living room had a fireplace at one end. The kitchen was a nice eat-in, with a lot of cabinets and enough space to fit a good-sized table. Two average-sized bedrooms and a small bathroom were upstairs.

He came out of the kitchen with a bottle of wine in hand, and Jenna stood directly in his path, admiring the view from the window. He moved up behind her and brushed the hair away from the nape of her neck. He trailed kisses up to her earlobe and whispered, "Would ye like to have a better look?"

"Hmm," she mumbled and leaned into his embrace. Her eyes rolled to the back of her head; she loved how his lips felt on her. "At what?" She was easily distracted from other thoughts with him so near.

He chuckled and moved aside. "The yard, silly. I'll get a blanket and meet ye out there." He grabbed the bottle he'd put on the table and started for the linen closet.

Damn, what a fine ass he has. She watched him step away until he was out of sight. Fanning herself, she headed outside to look around.

"Hey there."

She jumped, not expecting the unfamiliar voice behind her and turned around to find the source. "Oh, hello."

"Sorry, darlin'. I didn't mean to scare ye." The man laughed before bending down to pick a flower. He stood and gave her a once-over after handing it to her. "Peace offerin'. My name is Charles. Pleased to meet ye." He was an older man with thick, white hair, a slim build, stunning blue eyes, and a charming smile.

"Jenna," she said and extended her hand to shake

his.

He held it. "So how long have ye known Brady?"

"Not very long at all."

"I am in me wick," he murmured. "Ye know he normally doesn't bring his birds home. Ye must be somethin' special."

That made her smile. "You know Brady?" she asked. Whoever this charming man was, she certainly liked him, but she couldn't shake the feeling that she was missing something obvious. A familiarity, maybe?

He laughed again. "Aye, ye could say that." He looked past her for a minute, smiled, then held her hand to his mouth. "It was a pleasure, sweet Jenna." After kissing the back of her hand, he let it fall and headed in the other direction.

"We're all set," Brady announced.

What was it with men sneaking up on her today? Jenna had watched as Charles slowly made his way back to his house and hadn't noticed Brady behind her.

"Great. I like your neighbor, by the way."

Brady laughed. "That's no neighbor. He's nothin' but a pain in me hole." He said it loud enough that Charles laughed before he was out of sight.

She was appalled that he would say something like that about a man who seemed so sweet. "That isn't very nice," she whispered, and Brady laughed louder.

"Jenna, love, that's no regular neighbor. That's my da."

"I'm kind of glad I didn't know." She blushed and then laughed. "Parents are a big deal, and it would have made me nervous."

"No need to be, love. Now I've a throat on me, how 'bout some wine?"

As they sat out in the open, she couldn't remember the last time she'd had such a good time. It had been a while anyway, and she had no regrets coming to Ireland. In fact, she wanted to come back with Jayden sometime. He'd love it.

"Why the long face, love?"

"Sorry," she whispered. "I was just thinking about Jayden, my son. I miss him." Shrugging, she smiled at him shyly, and he gave her a curious look. She'd brought up her son a few times but hadn't really said much about him.

"So then tell me 'bout him, love. What's Jayden like?"

The simple question was difficult to answer. When it came to her son there weren't enough words to explain who he was or how much he meant. So how could she describe Jayden in just a few words? She gave it a try. "He's a typical four-year-old. He's amazing. Outgoing and carefree. He's sweet and loving. He has a way about him that draws people in. He's smart and unbelievably handsome, of course." She laughed. "But he's also a handful at times, very busy, and he gets into everything. A regular everyday pain in the butt sometimes, and he's my greatest accomplishment, the best decision I've ever made, and he's the love of my life."

"He's a lucky boy, and he's sounds just grand."

***

A half hour later, they packed up and headed inside. To Jenna's embarrassment her stomach growled, letting her know it was time for dinner. Brady told her to put her feet up while he cooked, so she curled up in front of the fireplace and admired him from afar. Soon the delicious aromas reached her, making her mouth water and stomach grumble again.

"Is there anything I can help you with in there?"

"No, love, but thank ye." He smiled, and her heart beat faster, just as it did every time he did that. With his piercing blue eyes that always made her hunger for just another look from him, he was a man who aimed to please, and she loved that about him. He not only cooked and cleaned but was considerate and dynamite in the sack. What more could a girl ask for?

He'd kept the meal simple with pasta and salad, and she insisted on helping him with the cleanup.

"The spaghetti was delicious, thank you."

He smiled again, took the last plate from her to dry, and shook off the extra suds. Drips of water and soap suds flew through the air, getting her wet in the process, and he laughed at her shocked expression.

"Oh really," she said, suddenly in the mood to play. She took the sprayer hose from the faucet, turned it on, and gave him a squirt with it. She laughed, and it was his turn to pause in shock.

She could tell by his expression that this meant war and made a run for it, laughing the whole way.

She made it into the living room before he extended his arms to catch her, and he swooped her up as if she was feather-light.

"Got ye."

They both laughed, but when she turned to face him, he became serious. She knew then that the games were over. He brushed a strand of hair from her face and pulled her toward him. As he slowly moved his face closer, his eyes sparkled and completely absorbed hers.

The kiss started out slow, and she wanted him to take his time with it. She held back a groan when he pulled his mouth away and yanked him tighter against her. Her adrenaline pumped faster, and warmth coursed through her body. There was no thinking twice about it; her desire for this man had consumed her.

She pushed him against the wall and kissed him hard, wanting him in that moment more than she'd ever wanted anything. She liked where this was going, liked being in control, needed it right then. She placed her hands on his chest and slowly moved them down his beautifully sculptured abs. "Stay," she whispered and took a step back so he could watch as she unzipped her dress. It slowly slid to the floor, exposing her bare breasts and her sexy black thong. She kicked it out of the way, pulled his shirt off, and pressed herself against him again, flesh against flesh.

"You're the first man I've wanted in a long time," she confessed, no longer feeling as vulnerable as she once had. "My first since Tyler left me."

"Jenna," he moaned and flexed his hips forward. Her confession seemed to shock but flatter him. "I'm staking my claim, love. Do you hear? Ye'r mine now, as I am yers."

She purred and rubbed her body flush to his to create friction against the heat of her core. Getting moister by the second, she lowered her head to lick and nip at his nipples and worked her way down his stomach toward the cock she ached for. She slowly tugged his zipper down.

"No underwear. What a pleasant surprise," she said and gently pulled him out for her wet mouth to taste.

She angled him where she wanted, and he gasped and moaned when she circled his sensitive head with her tongue. She took him as far back as she could over and over, swirling her tongue up and down his thick shaft, and hearing his rapid breathing and moans of excitement turned her on even more. She felt powerful and sexy as hell to be able to bring him so much pleasure.

"Feck yesss," he hissed. "Like that, oh, shite, Jenna…" He leaned back and closed his eyes, clearly enjoying the feel of her mouth on him.

She could tell he was close and cupped his balls while working him harder to take him over the edge. He placed his hands in her hair and flexed his hips faster and faster to fuck her mouth, so she relaxed her throat. His orgasm rushed through him, and he roared her name in delight as she sucked every last drop down her throat.

He took a minute to catch his breath before he swept her off her feet and into the bedroom. "It's time to return the favor," he murmured and dropped her in the middle of the bed. He playfully nipped her thong between his teeth and dragged it down her legs with his mouth to discard it. She moaned when he lowered his head, and he smiled against her glistening lips.

"Brady, please..."

She was breathless with need and lifted her hips as soon as his tongue made the first stroke. His slow, deliberate circles taunted her. As soon as she was close, he drew back and went lower. He slid his tongue through her folds, tasting, savoring, and then stroking in and out as he fucked her with it. She moaned again and then huffed as she reached out for him. She threaded her fingers through his thick, dark hair and gave it a little tug to guide him where she needed him most to end this sweet torture.

He chuckled before he obliged the silent demand, the tip of his tongue applying pressure against her clit with sure, confident strokes to take her over the edge. She massaged his scalp as she rocked her hips, then screamed his name as the powerful force of the orgasm took over.

They made love and cuddled the rest of the night. When she woke up the next morning, she was happier than she'd been in such a long time. They'd had an amazing time the day before, and she was still in Brady's arms. He was so attentive and treated her as though she was the only one that mattered to him. Realizing she'd developed strong feelings for him was a scary thought.

It can't be love already, can it? It was so soon. She felt a powerful connection to him, and being intimate had only ignited that spark a million times more. It was hard to explain, but she had never felt that type of chemistry before, not even with Tyler.

"Mornin'."

She smiled and pulled away from her thoughts. Having feelings like these for a man again was scary enough, but even worse was not knowing if he felt the same way while knowing she had to leave him eventually. She didn't want to think about it anymore.

"Good morning," she greeted, pressing her naked body against his. She sucked on his bottom lip and smiled. "I think it's time for more," she murmured, then kissed him, preparing herself for whatever he was able to give her.

Chapter Six

Her memories of the next few days were purely physical. It was as though once they'd started, they just couldn't help themselves no matter where they were. Her hotel room was no different.

"Brady, stop." She was short of breath from laughing so hard. She tackled him, pinning his hands above his head on the mattress, and straddled him.

She'd noticed his focus settling on the rise and fall of her breasts as she tried to get her breath back, and it made her smile. They'd been messing around like children, chasing, teasing, and wrestling each other, all in fun, and she was exactly where she wanted to be.

"Ugh, I wish you didn't have to go. I'm going to miss you," she pouted, then smiled when he rolled on top to give her a kiss.

"Ye could come with me, ye know. I haven't been to the boozer in a couple days. I'm bound to lose my job if I keep missin'."

"I know, and I would come. It's just that I

haven't seen Sam in a while. Caleb's going with you, leaving her alone, and I feel guilty for neglecting her. Although my time with you has been wonderful, and I hope to have much more of this before I leave."

"From now until ye have to go, ye can have 'em all, love, every moment."

She nodded and snuggled closer. "Will I see you later?"

"It'll be late, but if ye'll have me, I'll be back here as soon as I can."

"I'll be here." She kissed him and was reluctant to let him go when all she wanted was to tie him up and have her way with him again and again. He closed the door quietly in front of her after he quickly changed, and the room already felt empty without him there, but she'd made a promise to herself. It was time to see Sam now, and she couldn't wait to dish on how well her time with Brady was going.

Her friend was pretty quiet when she came to the door. Something was up, and it couldn't be good.

"Are you okay?"

Sam didn't answer. "No Brady tonight?" She flopped on the bed dramatically.

"Um, no, he's at work, but you knew that because Caleb's with him."

"I think I'm starting to regret spending so much time with Caleb," she whispered.

What the hell? She wouldn't even look Jenna in the eye. "Okay, Sam, spill it. None of this makes any sense. When I saw you a few days ago, you were on cloud nine and couldn't get enough of him.

What could have possibly changed in a matter of days? Has he hurt you?"

"Of course not," she snapped. "I guess I just miss our girl time. I think I need some."

"If you say so." Jenna helped Sam up, forcing her to get out of bed, "that's what I'm here for. You want to go see the guys at the pub, or would you rather do something else?"

"Something else."

They wound up taking a night stroll, sticking close to the hotel. Sam was still unusually quiet, and it was starting to piss Jenna off that she wouldn't open up, especially after how pushy Sam had been about getting her to talk in the past.

"Okay, Sam, this is ridiculous. Your silence is driving me insane, and you need to start talking."

"Jenna, you're the one that's being ridiculous. Like I didn't have enough to worry about, now I have to put up with your intrusion. I'm late. Are you happy now?"

She gasped. It was unlike Sam to snap or talk to her that way. "Late?"

"Yes, Jenna, late, as in my menstrual cycle. I've never been late before, and it's scaring the crap out of me. The condom broke that first night with Caleb, and, well, the last person before him had been quite a while ago, so I wasn't on the pill. I'm sure it's a false alarm. Hell, I'm praying it is, but I'm still freaked out."

"Oh, Sam." She wasn't sure what to do to comfort her. "Do you want to go buy a test?"

She shook her head. "I will, I swear, but I just want to wait a few days. Maybe by then 'Aunt

Rose' will make her faithful appearance and I'll have nothing to worry about."

"Well, have you told Caleb?"

"No, I'm afraid he'll be angry, although half of it is his own damn fault. It takes two to tango."

God, Sam was starting to sound like her mother. "Why don't you take the next couple of days to think about it? Talk to Caleb too. You shouldn't be going through this alone, and I'll be here for you, of course.

"On the bright side," she teased, "if you are…at least it'll take the pressure off me. You know Jayden has been bugging me for a brother or sister, or at least he did when Tyler was around. Now he could just borrow yours."

Sam smirked. "God, Jenna, I swear if I ever have a kid, I hope he's as great as yours."

"Impossible. Jayden is one of a kind." She was having a proud momma moment.

"Now isn't that the truth."

The night mellowed out after that. Sam looked a lot better and finally started having a good time. She talked about Caleb a lot and drilled Jenna about Brady. She wanted details, but there were things Jenna wanted to keep to herself. She wasn't one to kiss and tell, no matter how good it was.

That night she felt as though their roles had reversed a little. For such a long time Jenna had been a mess and Sam had always been there to help her through. Tonight, though, Sam needed her, and it was nice being the one needed, instead of being the one in need.

She just hoped everything worked out for Sam

and wondered how Caleb would cope with the news.

***

It was late when Brady got back, just as he'd said. She looked as if she'd just woken up and smiled at him as if seeing him again had been the best occurrence of her day.

"Hi," she said as she started to get up.

He smiled back and lifted her in his arms. "Hey yerself." He threw her back onto the mattress and enjoyed his view. Her wide smile was breathtakingly beautiful, and without further thought, he joined her. He captured her lovely mouth with his lips, needing to kiss her. He'd been thinking about her all night, and being away was driving him insane. He was addicted, just had to taste her, and it scared him shitless to need her that way.

While working at the pub, Brady had always gotten a fair amount of action. Hell, it was one of the reasons he enjoyed his job so much. But since meeting Jenna things had changed. When he'd gone in earlier, he'd gotten hit on several times. He always did, but tonight he found himself comparing the women to Jenna. Most of them were beautiful but artificial: fake boobs, fake hair extensions, fake fingernails, too much makeup, not enough makeup, and the list went on. None of them seemed to have Jenna's natural beauty or her charm.

Of course, first impressions could be deceiving, but he didn't want to know any of them better. He was ruined for everyone else, and he wasn't sure he was all right with that. Christ, Jenna was only visiting, and he seriously needed to get a grip.

So many things were going on in his head, and he groaned. Why the hell did he have to make things so complicated? He'd always been a chick magnet, and he would be again, damn it. He just needed to enjoy Jenna while he had her, and when she left, everything would go back to the way it used to be. The life of a bachelor was good. He liked no-strings-attached sex and being responsible for only himself. Besides, she had a kid to go back to, so she couldn't stay even if he wanted her to, right?

His kiss became eager the more he thought about it. It was a way to release the frustration of his thoughts. He needed it to come out somehow, and hell, he was feeling this way mostly because he needed her right then. But as she slid her hands down his body to work his pants off, he changed his mind, calling a stop to their intimacy temporarily.

"Is there something wrong?"

"No, love, it's late, and we should get going. Pack a bag. We're goin' to my place."

***

They were in his car, almost to his home when Jenna couldn't take the quiet anymore. Brady looked as though he had a lot on his mind and needed a distraction. "Can I ask you something?"

"Anythin'."

"Does Caleb ever say anything to you about

Sam?"

She'd caught him off guard, and he looked skeptical when he asked, "Why?"

"Is that a hard question for you? I'm asking because I'm curious. I think Sam's developing feelings for him, and I don't want to see her hurt."

"I see," he mumbled. "Caleb's a lucky man." He looked at her quickly and smiled.

"And is she a lucky girl?" She should have dropped it, but she wanted to know.

He laughed. "Ye know, despite what ye may think, we don't compare notes on the women we're with. But if I had to take a guess, I'd say that she was. They do spend an awful lot of time together."

Does he want me like I want him? She should probably just come right out and ask him. "What about me? Would you say I was a lucky girl?"

He sighed. "Well, what do ye think?"

"I don't know, but I hope I am."

"Look, Jenna, I think ye'r great, but do we need ta put a label on it? Ye'r mine while ye'r here. I've already said so. Seriously, love, why don't we just enjoy what we have while it lasts?"

"Yours, huh? Okay, forget it." She rolled her eyes. Obviously, she'd hit a sore spot. Brady clearly wasn't into discussing his feelings, and she'd obviously misread the connection they had. Or maybe it was all one-sided.

The thought made her uncomfortable. Maybe she should just take a cab back to the hotel and give him some space. Then again, he had a point. She was on a vacation and leaving soon. There no way what they had could work beyond that, and she should enjoy it while it lasted.

She opened the car door before he stopped and got out, anxious to get her bag back.

"Shite, Jenna, hold on." She said nothing as she waited patiently beside the trunk. "What's the matter now?"

"Nothing, Brady, everything is absolutely fine, just fine."

"Ye'r mad?" he asked, then he smiled when she crossed her arms and avoided looking directly at him in obvious annoyance. "Ye'r cute when ye'r angry."

"It's not funny, Brady. I should probably apologize before heading back. I hadn't realized talking about your feelings was hard for you. I shouldn't have brought it up."

"What the hell are ye talkin' 'bout? I said ye were great, didn't I? And who's goin' back?" He grabbed the bag from her hand and walked to the door to make his point. "Ladies first." He waited by the door after opening it, but she didn't move.

"Look, I've ruined the night. Maybe I should just give you some space."

"That's feckin' ridiculous and you feckin' know it," he snapped. "Ye surprised me, that's all, and what I'm feelin' is hard for me to sort through right now, but I don't want ye to leave." He pulled her into his arms. "Please, love, it's late. Will ye spend the night with me?"

She nodded and he kissed her. His lips moved against hers, slow and sensual. He nudged her lips apart, taking what he wanted until their tongues moved in synchronization and her need for him reached its peak.

"Ye'r a very lucky girl, love, very lucky."

***

"Wow, what's this for?" She leaned over to give him a kiss. "You're spoiling me."

He chuckled. "I just wanted to make sure I gave ye something to help ye with yer nerves."

"And why would I need help with my nerves?" *Uh-oh, what's he up to?* She took the wine he offered and swirled the glass around before taking a sip.

He looked at her carefully before answering. "My ma's quite jealous that you met my da and not her, so she wants us over for supper." He shrugged as though it wasn't a big deal, and she couldn't believe it. Her pulse quickened with anxiety. Parents were a big deal. She'd already expressed that belief to him. Now not only would she be seeing his father again, but she'd be meeting his mother, and he acted as though it wasn't a big deal. Was he crazy?

"Supper?" she squeaked "With your mother."

Her hands shook, and he took her wineglass from her to avoid spillage and placed it on the coffee table. "It's okay, love, take a breath."

"That's easy for you to say," she sulked.

"It's nothin' te worry yer pretty head about, love. 'Tis only supper and my ma's an angel. Ye'll love her."

She took a couple deep breaths to avoid a full-on anxiety attack. "I'm sure I will," she managed.

"Um, when are we expected?"

"'Bout an hour."

"An hour, are you kidding me?" She jumped out of bed as naked as the day she was born and quickly made her way to the bathroom to shower. The very least she could do was make an effort to look her best. Thank God she'd packed a dress.

He laughed as she scooted away. "Christ, I'm enjoyin' yer nervousness. I never imagined ye to be so comical."

"Ha-ha," she mocked, closing the shower curtain behind her. "So tell me this then, Brady. Have you always brought the women in your life to your parents' house for dinner? Because if so, I'm sure supper with your mom isn't going to be such a big thing."

"Actually, no."

"No?" That shocked her more. Was she the first? No, she couldn't ask him that. "Well then, since it's not a regular occurrence, I think I have a right to be nervous. I'm sure your parents are wonderful, but meeting parents is also a big deal. I've told you this before."

"Look, Jenna, if ye'r this upset 'bout it, I'll just cancel."

"Don't you dare," she snapped, peeking around the curtain. "You've already accepted, and I don't want you to. Parents are a big deal, yes, but they're also important. You're important, and I'd hate to hurt anyone's feelings."

He smiled and yanked the shower curtain open farther to kiss her. "Did ye just say I was important?" He looked flattered. "I like the sound of that."

"Hey," she shrieked and then laughed when he put her hand on his erection. "That will have to wait," she teased with a mock pout. "I'm meeting your mother. You have to give a girl some time to look her best."

He sighed and looked down at his stiff cock. "Damn, I should have said no when she invited us. What am I to do now?"

Jenna shrugged and laughed at his sullen expression. He had a tent pole in his boxers that he needed to get rid of, and there was only one way that was going to happen. "All right, then. Come here, big boy."

***

"Ye'r beautiful when ye fidget," he whispered and looked as though he was enjoying the moment.

His parents must have seen them coming. As soon as they approached the door, his father was there to greet them. She moved forward quickly to extend her hand. "Hello, Charles, it's nice to see you again."

"Likewise, my dear. I'm just glad his ma's naggin' finally convinced him to bring ye." He chuckled when Brady gave him an eye roll and proceeded to lead them to Sarah, his mother.

The back patio came into view, and Jenna could see her in the distance. She smiled at the sight of Sarah and took notice of Brady staring. She winked to let him know she was okay, but he surprised her when he tugged on her hand, bringing them to a complete stop.

"What are you doing?" she asked.

"I have to say that I'm a little disappointed. I thought I'd get to enjoy yer comical side some more, but ye seem so comfortable now. Then again, it's still pretty funny to see my ma so nervous."

Meeting Sarah was interesting. She was a lovely woman, tiny at a whole four feet eleven inches and slim, with shoulder-length salt-and-pepper hair and beautiful green eyes. She was also completely worshipped by the men in her life.

Brady was the youngest of three and a momma's boy. Having one of those herself, Jenna admired him for it. His two older sisters were both married and living abroad. They all seemed to be close, and Jenna was proud to be a part of this family even if only for a short time.

They had just finished eating when Sarah asked, "So where are ye from?"

"Staten Island."

"Interestin', I can't say that I've ever been—"

"So tell me, Jenna," Charles said, "have ye ever considered movin'?"

"Da," Brady snapped, giving his father the evil eye. "'Tis no time to play cupid."

Jenna tried not to smile at the obvious setup. Ignoring Brady, she answered for herself. "It's a little complicated, but I've honestly never really thought about it before. Staten Island has been my home for the last six years."

"But 'tis not a no."

Brady groaned his embarrassment and Jenna chuckled.

"So tell me 'bout the complications, me dear." Sarah patted Jenna on the arm and ignored her son's next protest. Jenna was having a blast watching Brady squirm, and they were all innocent enough questions.

"Well, I have a four-year-old son. It would be complicated mostly because of him, and my parents are not that far away if I need them."

"And the boy's father?" she questioned, then hushed Brady again.

Another innocent question, but a painful one. Jenna's face flushed, and she tried to keep it together. "He died. Um, will you excuse me, please? I think I need to use the ladies' room."

She needed a minute and didn't wait around for their answer before leaving the table. Their house was so huge that it took her a few minutes to find the restroom. She'd just finished splashing her face with cold water when someone tapped at the door.

"Jenna, love, it's Sarah. May I join ye in the jacks for a moment?"

As soon as the door opened, his mother pushed her way in to embrace her. "I'm sorry, dear. I had no idea. Please understand I only asked ye because I had to know for my son's sake that there was no one else in yer life. I think Brady loves ye, and I don't want to see my boy hurt."

Jenna stiffened and went over what she'd just said. *I think Brady loves ye* played over in her head, and it took her a moment to respond. "No, I'm sorry. I shouldn't have gotten emotional. It was just so hard for such a long time. Tyler was a good man, and I still miss him, but it's time to move on, and being with Brady has shown me that I can."

"Of course ye can, love."

Jenna smiled and hugged Sarah again. "Thank you for checking in on me. You're very understanding, and that means so much. Believe me, I can understand having the best intentions when it comes to a son, and I admire the closeness you obviously share."

"Well, that's a relief." Sarah guffawed. "And I'm glad all can be forgiven, but we better get back, my dear, or my poor son will soon die of a heart attack waitin'. He was not very impressed when I came after ye myself. He's worried I'd upset ye."

Jenna nodded. "Wait, just one more thing…"

"Well, come on then, out with it."

"He loves me?"

Sarah laughed loudly for such a small woman, and it made Jenna laugh with her. "Aye, my dear, I believe he does, and I believe ye love him too."

***

"So what did she say? Are ye all right?" They were halfway back to his house when Brady stopped to give her another hug.

"I'm fine, Brady, really." She stepped back and held his hand. "She mostly came to see if I was okay. She was concerned she'd upset me, like you are. We both agreed that having a son is a blessing." Okay, that hadn't actually been said out loud, but it was there through the mutual understanding they'd shared. Sarah loved Brady in the same way Jenna adored Jayden. She cupped his face. "And she told me she thought you loved me."

"What?"

They were in the house by then, and she could tell he was shocked and embarrassed. He obviously wasn't expecting one of his parents to declare his love.

"Feck!" He began to pace, raking his fingers through his hair. "If I loved ye, I could damn well tell ye myself, when I was ready. Bloody meddlin' parents need to shut their holes," he muttered.

"So then you don't?" she questioned and raised a brow. She was curious now that she'd brought it up. Her feelings for Brady were only starting to surface, although she was just beginning to admit them to herself. But love?

"I don't know." He sighed. "I care about ye a lot, and it scares the shite outta me 'cause I've never cared like this before. I'm confused, love, but when I figure it out, I'll be sure to let ye know." He shrugged. "Christ, I hope that's enough for ye right now. I'm not ready to let ye go yet."

"Well, at least you're honest." She was still not sure about her feelings, so how could she expect anything more from him? He cared, and that's what mattered.

"So we're okay, then?"

"Yes." She took a step closer. "And you finally believe that I'm all right?" He nodded and she moved closer yet again. "Good, because I want to show you how good I feel." She stood in front of him now. "Or better yet…" She brushed her lips across his. "We could show each other."

Her kiss was sure. She tasted him easily and

eagerly. She slid her tongue against his; their breath was hot, and her excitement skyrocketed. The dampness between her legs increased with each passing moment.

He gave her an approving growl and hiked up her skirt before he lifted her onto the kitchen counter for easier access. As he moved her underwear aside, his need seemed to become desperate and feral.

Jenna moaned with pleasure when Brady stroked her moist center, then arched her hips forward and nearly climaxed when he entered her. He wasn't gentle as he pumped her hard and fast. He grazed the hollow of her throat and took a bite while he rammed her as hard as he could. She gasped and panted for air, then did something she'd never expected.

Acting on instincts and without thinking it through, she pressed her lips against his ear and whispered, "I love you."

Chapter Seven

Her words just sort of slipped out unintentionally. He'd been so eager and insatiable, and she couldn't seem to get enough of him, either, so it felt good to think that they shared the same need for each other. Damn, but why did she have to go and say the *L* word? What the hell was wrong with her? She felt like an idiot.

His whole body went tense as soon as she said those three stupid words. His only reply was a kiss, and she assumed it was meant to keep her occupied so he wouldn't have to answer. She loved him, had said it, and knew he was pretty sure that she meant it. Christ, he should be happy, so why was he freaked out?

He obviously wasn't ready to say it back and didn't want to hurt her. *Damn it.*

Brady began to give it to her harder. Despite the minor disturbance her words had caused, and his lack of response, she was still wet, and he felt so good while he impaled her. *Here we go, oh yeah.*

"Jennaaa," he moaned, shuddering his release,

and she wasn't far behind in joining him.

As he carried her upstairs to his bedroom in the awkward silence that followed, she clung to him, laying her head against his shoulder. She could feel the heat in her cheeks.

He laid her gently on his bed and brought her chin up so he could look her in the eye. "Are ye okay?"

Jenna nodded but turned over. God, she hadn't been this embarrassed in years. This was worse than walking in on Sam and Caleb. "I'm fine. Just a little tired, that's all." She pulled the blanket up to cover herself more. Shit, she should probably just leave to save face but couldn't.

"Jenna, I..." He seemed to be at a loss for words right then. Was he going to pretend as though it hadn't happened, or would he finally face it?

She felt the mattress move as he joined her and cuddled her close to him. "It's okay, Brady. I'm fine." She patted his hand and closed her eyes, hoping sleep would soon consume her. She needed a break from her conscience and an escape from herself at the moment. Tonight had been one hell of an emotional clusterfuck.

"Are ye asleep yet?" he asked after a few minutes of silence.

"No." She laughed. "Sorry."

He lifted up on his elbows to give her the full effect of his hypnotic glare. God, this man had the most beautiful blue eyes she had ever seen.

"What?" She couldn't bear to have a staring contest, so she pulled the blankets over her head. "I hate when you do that. You drive me insane when you get that intense look. What are you thinking about?"

"I'm thinkin' 'bout ye, actually." He laughed. "Feck, I don't know how to explain."

"Then don't, but please for the love of God, get that serious look off your face. I mean, I love that you look at me and that you want me around—what woman wouldn't? But that look—gah!" She threw the blanket off and cuddled up to him.

He laughed harder. "Do I make ye nervous, love?"

"Sometimes."

"Am I makin' ye nervous now?"

"Yes."

"But ye love when I look at ye and bein' here with me?" She nodded. "Ye sure do love a lot of things, don't ye?"

"Brady, I…I…" She was at a loss for words and wanted to cry. Even better, she wanted to crawl in a hole and disappear. "I guess I do," she whispered and got out of bed.

"Hey, where ye goin'?"

"Downstairs. I need to find my clothes." She began to cry and had to get out of his sight to pull herself together. *Shit, shit, shit.* She just had to go and ruin everything with her stupid declaration. Why did she have to tell him that she loved him, why?

"Ugh, Jenna you're an idiot," she mumbled and slapped her palm against her forehead as she left the room to go down the stairs.

"I disagree."

She jumped at the sound of his voice. She'd been

so wrapped up in her thoughts she hadn't heard him follow behind her. She found her clothes and her overnight bag and still debated if she should go.

"Ye'r cryin'," he said, and she looked back at him quickly before continuing what she was doing. He looked appalled, and she hated herself for it.

"I'm fine."

"Jenna, please, love. I'm sorry if I hurt ye."

"No, I'm sorry for ruining everything. I told you that I loved you, and you threw it back in my face." She did the best Brady impression she could. "Ye sure do love a lot of things, don't ye." She grimaced. "I think it might be best if I just go before we both say things we might regret."

"Probably." He nodded. "I really am sorry if I hurt ye."

Jenna nodded back after grabbing her bag and headed toward the phone to tear a page from his phone book. She needed a cab, and she wasn't about to wait for one there. "Well, you just did," she whispered, and with that she slammed the door behind her and ran into the night.

"Jenna, wait. Jenna, please—shite, feck."

She stopped when she was far enough away and watched as he banged his head against the doorway as if in frustration and then closed it behind him after going back in again. Would he come after her?

She waited at the end of his parents' driveway and hoped she was out of sight of either house. Thank God she had brought her cell phone. She called for a cab, gave the dispatcher the address, and told them she'd be waiting outside.

The sky looked so beautiful at night. Jenna sat in

the dirt, rested her hands loosely over her knees, and admired the stars. God, it was amazing and so peaceful here. She wished she had a camera. You couldn't get this view in the city where she lived, and you definitely couldn't get the quiet in New York. She sighed, wondering how her life had gotten so screwed up. She missed Jayden, Tyler was gone for good, Sam was going through enough stress of her own, her parents were far away, and she'd gone and screwed things up with Brady.

From the corner of her eye saw Brady's door open and close again. He was fully dressed and headed toward his car. *Damn, where is that taxi?* She leaned farther into the bushes, hoping he wouldn't see her, and watched his tail lights fade as he drove by. She was in the clear to come out of hiding, and it didn't take long before her taxi finally pulled up, but now what should she do?

***

No one seemed to have noticed that she'd camped out in her hotel room for the last two days. Brady hadn't called, and Sam didn't stop by until the third morning.

"Jenna, open up. It's Sam," she called while banging on her door. Jenna felt like groaning as she opened it, and did when she was greeted with, "You look like shit."

"How very flattering, Sam," she snapped and slammed the door after her friend walked in. "Why thank you for the comment, and if you must know, I feel like shit. So I think I'm entitled to look like it too, considering I've been here for two days and nobody's cared to notice."

"Two days?"

Jenna nodded and was about to break down again. God, she hadn't cried this much since the night they'd decided to take this trip, and it didn't feel very good.

"I'm sorry, Jenna. I just assumed you were with Brady. I only realized you were here because Brady asked how you were when he came to pick up Caleb to head to the pub."

As soon as Sam mentioned Brady, Jenna started bawling like a blubbering idiot. "And what did you say?" She sniffed away the snot that was trying to leak from her nose and wiped her eyes.

"Nothing. What could I say? I told him I hadn't seen you in a few days and thought you were with him. He looked like he felt guilty, and then I knew something was up. I'm sorry, Jenna. Do you want to talk about it?"

"No," she said, then changed her mind. "Yes. I finally opened up, Sam, and he threw it back in my face. We were great together, and I screwed it up."

"Aw, Jenna, it can't be that bad, hun. Tell me about it."

"We spent the evening at his parents' and had a lovely time. Anyway, they asked me about Tyler, and I got choked up for a minute, so I excused myself and then had a wonderful heart-to-heart with his mother when she followed me. We went back to his place after our visit, and he was genuinely concerned about me, fearing that his mother might have upset me, and then, I don't know, I acted on impulse. While making love I told him I loved him, and he couldn't return the sentiment. Instead, he tried to ignore it and then made a comment that I seemed to love a lot of things. I'm such a dummy; I wasn't thinking."

"Oh, Jenna, I know that must have been hard for you, and I'm sorry it didn't turn out as you'd hoped."

Now that is an understatement. "It never does, Sam, it never does."

"Would it make you feel better to hear some good news?"

Jenna managed a small smile. "Good news, of course."

"Well, it was a false alarm," Sam announced, beaming with happiness. "I swear I've never been so happy to have a period in my whole life. And Caleb, that sweet fool, he proposed anyway."

"Oh, Sam, that's wonderful. Wait. What?" Jenna did a double take. "He proposed?"

"Yes, and I'm a fool too, for accepting. Oh, Jenna, I love him, and when he asked, I couldn't help but accept. Just because we're engaged doesn't mean we have to rush the wedding, right? He's going to go back home with me for a bit, and then maybe we'll come back and settle here."

Jenna began to cry again and couldn't help but feel selfish. She wanted to say, "Great, now not only am I not lovable, but I'm about to lose my best friend too." Instead she said what she knew she should've been thinking. "That's great, Sam. I'm so happy for you."

"Aw, come on, Jenna, it's time to socialize

among the living again. So wipe those tears, go get a shower, doll yourself up, and get ready."

"Ready for what?"

"We're going out, silly. I have some celebrating to do, and you, my dear friend, look like you could use a drink."

Jenna dried her eyes, washed her face, and went to grab a shower. An hour later, she actually looked presentable for the first time in two days. She had her hair done up, a bit of makeup on, and had even agreed to wear the black halter top and slim-fitting hip-hugger jeans Sam had picked out.

"See, now you're beautiful." Her friend pushed her toward the mirror for one more look at herself.

Jenna rolled her eyes and laughed without humor. Her dark hair was loose, the layers accentuating her heart-shaped face. Her full lips were pouty, and her green eyes were glossy from the crying she'd done earlier. Thank God they weren't as puffy as they once had been. Now that she was ready, she actually looked forward to going out.

"Bring on the alcohol. I can use it."

"I'll bet." Sam ushered her out of the hotel room. "Tonight is for celebrating good times, my engagement, of course, and to you not wasting away in that room. Lord knows you've done enough of that."

"To not wasting away," Jenna seconded.

Sam seemed to be on a mission and there was no stopping her.

***

"Whelan's, Sam?" Jenna hissed. "You did this on purpose. You know Brady's in there and I haven't seen him in days. Hell, he probably doesn't even want to see me. Otherwise I would have heard from him by now."

"Nonsense, Jenna, let's go." Sam tried pulling her forward, but Jenna wouldn't budge.

"No way," she argued. "And I'm not impressed, by the way. I thought we were supposed to be celebrating."

"We are. Why would I want to celebrate anywhere but where my fiancé is? Come on. It's busy in there; you may not even see him." Jenna still didn't move. "Okay, fine. I can see it's time for some tough love. Here it is. I'm going in, Jenna, with or without you. So you can stand out here and pout, or you can come in and celebrate with me."

Still not moving an inch, she watched Sam carefully, thinking about what she'd said.

"Okay, here I go." Sam walked forward, then stopped again and turned to look over her shoulder. "You're my best friend, Jenna, and you're ruining this for me. Please?"

"Fine!" Jenna snapped and walked ahead of her. Whether Brady wanted her there or not, she was there for Sam and Caleb tonight. So let the good times roll. The place was packed, and at least she had comfort in that.

"I need a drink," Jenna shouted over the band and didn't wait for Sam to answer before heading straight to the bar. After drowning in a few shots and grabbing a bottle of beer to go, she realized Sam was gone. Jenna moved around the pub looking for her but found Brady instead.

He stood about five feet away by the stage and didn't seem to have noticed her yet from where she stood, so she admired the graceful way he mingled with the others in the bar.

"Careful, love, he gets that all the time."

Huh, what the hell? Jenna turned around and recognized the older woman from the first time she came to Whelan's. She'd brought Sam and Jenna their complimentary drinks that night. "I'm not sure what you mean."

The old lady laughed and gave her a knowing look. "Ye'r lookin' at Brady, aren't ye? He's quite the catch, ye know. I'm not even sure why he bothers with this place. The boy probably doesn't have to work a day in his life. His family, they're well off, but he's probably here for the women."

She rambled on, surprising Jenna. "If I were a few years younger…" She let her sentence trail off and gave a cat call, which made Jenna laugh and instantly like the woman. "But ye have to get in line," she continued. "There are a lot of locals that have been tryin' to snag him for years."

She shrugged and Jenna blushed. The idea of a bunch of other women doing anything to Brady made her want to jump out of her skin.

"My name is Jenna. It's a pleasure to meet you." She extended her hand, liking the spunk in this sweet older woman.

"I'm Molly, love," she said, taking it. "It's nice to meet ye too."

Before they could finish the interesting conversation, Brady climbed onstage. "Can I get yer attention? I've got an announcement to make, so shut yer holes."

There were a few snickers, but everyone quieted down, and he held up a drink. "So tonight I found out somethin' pretty special. My best friend and brother Caleb has decided to settle down. Ye all know Caleb, don't ye?" There were cat calls and whistles, and Jenna laughed when Caleb and Sam climbed onstage to join him, so she moved closer. "Well, turns out that this woman has finally tamed the beast." Brady roared, pointing his bottle of beer toward Sam. "And they're gettin' married, so please join me in their celebration as we all offer our congratulations to the happy couple." He raised his bottle, downed the rest of its contents, and looked out into the audience as Sam and Caleb sealed the announcement with a kiss.

Their eyes locked as soon as he saw her and held as he made his way off the stage. For a moment, everybody else in the room disappeared, leaving only the two of them.

But that fantasy came to a screeching halt when Brady got sidetracked by a voluptuous redhead, who began to rub her large breasts up against him. He broke eye contact with Jenna, and Red was on him like a bitch in heat.

At the sight of her Jenna stopped walking, but unfortunately she was close enough to be within hearing range.

"Brady, I missed ye today," Red said in an annoying squeak. "I never did get a chance to thank ye for the other night." Before he could answer, she kissed him. A full, openmouthed, sloppy, spit-swap type of kiss.

Jenna dropped her beer in shock, and Brady turned at the sound of the shattering glass.

"Jenna." He reached out to grab her, but she backed away.

"No." She turned to look for a place to run.

"Jenna, wait, love."

He pushed the redhead away to chase after her. The exit was in the other direction, and Brady was catching up, so she ran into the ladies' room.

Damn. She knew she couldn't wait in there all night and tried to figure out a way to get past him unnoticed. Just as she hoped he wouldn't follow her, she heard him.

"Everybody out. This jacks will be outta service until I say so."

"Well, where we supposed to piss, then?" One of the waiting women muttered crossly.

"Go use the other, there's no line in there." After a few protests, and angry words he managed to get everyone out and locked the door to ensure privacy. She was trapped now with no other choice but to listen to him.

"I'm not leavin' 'til we talk," he warned as he looked under each stall to find her. "Please, Jenna, ye can at least let me explain."

"So explain," she snapped.

"Jenna, I'm sorry."

He must have been standing on a closed toilet seat, because she spotted him leaning over the wall between her stall and the one next to it. She sat on the closed toilet with a ball of tissue in her hand to wipe her eyes, and to make matters worse, she knew she looked awful. Her eyes were sure to be red-rimmed and puffy. Plus, how attractive was a runny nose? After grabbing more toilet paper for her face, she stormed out of the stall.

"Oh, save it! If you were sorry or if you even cared, you would have come to see me instead of avoiding me like I had something contagious. Geez, Brady, I told you I loved you, and you threw it back in my face. I felt ridiculous afterward, and you let me leave. It's been two days, and you've already got someone new, for the love of God." She laughed humorlessly at her stupidity.

"I don't," he said, and she couldn't believe her ears.

In her most annoying nasal voice, she mocked the voluptuous redhead. "Brady, I missed ye today. I never did get a chance to thank ye for the other night."

"Nothin' happened, Jenna."

They were interrupted by a knock on the door, and Brady cursed as if he knew no other words.

"Don't ye start using that type of language with me," Molly snapped. "I don't care what yer doin' or who ye got in there, but it's time to get out. Ye hear?" She banged again. "I'm not gonna stop. There are ladies out here that need to use the jacks. Now get."

"Feck," he snarled, and slung Jenna over his shoulder before she could utter another word, or even better, escape. He unlocked the door with her screaming in protest. "Ye'r not getting' outta my sight 'til we talk this through, so get used to it, love. Ye'r gonna hear me out if it kills me."

"Brady, let me down!" She thrashed, but his grip was too strong.

Molly and a few other women laughed as they went by, only making Jenna's anger worsen. Everyone was staring as he moved through the bar, and when they exited, she was fuming. He tried to put her down gently, but he stumbled as she pushed him away.

"Okay, now that you've caused a scene, what do you have to say?" she snapped.

"I said nothin' happened, didn't I?"

"What a load of crap. Nothing happened. It didn't seem that way to Miss Big Boobs in there, and that nasty kiss was nothing? How would you like to see me kissing someone else like that?"

He ignored that question. "Look, she was in the bar the other night and had a bit too much to drink. She and a friend were hittin' on me and Caleb, and we gave 'em a ride home. That's all it was, nothin'. We didn't even go inside with 'em. Honest. Come on, love, it's been hell without ye. I was plannin' on seein' ye tonight. I swear it."

He tried to pull her into his arms to kiss her, but she turned away. "Brady, please, your lips were just kissing another woman."

"No, she kissed me," he corrected. "I love ye, Jenna, and I've been a fool for not tellin' ye sooner. From the first moment I seen ye, I fell, darlin'. I've been goin' crazy since the night ye left me. I can't get ye outta my head, and I swear to ye that I was comin' to beg ye for forgiveness. What do ye say?" He got down on both knees before gathering her closer. He wrapped his arms around her waist and pressed his face into her stomach.

She couldn't take any more and followed what was in her heart as she stroked his hair. "Brady," she whispered, glossy-eyed. He loved her, and when he looked up in response, she finally kissed him.

Chapter Eight

"So have you thought about what we're going to do when I leave?"

They'd been too eager to make it to Brady's bedroom once they got in and had just finished making love right there on the living room floor. They sat in front of the fireplace wrapped up in nothing but the decorative blanket he used to drape over the sofa.

"Nah, I don't like to think of it."

She nodded and cuddled closer. "Come with me," she whispered. She had to take a chance; it was the perfect solution.

"Stay."

She rolled her eyes. *If only it were that simple.* She had obligations to go back to. "I'm not asking for anything permanent, Brady. I guess I was just hoping you'd think about coming with me so I could get things settled at home. Prepare Jayden for whatever may come of this." She paused and looked up at him. "So tell me at least this much: if I did say yes to returning eventually, where would Jayden and I stay?" She knew his probable answer and hoped he'd say with him, but then again he hadn't exactly made the offer.

He brushed his lips against the side of her throat and trailed kisses along her jawline and then up to her lips. "With me," he said, smiling like an eager child on Christmas Morning. "We could make this work, Jenna. There's an extra room for Jayden, and ye could register him for school."

"And you're prepared for an instant family? Things may get worse before they get better; I have no idea how Jayden's going to react. I was a mess before I came here, and now I'm going back with a lot for him to deal with. There's you and now a potential move."

"So 'tis a no then?" He looked disappointed, hurt even, and she could tell he was prepared to argue.

"It's not a no, Brady. I just want you to be aware of the possibilities. Jayden will come around eventually, and who knows, maybe he'll be okay with it from the start." She smiled at him and then sighed because the answer should have been obvious. "My answer is yes, but first you have to agree to come back with me, just long enough for me to sell the house and make arrangements. Not to mention, it may make things easier for Jayden to meet you first, and then there's my parents."

"Parents?"

"Yes, parents. Now that I've met yours, I think it's only fair that you meet mine." She shrugged and studied his reaction, but his was nothing like hers had been when he'd first told her about meeting his parents. He was so calm and collected.

"So in order for ye to eventually stay, I have to go back with ye for a little while to meet Jayden and face yer parents. Is that right?"

She nodded, thinking the terms were fair.

"And if I don't agree?" he teased. "Then what?"

"Then I'll have to say no."

Okay, enough of this, she wanted his answer. She caressed his torso with her palm and moved herself beneath the blanket. She gripped his shaft, which was already thick and ready for action, smiled, and began to pump it up and down. "So if you don't want me," she whispered, "then just say no." She leaned down and replaced her hand with her mouth, and he moaned with appreciation.

"Jenna, oh, love, take it all. Take it all!" he shouted, and in just a few minutes she worked him to a climax.

"Christ, love, that was—ye'r amazin'."

"I'm glad you enjoyed it." She giggled. "But you still haven't given me your answer. So will you come back with me temporarily?"

He nodded. "Aye, Jenna, we'll have it yer way. I'll go back with ye."

"You do love me," she teased.

"I do."

***

Her nightmares started that night, and she couldn't figure out why. Her time in Ireland had been incredible, and she'd accomplished what she'd set out to do. She'd managed to find the woman she used to be as well as a happiness with Brady she never thought she'd find again.

The horrible dreams started out with flashbacks—vivid glimpses of her life with Tyler from the time they met until the day before their accident. She experienced the happiness she'd felt, and the love they'd once shared. Then it seemed as if someone hit the Fast-Forward button.

Bright lights were coming straight for her. She fell back hard, and everything went black. She was floating, light and carefree. When her eyes adjusted, she stood in the rain, drenched. Her car was there, and she could see Tyler within reach.

"Tyler," she screamed, needing to warn him somehow, but she couldn't move and something was coming. Oh God.

Screeching tires echoed, the car door opened before the truck collided with it and threw the body left inside like a rag doll.

"Tyler, No."

***

"Jenna? Jenna, love, wake up."

She gasped for breath and went wide-eyed before she began to cry as she clung to Brady for dear life.

"Shh, it's okay, love. I've got ye, ye'r safe," he soothed and held her close to make her feel better.

***

The sunlight beaming through a crack in the

curtain landed right on Jenna's face. "Ugh," she groaned and opened her eyes. After being awakened from her nightmare, she had taken a long time to fall asleep again. "What time is it?"

She was alone.

"Brady?" Jenna got up and headed downstairs. When she didn't find him in the house, she checked out in the yard, but he wasn't there either, and now she'd run out places to search. Knowing he couldn't have gone far, she decided to enjoy the beautiful day while she waited for him to return.

She curled up in an oversized wicker glider and admired her surroundings. The day was beautiful, the sun was shining, and the slight breeze flowing in from the north made the yard smell like wildflowers. It was heaven, but last night was one hell of a night, and she was moving forward. Brady was now her future, but that dream had felt so real it scared the crap out of her.

"Jenna."

She was so absorbed in her thoughts that she hadn't noticed Brady approach.

"Are ye all right, love?"

"I'm fine. Actually, I was wondering where you were, and it was such a lovely day, I waited out here," she ended with a shrug.

"Aye. Have ye been up long? I should have left ye a note or somethin', but we sure made my ma's day."

"We made your mother's day?" she repeated. "So then you were at your parents'. I wish I had known; I would have joined you."

"Sorry, love. Next time, I promise." He laughed.

"I told ye I had to start planning, remember? Well, I took care of it this mornin'. I went over there so I wouldn't wake ye, but I also figured my parents should know why I won't be around for a while."

"So they're happy, huh?" She smiled. She liked his parents, and it meant a lot that they approved.

"Oh yeah, she's plannin' the party as we speak. Callin' my sisters and the rest of the family to gloat that I'm finally settlin' down. She loves ye, Jenna, but be prepared for when we return. She's plannin' a large family gatherin' to introduce ye to the lot of 'em."

She gasped in shock and tried to tell herself it was too early to feel nervous.

"It won't be that bad, Jenna. I honestly think it's just because everyone's in disbelief. She feels like she's got som'thin' to prove." He shrugged.

Jenna giggled. "I'm a very lucky girl."

Brady moved closer and brushed his lips against hers. "I'm the lucky one, love, so what do you say we press our luck a bit more?"

She screeched with laughter as he threw her over his shoulder again and rushed her over the threshold, upstairs, and into the bedroom.

***

She was in a black room, sitting with a bowl of popcorn, waiting for a movie to begin. Only it wasn't a movie; it was Jayden on screen.

He lay quietly in his bed, waiting patiently for his favorite story. She gasped when instead of her telling it, she saw a bloody Tyler standing next to his bed.

Jayden looked scared and called for her, but she couldn't answer or reach him. Tyler started telling the tale, and when he was finished, he leaned down to give Jayden his nightly kiss. As he stood up again, Jayden began to cry.

"I want Mommy," he whimpered.

Tyler sat next to him. "Mommy's not here, Jayden."

"Is she coming back?" he whispered.

Tyler shook his head. "You can't come back when you're dead," he said and looked right at her with a smile. It was terrifying.

Tyler stood up and walked out of the screen to stand in front of her. He placed a hand on her shoulder and said, "We need to look at this."

The images on the screen changed to her memories with Brady. Starting at the very beginning, there was their first glimpse of each other at the airport, every date they'd gone on, the few arguments they'd had, and every time they'd made love.

She looked up at Tyler, overwhelmed with grief at the state he was in.

"You've moved on," he whispered.

She began to cry. "I'm sorry," she finally managed to whisper.

Tyler smiled. "I'm happy for you," he said, but then blood started to gush from his mouth. "But what does it mean for the two of us, Jenna?"

She didn't know what to say. Why was he torturing her? He was gone. Didn't he want her to be happy again?

He leaned in to kiss her, and she gasped in horror. There was so much blood. She tried to move away, but she wasn't fast enough. She gagged and tried to push him off, and as she frantically tried to wipe the blood off her, he screamed, "What happened to me, Jenna? What did you do?"

Jenna sat up, shaking and dripping with sweat. That action alone woke Brady and he was there for her in an instant.

"Shh, it's okay, love. I've got you."

The dream had been worse than the others, and she felt as though she was about to hyperventilate. She'd begun sobbing as soon as Brady put his arms around her.

"What's wrong, love? Talk to me."

That was the million dollar question she'd been trying to answer herself. What was wrong with her, and where were these dreams coming from? As embarrassed and upset as she had been after the previous nightmare, she hadn't been able to give an explanation then, and she knew she needed to now.

"I'm sorry about last night. I freaked out a little, and you're probably thinking, 'Oh great, I picked a crazy one.'" Teasing him took the edge off.

"No, not crazy, love, but I am curious about the sudden night terrors. What is it that yer dreamin' about?"

She sighed, feeling self-conscious. "It was Tyler; he didn't look very well. He was pretty banged up, and there was a lot of blood gushing out of him. We were in a dark room, and it was like we were watching a replay of everything that's happened between you and me." She tried to smile to reassure him; that hadn't been the bad part of the dream. "When it was done, he said he was happy for me but then asked me what about him. Before I could say anything, he leaned forward to kiss me. I pushed him away and was full of his blood afterward. It was all really disgusting. Then he yelled at me and asked what had happened to him. He asked me what I did to him. I'm sorry, Brady. It was a silly dream, and I shouldn't have gotten so upset, but after it I felt so terrified."

"I can see why ye were so scared." He took her hand in his. "Jenna, I know ye blame yerself, but it wasn't yer fault, love. What happened to Tyler was very tragic, but there was nothin' ye could do. Are ye feelin' guilty about us?"

"I don't think so," she answered honestly. She shouldn't feel guilty, right? Tyler would have wanted her to move on. He would have wanted her to be happy again. Wouldn't he?

"It's all right, love." He pulled her onto his lap and into his embrace. "I love ye, Jenna."

***

Brady

"Make love to me."

"Gladly, darlin'." He chuckled. She didn't need to ask him twice.

"Please, Brady, I need you now," she whispered, looking vulnerable.

He understood so much more after their talk that

97

morning, and he was troubled to know she felt guilty. Was it his fault for loving her? Had the dreams been triggered because of him? He was willing to do anything to keep her from her fear. Especially if that involved making love, because loving Jenna was no chore at all.

Jenna Baker had to be the most beautiful woman he'd ever seen. She was precious to him, and tonight he wanted to show her, wanted her spread before him, glistening and aching for him to have a taste.

He literally swept her off her feet and carried her to the dresser, then set her down on top of it. "Lean back, love," he whispered. He moved his hands up her calves and cupped them behind her knees before spreading her to get where he wanted. "That a girl."

She leaned back on his low dresser and tried to angle herself so she could see everything from the mirror at the other end of the room.

"Ye'r so lovely," he whispered, admiring his view. She glanced between his expression and the mirror, probably to see how she looked. He followed her gaze with a lazy smile. "Now watch how much I love ye. How much I can't get enough of ye," he murmured.

He dropped to his knees and teased her with his tongue, savoring the moment before he treated himself to her unique and addicting taste.

"Yesss," she hissed and arched her hips forward.

He finished kissing and licking each side of her labia. With a long lick down her center, he swirled his tongue and applied pressure when he reached her clit. He repeated the motion over and over again until she shivered with desperate need. Jenna guided him to the right spot with a grunt and held him there, only shouting his name as she came. Her pussy pulsed around his tongue, and he worked her until every last one of her shudders subsided and she was left limp.

"I think I saw stars," she said, and tugged on his arm to make him stand from the floor and up closer to her. "Please, Brady, I need to feel you."

He smiled before kissing her belly and carrying her to the bed. "If ye insist," he teased while laying her down. Her smile lit up as he moved on top of her, and he wanted to look into her eyes as they made love. He wanted to see every expression, hear every noise, and touch and taste every part of her body over and over again. He placed one of her legs over his hip while he held on to the other so he could thrust deep.

"Ye'r so beautiful," he whispered and leaned in for a kiss. "I can't get enough."

She clutched him closer as she broke the kiss. "I love this, Brady. Everything about you. I can't wait to learn more, but right now I want to come again, to pulse around you until your climax hits and you scream my name. I love you, and I want to continue to show you how much every day."

She rolled over to straddle him, taking control. He admired her directness and confidence, and loved that she was a woman who wasn't ashamed to fulfill her needs. Her take-charge attitude was one of the things he loved most about their lovemaking. He watched as she slid her hand down to where they were joined and worked her fingers in slow circles around her nub. Her pace quickened, and she quickly worked herself into her second climax.

He was close, and watching her pleasure herself heightened his own excitement. "I love when ye do that for me, Jenna. Christ, ye'r so sexy."

She was breathless and looked too close to the edge to reply. Her breath hitched, her pace quickened above him, and she bit into her lip as her own climax hit hard.

Her fingers still lingered between them, wet with her juices, and she shocked him further as she flicked her tongue out to taste them. That did it for him. He flexed his hips to match her, making his movements more frantic and primal.

"That's right, love." He thrust harder and was so turned on he could barely contain himself. *Fuck it.* He let go, and his cock jerked inside her. His release mixed with hers, made her soaking wet around him. He smiled with satisfaction.

Yep, he was one lucky guy all right.

Chapter Nine

Jenna

"Are you ready for this?" Jenna asked on the night before they left. She was curious if the thought of meeting Jayden and her parents made him nervous at all. She was looking forward to it.

"I think I am, actually." He seemed so confident when he answered and smiled down at her. "I can't wait to meet Jayden. I just hope he likes me. But I'm mostly lookin' forward to bringin' ye both back here forever." His brow creased for just the slightest second with uncertainty.

"Forever. I like the sound of that, and try not to worry about Jayden. I'm sure he'll come to love you as much as I do."

Forever with Brady. Someone needed to pinch her to make sure she wasn't dreaming. Speaking of which, she hadn't had a nightmare since her last bloody Tyler dream. It was such a relief.

She yawned and snuggled closer to him. "I think you've worn me out." They'd been so busy the last couple of days. Between spending time with his family, making arrangements with his job, and seeing Sam and Caleb off the day before, she was exhausted. Not to mention all of the packing, planning, and lovemaking in between. Okay, the lovemaking didn't count as a chore. That was a huge bonus.

"Bet ye saw stars. I tell ye, love, ye do wonders for my ego." He grinned proudly.

"I'm sure I do." She gave him a sleepy smile. She drifted off in his arms and was still there when she woke up the next morning. She'd set the alarm to go off early, hating the idea of not having enough time to do some last minute errands. Sighing heavily, she slammed the Snooze button to turn off the annoying sound. Didn't people wake up to the radio going off anymore instead of that incessant beeping?

"Brady." She nudged him awake. "It's time to get up, honey, come on." His gorgeous muscular ass was within reach, and she couldn't help herself. She gave it a light tap before getting out of bed. "Very nice."

He groaned and stuck the pillow over his head. "I'm comin', I just need a minute."

She hurried downstairs and was putting the coffee on when a sudden burst of nausea hit. She felt stiff and really sore and couldn't understand why her joints ached so much. Maybe she'd just slept weird or something, but the pain was starting to go beyond her comfort level.

She tried moving her head around to relieve some of the pressure and stretched to loosen up her muscles, and that's how Brady found her.

"Good mornin'."

"Hey," she said, trying to hide her extreme discomfort. "Coffee?"

"Not only a woman who has my heart, but she's one that can read my mind," he teased and placed a hand to his heart. "Coffee sounds wonderful, love." He kissed her forehead and went to sit at the table with yesterday's morning paper. "Mind tellin' me what happened to yer leg?"

"My leg?" Jenna looked at him as though he was crazy, then gasped when she saw that her entire calf down to her ankle was bruised and swollen. "What happened?" She began to panic. "I mean, I don't know." She'd been fine when she'd fallen asleep last night.

"And yer arm. Are ye gonna tell me ye don't know where the scratches came from either? Come on, love, I need ye takin' care of yerself. I'm sure ye left to come here in top shape, and now we're goin' back and ye'r bruised and scratched up. What will yer parents think?"

She gave herself a once-over and couldn't believe her eyes. Injuries were coming out of thin air. One minute she was fine, and the next she was stiff, bruised, scratched, swollen, and so very sore. "Oh my God, I don't know."

The mugs of coffee crashed to the floor as flashes of images blinded her. It looked like her car accident again, but everything was passing by so quickly as it surrounded her.

"Jenna?" A concerned Brady said in the background, and the sound of his voice pulled her away from whatever it was. "Talk to me, love." He wrapped his arms around her and pulled her close.

"I'm fine." She wanted to believe the words, but she didn't know how to explain what was happening. She bit her lip hard to keep from moaning from her discomfort. *What the hell was happening here?*

"Here, let me help ye, ye'r bleedin'." The salty tang of blood hit her lips, and he grabbed a rag to clean her up. She'd obviously been preoccupied in thought this morning, but something weird was happening, and he was trying to fix it.

"I'm sorry about the coffee." She flinched and cried out in pain. Bright light, the light was so bright. She fell to the ground and was blinded by more images. Only this time she felt as though she was actually living them.

The flashlight shone on her face as a strange voice called out to her. "Jenna, Jenna can you hear me?" Her vision was blurry. She could feel herself blink to try to focus and hear herself as she wondered where she was. Her body was warm and felt heavy as she lay there, unable to move. It became dark again, and the voices reappeared.

"We have a woman here, age twenty-seven. She looks awake but is not responding. We'll have to be very careful pulling her out. There is a lot of blood, and I can't tell the extent of her injuries from here." The bright light shone in her face again. "It's gonna be okay, Jenna. We're gonna get you out of here, and I need you to remain as still as possible. Blink if you can hear me."

The image faded and was replaced with Brady's panicked expression.

"What's happenin', Jenna? Ye'r fadin' in and out of consciousness, and ye have a head wound that appeared out of nowhere. I need ye, love, and ye'r scarin' me. Please don't leave me."

She heard sirens, and strange people barged into the kitchen with a gurney. *Wait, when did he call an ambulance?*

Pain, there was so much pain. A sharp, stabbing sensation like hot knives piercing her entire body over and over. "I love you, Brady. Please don't let me go." She reached for him.

She heard sirens, her breath was heavy, and she could barely open her eyes. "I'm slipping. Maybe if I just sleep a little." She was in an ambulance strapped down to a very uncomfortable gurney, but she couldn't fight anymore. Her eyes opened and closed before everything went black as night.

"Jenna, try to stay with us, honey. We're almost there." A soft pressure touched the side of her face. It was cool compared to the fire burning the rest of her. A man close to the same age as she was hovered over where she lay. She tried to laugh, and would've expressed that it was easier said than done, but her mouth just twitched and she became frustrated.

"That a girl," he teased. "This one's a fighter."

The doors of the ambulance flew open, and an entourage of medical personnel waited to wheel her away.

Still holding her hand, the paramedic gave them

the rundown as they ran. She was watching the lights on the ceiling rush past when she finally heard a familiar voice. A voice she thought she'd never hear again, and it made her panic inside.

"Jenna, Jenna, I'm here." He tried to push his way through, and her eyes moved in his direction. She felt the wetness of her tears.

"Tyler?" She could see his face clearly above her. What the hell? "Are you really here?"

Her heart began to race, and she felt really weak as the images faded once more and she was in Brady's arms again. "I'm so sorry," she whispered. "Stay with me, Brady, I don't want to go. Please, just don't leave me."

She was slipping away, and she knew it. But to where? And why?

"Oh, Jenna," he whispered in grief. "Ye'r scarin' me, love. I love ye and I can't lose ye now."

She could feel his lips press against hers and more wetness on her cheeks. Was he crying or was she? "I love you too," she breathed before everything just disappeared and she was back in that blank, peaceful place where she felt light and carefree again.

Chapter Ten

Jenna felt as if she'd turned back time and had become lost. She couldn't feel Tyler near her anymore, she hadn't for a while now, but more importantly, where was Brady? And where was she?

She was floating. The heaviness faded, and she wasn't with her body anymore. There was nothing left but her own thoughts.

So was she dead? She couldn't see, couldn't hear, and couldn't feel anything or anyone around her. She was in an empty place, but she still had this strange feeling of being safe, and she kind of liked it. Content with no emotion, it was amazing and stress-free. There were no worries or sadness wherever she was, but then Jayden came to mind, her parents, Tyler, or at least the memory of him, and Brady. She remembered her love for them all and had to fight. She let go of the tranquility and fought to go toward the light again to see what would happen. Suddenly she could hear again; it was her mother's voice, pleading.

"Jenna, wake up. Please, baby, just wake up. Come back to me."

The closer she drifted toward the sound, the more painful it was. Her body was so stiff and in agony. She could barely move. Her finger twitched, and she could feel someone clutch her hand. She opened her eyes quickly only to close them again.

"Jenna?" Her mother gasped. "Open your eyes, sweetheart."

"Too bright," she managed to whisper and heard a chair beside her squeak.

The lights dimmed. "The hospital. Déjà vu." It felt like she was reliving the beginning when she'd woken up to find out that Tyler had died. "What put me in here this time?"

"There was an accident."

Jenna looked around the room, examining the machinery and tubes sticking out of her. Her mother was crying and trying to speak. Looking up, Jenna tried to smile, but that hurt too much and she grimaced.

"What—what's wrong?" Her mother looked panicked. "Do I need to get someone?"

"It's okay, Mom. Everything is fine. I just need to remember that it hurts to smile. In fact, everything pretty much hurts right now."

"Oh, Jenna, you had me so worried. For a while there it was touch and go, and we weren't sure if you were going to make it."

"And Tyler didn't make it, right?"

She'd already lived through this chapter in her life, and the words had just slipped out. Her mother was silent and stared at her in disbelief.

"Where's Brady? Mom, please, tell me he wasn't with me when whatever happened. Brady's okay, right? I can't lose him too."

This could not be happening a second time. She hadn't done anything bad enough for life to be this cruel to her. But the more Jenna spoke, the more confused her mother looked. She panicked further. "And Jayden?" Her hospital monitor was going crazy.

"You need to relax, honey. Jayden is fine. He's with Dad." Her mother smiled and wiped her face dry. "We'll bring him by shortly to see you, all right?"

"Mrs. Baker, it's nice to see you awake." Her nurse smiled as she entered the room. She checked Jenna's chart and jotted something down before checking the machines. "Hmm," she hummed, looking at Jenna with disapproval. "Mrs. Baker, I understand that in these circumstances emotions can run high, but you have to keep yourself calm." The nurse looked at her mother. "And I'll expect your family to abide by making things as stress-free as possible for you in the meantime." Jenna and her mother nodded in unison. "Okay then, I'll just let the others know you're awake."

Once she was gone, Jenna had to know. "Where's Brady, Mom?"

"Brady?" she repeated. "Jenna, I don't think I know who you're talking about."

"Brady, Mom. The one I met in Ireland, the one who helped me move on. The last thing I remember was just before we were going to come back here." It was all so fuzzy for her now, but she had to jog her memory.

They were both silent, and Jenna patiently waited for answers while her mother opened and closed her mouth a few times as if she didn't know where to start.

The door opened and her dad entered, distracting them. "Jenna," he cried in relief.

This had to have been the first time she could remember ever seeing her father shed tears for anything.

"Hi, Dad," she gasped, and then cried out in discomfort when he hugged her.

"Sorry." He winced and pulled himself away. "It's just so good to see you awake. You're going to be okay." He turned to his wife. "Our little girl's okay," he whispered as if he was finally able to breathe again.

"Aw, Daddy, don't cry," Jenna pleaded. "You're making me cry and everything hurts, including that." She laughed and then groaned loudly in pain just as the door opened again. She smiled then, not caring how much it hurt. "Jayden," she squealed, as much as she could under the circumstances. She'd missed him so much, and it felt like forever since she'd last seen him or had him in her arms.

Her joy turned into a stunned silence when she saw who was with him. It was a living ghost.

Jayden rushed to her side, and out of instinct she extended her arms to hold him close.

"Tyler?" She looked at her mother with wide eyes and then back to Tyler again. "I-I don't understand."

Her husband smiled at her and looked just as

relieved as her father had. He closed the distance between them. "Oh God, Jenna, I thought I'd lost you," he whispered and kissed the top of her head.

"This can't be happening," she cried and began to shake in panic. "Oh my God, I'm dead, right? I mean we all are. We got into the accident together."

The machines in the room blared. Her father rushed out to get help, and by the time he got back she'd become hysterical. Everyone in the room stood there wide-eyed, stunned, and looking at her as though they weren't sure what to do next while poor Jayden cried and looked terrified at the scene in front of him.

"Tyler?" She couldn't believe her eyes.

"Jenna, please," he begged. "I just got you back."

She closed her eyes and could feel his lips on her forehead. "But you were dead," she whispered. "You died, and I was forced to move on without you."

"Jenna, please?"

She nodded and tried her best to calm down, but she just couldn't. "Just tell me one thing," she pleaded. "We're dead, right? We all died that day?"

Her eyes became heavy before she could get her answer, and she couldn't fight it. She heard Tyler yell, "No, please, just give her a minute." But it was too late, and the darkness took her again.

***

She was standing in a beautiful field of wildflowers, a completely open space. The sun was shining in the beautiful blue sky, and it reminded her of Ireland. She could see somebody approaching in the distance and smiled with excitement as soon as she recognized his amazing face.

Filled with joy, she laughed and ran toward him. When they were face-to-face, she smiled and traced her hand down his chest to those beautifully sculptured abs. "Where have you been?"

"I'll always be with ye as long as you let me. I love ye, Jenna."

She smiled blissfully. "And I love you, Brady."

Someone cleared their throat behind her and interrupted their moment. Brady looked up with an annoyed expression before she turned around.

"Tyler!" What was he doing there?

He looked at her quickly, then back toward Brady. "Jenna, what's going on?" he asked without taking his eyes off Brady and directed the next question toward him. "And why are your hands on my wife?"

She was so confused, standing between the two of them, looking back and forth between their two faces. "I don't understand. How can you both be here?"

Tyler smiled and answered with a question of his own. "Is it true, what you said? Do you love him?"

She couldn't look Tyler in the eye when she answered, so she concentrated on Brady and spoke the truth. "I do."

Brady smiled and she turned to Tyler. "But I love you too."

Looking between them again, she could see the

anger in their expressions as she confessed her love for both of them.

"Jenna," Tyler said and reached for her.

"Jenna." Brady held his hand out as well.

She didn't move and wished she could split in two. She hated hurting the people she loved the most in this world, but she didn't know what to do.

"She's my wife, She's coming with me."

Brady narrowed his eyes. "Things change, Tyler. We have a connection that just can't be broken."

Both angry men charged at each other and pushed Jenna out of their way.

She woke up with a start and whimpered in agony. It was night, but she could see Tyler sleeping in a chair beside her bed.

"A dream," she whispered in relief. "It was just a dream."

But nothing felt like reality anymore, and she couldn't sleep. She lay there watching Tyler sleep instead. He looked so peaceful. She stretched her hand out as far as it would go. She had to touch him to make sure she wasn't dreaming again. He felt so real. Could he actually be alive? She wanted him to be. Her husband was actually there with her, physically beside her, and not just ashes in a container. He was warm and soft, with drool coming out the side of his mouth as he slept, and she was in complete awe.

"You're awake," a woman whispered as she entered. "And relatively calmer. That's good."

"I'm quite sore, though." Jenna tried giving her a friendly smile but grimaced instead.

Her nurse laughed. "I can give you a little something for the pain. It should make you feel better." She left and came back with a syringe a minute later.

"Please, I don't want to be knocked out again," Jenna told her. She'd just woken up and hoped to be alert for a while.

"It's okay, Mrs. Baker. It's not quite as strong as that, just something for your discomfort, that's all," the nurse assured her and administered something to one of Jenna's many connecting tubes.

"Thank you."

"Well, my name is Eleanor. If you need anything, just press that button beside you, okay?"

Jenna nodded as Eleanor left and focused on Tyler again. The next time she smiled, it didn't hurt as much.

***

"I don't understand why she was so worked up, and why is she convinced that she's dead?"

"I'm not sure…I think it may be because she thinks that you're dead."

"What?" It went silent for a second. "Who convinced her of that? That's ridiculous…I mean, I was never—although I probably should be after saving myself and not her."

"Oh, Tyler."

Jenna didn't like where the harshly whispered conversation was heading and wondered if she was dreaming again. She opened her eyes to see Tyler and her mother across the room. "Mom?"

They both jumped and exchanged worried looks. "Hi, honey, have you been awake long?" Her mother approached the bed. "We didn't want to disturb you."

She shook her head, not wanting to give away her eavesdropping. "You guys could never disturb me."

Tyler stood on the other side of the room, looking uncomfortable and not sure if he should approach, but who could blame the guy? His wife thought he was a ghost, and the last thing he would want to do would be to upset her.

"Tyler." Jenna extended her hand, wanting him to come closer. "Come here." She needed some alone time with him. "Mom, would you mind giving us a few minutes?"

"Sure, honey."

Jenna waited until the door clicked behind her. "So we're not dead?" she asked with a smile and tried to apologize for her initial behavior. "I'm so sorry, Tyler."

He shook his head and finally approached her. He reached for her hand but pulled back before making contact. It hurt her to see him be so hesitant. "What's the matter?" she asked, because what she'd heard of his conversation with her mother didn't make any sense to her. He blamed himself for her being there, and she couldn't shake his expression of remorse.

"Everything's fine, Jenna." His eyes were glossy, but he forced a smile, and she could tell he was struggling with his emotions.

Jenna narrowed her eyes and tilted her head to

the side, catching him in a lie. "Come here," she urged. He stood directly in front of her but still wasn't within her reach.

"I am here, Jenna."

Sighing in frustration, she pressed her hands down on the mattress to wiggle over, giving him enough room to sit on the bed with her. She winced at how much the movement hurt but was determined to have him closer.

"What are you doing?" he snapped, and it just made her roll her eyes and repeat herself.

"Come here." Tapping the space beside her, she continued, "I've missed you, and so help me God, Tyler, if you don't come here, I'm going to endure a lot of pain when I come and get you."

"You wouldn't," he said but sat beside her just in case.

"Not close enough."

"Geez, Jenna, how close do you want me to be? I'm afraid I might touch something I'm not supposed to, and I don't want to hurt you."

"I'm fine. The nurse gave me something amazing." She lied a little. The medication was starting to wear off, but she didn't care. He was there, and if she had to endure being uncomfortable for a little while, then she'd gladly take the trade-off.

"You woke up before?"

"You were sleeping in the chair beside me, and I held your hand, or at least I tried to. I must have dozed off again." She sighed and felt as though she'd been asleep for too long now.

He looked at her and finally smiled. His spirits

seemed to lift a little bit, so she pushed her luck. "Kiss me."

"Seriously?" He moved his face away as if the thought of it made him nervous and looked at her from head to toe.

"Do I look that awful?" she teased. "Kiss me."

"I don't know, Jenna," he started to argue, but she wouldn't give him the chance. She pressed her hands down again to move forward. If he wasn't coming to her, she was going to him.

"Are you crazy?" he exclaimed and pushed gently on her shoulders to get her to lie back. "You're as stubborn as ever, and I'd like you to heal so that I can actually take you home one of these days."

She laughed. "Yeah, but mission accomplished. You're touching me; is that so bad? Honestly, Tyler, I thought I'd lost you. Is it so terrible that I want a kiss?" She looked away, feeling rejected and self-conscious. She hadn't looked in a mirror and began to wonder if she really did look that terrible after all.

The bed moved a little as he came closer and smiled. "No, it's not half as bad as it was."

"I missed you," she whispered. "And I'm so glad you're here with me." She held his face as he moved closer to feel him against her again. Their lips finally touched, and she began to cry. She thought she'd never be able to do this with him again, and there they were. He pulled away way too soon. "Not done yet," she whispered.

He chuckled and obliged. His tongue outlined her bottom lip for entry. A moan sounded from deep within his throat, fueling her desire to keep kissing him. Tyler, her husband, was actually alive and well, had come back from the dead.

"Oh!" Her mother gasped from the door, and they both laughed at her embarrassment.

"Ouch," Jenna said between giggles. "I think it's time for more pain meds. Can someone get the nurse?"

"Are you all right?" Tyler asked.

Jenna nodded. "But I'll be better once I get a little more of whatever they gave me earlier, though. Can you stay with me for a while?"

"There's nowhere else I'd rather be."

Once the nurse had administered her magic and her mother had been assured that Jenna was doing fine, her mother left them alone for the day.

Drugged and comfortable, Jenna still had a lot of questions. She needed answers, and this was her opportunity to get them from him. "So what happened?"

"Do you remember anything at all?"

"We were on our way to pick up Jayden, and it was raining, right?"

He nodded. "We left early, and it started to rain. I pulled over because we could barely see through the windshield." He smiled, but it looked strained. "You were bored and feeling a little uneasy with the weather." He looked away and cleared his throat.

"Tyler, what happened? I remember that part. I want to know the rest." She needed to know.

"I'm so sorry, Jenna. It all happened so fast. We could hear tires squealing close by, and the headlights came for us fast. It was a delivery truck.

The man swerved out of the way thinking he saw something in the road and didn't see us clearly until it was too late. As soon as I could make out what was happening, I tried to pull you along with me. I managed to get the door open and jump out in time, but the car was crushed. I could see your body fly inside of it. You almost didn't make it." He stood up and started to pace. "If anything had happened to you…I mean if it ever came to that…" He looked away again. "I just don't know if I could live with myself."

"Now who's being ridiculous? You should know better than anyone that I'm too stubborn to die. There's just too much to live for." She smiled, hoping that by teasing him she could get him to smile with her. She hated that he blamed himself. What happened had happened. She was still just so relieved that he wasn't dead.

He sat with her again but stayed silent.

"So is this a bad time to ask more? I mean, what am I dealing with here? How bad am I?"

From what she could see there were a lot of tiny scars and tender spots all over her arms and legs, though her right side was the more damaged. Her lower calf and all foot were bandaged. Tyler watched as she tried to examine herself. She slowly traced her fingers across her face, and it didn't feel that bad. Her lips felt really dry, and the top of her head was tender, but otherwise she didn't feel too many scrapes and bruises there.

"You're beautiful."

"Liar." She smiled, knowing she must have looked awful, but he was still sweet for denying it.

"You have a minor head injury; that's why you're probably still feeling uncomfortable," he said, tracing his finger across the top of her head. "When the truck first made impact, your body flew forward, and you hit your head on the dashboard. A lot of the cuts and bruises were caused by the shattered windshield. The car was pushed from the impact. It zoomed a few feet away before crashing into a streetlamp. When it did, you flew to the backseat again. They wouldn't let me see you. They insisted that I get checked out no matter how many times I told them I was fine."

He cleared his throat, and she could tell he was trying hard not to cry. "When they brought you to the hospital, they rushed you right in. You were far worse off than my worst nightmare. I ran to you as they rushed you down the hallway, and you whispered my name before you passed out." He smiled and then exhaled before looking away again. "You'd lost so much blood, and I could see the glass fragments all over you. While they tried to clean you up, they noticed some unusual discoloration and swelling around your stomach and found out there was some internal bleeding. The lining of your spleen was torn. They rushed you into the ICU and gave you an IV for fluids. You had to wear an oxygen mask, and you had a few blood transfusions. They tried their best, but it wasn't working out, so a couple days later they decided to finally operate to try to repair what they could."

"That sounds like my kind of luck, but what happened to my ankle?"

"You sprained it," he whispered, then sighed. "I

have never been so afraid in my life, Jenna. Things seemed to go well after the operation. Well, the bleeding stopped anyway, but then you got sick. They told me an infection had developed, and they had to keep you out of it until the treatment worked."

"So exactly how long have we been here?" She said "we" knowing he'd been by her side the whole time.

"A little over a month."

"More than a month?" It felt longer, or at least it'd been so much longer when she'd thought Tyler was dead.

It was a lot to take in. She was happy to be alive, of course, and that her husband was alive. She loved him, but she also loved Brady, or thought she did, even though logic told her he couldn't be real. She wanted him to be. All of it had seemed so real at one time. It made a girl wonder, and she began to second-guess herself. Was she a horrible person to be in love with two men at once, knowing that one may be no more than a figment of her drug- and illness-twisted imagination?

Chapter Eleven

"Are you okay?"

She nodded. "It's just all so overwhelming and nothing like I woke up thinking. How is Jayden?"

"I wondered how long it would take before you asked about him," Tyler said with a smile. "He's always been a momma's boy."

"And I love that fact. Let's hope that hasn't changed," she said as her stomach knotted with anxiety. The first time she'd seen him, she'd freaked out. She hadn't seen him since, not that she blamed them for keeping him away, but still, she really missed him.

He gave her hand a reassuring squeeze. "Not a chance. It's been hard on him, but he's a tough little boy, and now that you're doing so well, it'll only get better. He's been with our parents a lot. They take turns watching him, and I've gone to see him whenever I could. The house has been pretty crowded since your parents temporarily moved in, and I can't wait to get you home so things can get back to normal."

"I imagine you've probably spent most of your time here, right?"

Tyler smiled. "I hate when I have to leave, but it gets stressful, and your mom has kicked me out a few times."

"She has?" That shocked her but made her laugh too. "It was probably for your own good."

"Probably. It gave me the opportunity to spend time with Jayden or help out at work. They've got to where they're not as shocked to see me as they were at first. I'm on a leave of absence, but on the odd occasion, Alex would let me help her out. I needed that escape. She's working an interesting case involving a minor in an armed robbery, and I helped her put together some of the defense strategies."

"Sounds interesting, and I bet its killing you that you've been away for so long," she teased, knowing how much Tyler adored being a lawyer. He was a man who loved a challenge and a good argument.

He laughed, but she sensed there was something he wasn't telling her. "Is there anything else?"

"No, why?" His laughter died, his face flushed, and he became serious suddenly. She could tell he was being evasive but didn't have it in her to argue. It was probably something small that he thought would upset her to learn about while she was recovering. She changed the subject. "So this Alex is a woman, huh? I don't think I've met her. Is she new?"

"Not really."

Maybe teasing him would take the edge off whatever he wasn't saying. "So then she's pretty.

Should I be worried?"

"That's ridiculous, Jenna, for you to even ask that," he snapped. "I mean I can't believe that you would."

Her being in the hospital for so long had to have been stressful on everyone and it was beginning to show in Tyler. She was still annoyed, though. They used to be able to tease each other. What was the problem?

"No need to get so worked up. Geez, Tyler, lighten up."

She watched as he studied her and felt the bed shift as he came closer. "I'm sorry, Jenna. Everything's just been so hard, and I guess I just needed to vent a little." He sighed, running his hands through his hair. "Okay, so she's pretty, but she's nothing compared to you."

"I must be so appealing right now, huh?"

"Very." He leaned in for a kiss. "I can't wait to get you home. I'll be able to properly show you how pretty you are then."

"Now that's appealing." Going home was something she looked forward to. "I need to see Jayden," she whispered. She could feel the lump in her throat and couldn't help the tears. She was still worried about her little boy.

Tyler nodded and wiped the tears from her face. "That's a good idea. He misses you just as much."

When her mother walked in, Jenna asked, "Mom? Where's Jayden?" She pictured him running in with excitement.

"He'll be up in a minute. He suckered your dad in when they passed by the gift shop. Now let's hope they don't buy the whole store."

Jenna smiled but was impatient for his arrival. She hadn't even had the chance to hug him the last time she'd seen him.

"He's coming, Jenna, have patience." Tyler smiled and laughed when she childishly stuck out her tongue.

When he came in, Jayden hid behind a large bouquet of flowers but remained by his grandfather's side. Jenna's smile soon turned into a look of concern. "Jayden?" She reached out to him, trying not to show how much his reaction hurt.

He didn't move.

Tyler got up and spoke to her parents. "I know you just got here, but could you give us a few minutes?"

"Sure, we'll go grab a coffee," her father said.

He lifted Jayden into his arms and walked to Jenna's bed. "Jayden, don't you want to see Mommy?"

His little head bobbed, and he peeked at Jenna from behind the flowers before hiding his face again.

"It's okay, honey. Are you feeling afraid?" Jenna asked.

He nodded and finally looked at her. "Mommy, are you going to die?"

"No, Jayden, I'm not going anywhere. Why would you think that?"

"Because last time you said you were dead."

She laughed humorlessly at her stupidity. "I did, and I'm sorry. Mommy was overwhelmed and a little afraid at the time, but I was never dead,

Jayden, and I shouldn't have said so." She felt terrible. What kind of mother put her child through so much trauma? It was unspeakable. "I missed you."

"I missed you too, Mommy." Jayden leaped into her arms and cuddled close, and the flowers he held were in her face, but she didn't mind. "When are you coming home?"

"Soon, baby, I promise." She took the flowers he offered and put them next to her bed. "Thank you, they're beautiful, and I feel so much better already, especially having you here with me. I love you, Monkey." She had to make it up to him and was now determined more than ever to go home.

Her father poked his head in the doorway to make sure the coast was clear. "Did we come at a bad time?"

"Perfect timing, come on in." Tyler got up to socialize across the room with her parents, giving Jenna and Jayden some much-needed bonding time. Visiting hours came to an end way too soon, and nobody but Jenna thought it was good that Jayden stay with her through the night. She couldn't help but be selfish, though.

Jayden cried and clung to her. "No, I want to stay with Mommy."

She needed to reassure him before he left, but her mother acted too fast and tried to take him away. "Give me a minute," Jenna snapped. "Everyone out, please, I need a few minutes with my son, and I would appreciate the privacy."

Ignoring their protests, she concentrated on calming him. "Jayden, I need you to know that

Mommy isn't going anywhere. Do you understand? I need you to know that you can come see me anytime now that I'm feeling better, and I need you to understand that I'm going to be coming home soon. So I don't want you to be afraid, because there is no reason to be. I'll be there as soon as I can. Okay?"

"But why can't I stay?" he whined, and it made her laugh.

"Because it's almost bedtime, and Grandma needs you to stay with her right now. She loves when she visits you, and she knows I'll be coming home soon. When that happens, Grandma and Poppa will be going back to Cornwall."

"But it's not the same when Grandma puts me to bed. She doesn't tell me any good stories, and when she tries she never says them right."

She laughed again and tried to picture it. "Okay, my tired boy, I will tell you your bedtime story tonight if you promise me that you're going to be brave for me. After the story, you'll have to go back with Grandma for the night, and I'll see you in the morning. So remember the faster you go to sleep, the faster we'll see each other again. Okay?"

He nodded.

She stuck to one of his favorite stories and sighed when it worked because it didn't take long for Jayden to fall asleep beside her.

Tyler walked in on an already sleeping boy. "Are you ready to part with him until tomorrow?"

She nodded. "I don't think he'll be putting up much of a fight anymore."

"I'm not surprised." Tyler chuckled. "It was

quite a day, and he always felt safest with you."

"Momma's boy," she whispered with more confidence than earlier. She just had to make up for scaring him so badly. She watched as her Tyler picked up their son and left.

Tyler chuckled when he returned a few minutes later. "I was impressed, by the way," he said. "I don't think I've ever seen your mother speechless before."

"It wasn't my intention to upset her." The last thing she needed was more guilt. "It's just that Jayden has a fear of losing me, and I needed a few more minutes to calm him down."

"I understand why you did it, Jenna, and you don't' have to justify yourself. I honestly thought your mother would've known better than to try to come between you and your son. Hell, I even know better than that."

She laughed at his teasing tone. "What can I say? He's the love of my life."

"Well, I hope that I'm still on that list," he said while walking toward the bed and sitting down.

She cradled his face to bring him closer. "Of course," she whispered, and her heart raced as she brushed her mouth against his. His lips were full, delectable, and waiting for her to taste. Her lips moved and re-explored the lips she never thought she'd touch again. Their tongues caressed in perfect synchronization, and his erection pressed against her side, aching for release. She pulled away. It had been way too long without Tyler's touch, but unfortunately for them both now just wasn't the time for anything more.

It wasn't until two weeks later that Jenna happily saw the hospital fading in the background as they drove away. She was on her way home, and there was no sweeter feeling than to be free again. She missed her life.

Chapter Twelve

"It's good to be home." she whispered before taking a deep, relieved breath as she stepped out of the car. The day was beautiful and so was the view. The ride from the hospital seemed to take forever. Although she appreciated Tyler's thoughtfulness, he drove like an eighty-year-old woman after church on Sunday. In any other circumstance, she probably would have laughed or gotten frustrated with him. Instead, she was touched.

Home—she was finally home, admiring Tyler with Jayden in his arms. The sight of their faces lit up with excitement made her smile. It felt like a dream; too good to be true. She took in her surroundings as if seeing them for the first time. Her square, average-sized, brown-brick home had never looked better, and she jumped when Tyler wrapped his arms around her.

"Whatchya thinking about?" His lips were close to her ear, and his hot breath felt like a caress to her whole body, making her go weak in the knees.

"Hmm, I'm thinking that it feels like a whole

new beginning, that I'm so glad to be home, and I was admiring you with our son." She laughed, looking around. "Where is our little monkey?"

"He ran off." Tyler shrugged. "It's so good to have you back, Jenna."

His eyes turned glossy and she couldn't stop her need to comfort him. Leaning forward, caressed the side of his face and embraced him. The need to feel his lips against her own was overwhelming. "I love you," she whispered, breathless. Tyler was still alive, she was actually home with Tyler, and it still wowed her.

"Geez, Tyler, she's been home all of two minutes and already you're hogging her."

Jenna chuckled happily at the sound of her best friend's voice. "It's great to see you, Sam." She turned to see Sam holding Jayden's hand and her parents standing behind them, waiting patiently for her and Tyler to go inside.

"Damn straight," her husband remarked. "And I'm not sure that I want to share." He pulled Jenna toward him, winked playfully, and kissed her good before letting go.

"Later." She winked back and laughed as he swatted her butt.

"That's a promise. Welcome home, Jenna."

She was coddled, loved, and completely pampered the entire day. It wasn't surprising, but it was tiring. She'd been in the hospital for too long, and it was time to fend for herself and take care of her family as she had before. One day wasn't going to kill her, though, so she bit her tongue and spent some quality time with her favorite people.

"It's great to see you, Sam. I missed you at the hospital."

Sam looked guilty. "I went to see you once. It was after your surgery, and you looked awful." Jenna laughed and Sam smiled apologetically. "Sorry, I didn't mean it like that. It's just…I couldn't handle it. There were complications, and you looked so lifeless. I should have been there, but I couldn't. I got updates about you, but I just preferred to remember you full of life. Can you forgive me?"

"There is nothing to forgive." Jenna knew Sam cared and could understand. Had their roles been reversed, she might have preferred not to have haunting memories of a lifeless Sam. She looked around to make sure the coast was clear. "Um, can you join me on the porch? I have some questions, and I'd prefer if we could keep them between us."

"S-sure what's up?" She followed Jenna out.

Fall was approaching; the nights were beginning to get cool, and she shivered. Jenna needed to get to the point. She was confused and searching for some kind of rational explanation for how she had "dreamed up" Brady and all that time in Ireland in such believable detail.

"When you were in Ireland did you happen to go to Dublin?" It was a stupid question, of course Sam had, but she was nervous and had to break the ice somehow.

Sam nodded, looking confused.

"The pictures you brought back, I know I saw them, but what were those places? Where they, by chance, pictures of St. Stephen's Green, Merrion

Square, Saint Patrick's Cathedral, or the Four Courts, to name a few?" These were places she'd seen, or at least thought she had, and she needed to know if she'd pictured them subconsciously because she'd already seen them in photographs. "Please, Sam."

"Some of them are," Sam answered, looking puzzled.

Jenna nodded and felt so frustrated that she wanted to cry. Ireland was a place she'd always dreamed of visiting. At least that part made sense. Her familiarity with the country was the result of Sam's experiences mixed with her daydreams of one day visiting. That had to be the explanation, partly at least.

"Sam, did you ever visit a place called Whelan's? It's a pretty popular pub, I think."

"I've heard of it, but no. I was too busy, and besides, I'm not one to go out by myself. I'd feel kind of silly. Why are you asking me this?"

She didn't answer and continued. "Did you happen to meet anyone named Brady or Caleb while visiting, whose picture I might have seen? Both are tall and extremely handsome."

"Hmm, I wish I had. It would have definitely made the trip more interesting, but I'm not really sure if I could handle two men at one time." She winked and smiled. "Why the sudden curiosity about Ireland and the handsome Brady and Caleb?"

The front door opened, distracting Jenna from her disappointing conversation.

"Dad and I are leaving now." Her mother looked out the door.

"All right, Mom, thank you for coming today."

"What's going on here?" She glanced between Jenna and Sam.

"I was just asking Jenna the same thing," Sam said. "I'm calling it a night too." She stretched and forced a yawn. "You and I need to talk soon," she whispered as she hugged Jenna. "And then maybe you can explain this conversation."

"Thanks, Sam."

Several hugs and kisses later, Jenna and her two favorite men were finally alone in the house.

"Okay, Jayden are you ready?" Tyler asked while swinging him up into his arms.

"Ready?" he repeated.

"Yes, Monkey, it's time for a bath, then bed."

"Aw, no fair," he whined, and Jenna bit her lip to keep from laughing.

"That's tough, little man. We've all had a long day, and your mamma needs her rest." Tyler looked adoringly toward his wife and son and helped Jayden up the stairs for the nightly ritual of bath, bedtime story, tucking him in, and a kiss good night.

***

"He's finally asleep," she announced, joining Tyler in the living room again. Jayden had been abnormally hyper throughout the day, and putting him to bed took longer than usual.

"That's a miracle. I thought he'd never sleep." He moved over on the couch to make space so she could sit beside him. "How are you feeling?"

Tyler still looked worried, and she knew he wouldn't take any chances with her recovery. "I'm fine; you can stop asking. I promise to let you know if I'm not." She plopped on the couch and snuggled as close to him as possible. "And if you promise to be gentle with me, I was hoping we could catch up a little."

"Are you serious?" He moaned. "It's been way too long without you, and there is nothing more I would rather be doing right now. It's all I think about. Hell, I've even dreamed about it."

Tyler shifted uncomfortably in his seat and tried adjusting himself to get more comfortable. He was definitely sporting a chubby, and she leaped at the chance to have him inside her again, so she was on top of him in no time. When she covered her mouth with his, he immediately responded. Their tongues wrestled and played with each other, and she moaned in desperation while wrapping her arms around his lean, muscular shoulders to deepen the kiss as far as they could. She had to touch him. She trailed her hands down his torso. She was on fire for him and had to feel him in her hands. She wanted him in her mouth, and then she wanted him inside as deep as he could go. She stroked his straining cock several times and lifted her hips to feel the friction against her.

"Easy now, Jenna. Any more of this and it'll finish before it starts." He was breathing hard and spoke through a clenched jaw to control himself.

"Now we wouldn't want that."

He growled his impatience, scooped her up, and carried her to the privacy of their bedroom.

"Tyler, wait." She was breathless, and self-consciousness swept through her as he undressed her. Her body wasn't the same since the accident. She was thinner from the horrible hospital food and being in a coma. She had scars from her surgery, and she was still tender in other spots, even though she didn't look half as bad as when she'd first come to.

"What is it, Jenna?"

She blushed and felt a little silly all of a sudden. Since when had she ever been shy with him? The answer was never. "I'm different now," she whispered. "With the scars, it's probably not going to be very pretty to look at."

He didn't answer. Instead he continued to undress her until she stood before him completely nude. "Come with me." He moved her in front of a long mirror and lifted her chin so she was forced to look at herself. "You're beautiful, Jenna."

His lips were close to her ear, and his breath was warm and soothing. It gave her a chill as she leaned into him. "I'm glad you think so."

"You're trim." He continued trailing his hands from her hips up to cup her breasts. "And perky, perfect. God, Jenna, your breasts are just right the way they lay in my hands." He tested their weight in each as he fondled them, stroking his thumbs across her hardened peaks.

"Tyler, don't stop." Breathless, and weak in the knees, she leaned into his embrace while he teased and tweaked her nipples. She reached back to stroke him, but he moved to stand in front of her instead. Starting with her feet, he gazed up her entire body with lust. Once he reached her eyes again, he said, "The scars are still healing and barely noticeable. You've been through hell, and you're still so damn sexy."

Before she knew it, the back of her legs hit the side of their bed, and he was lowering her onto it. He slid down her slick body, teasing her with his tongue until it finally hit her sweet spot, and she arched her hips forward with a moan.

"Yes, Tyler, yes." She tightened her hands in his hair with a demand to make her come. She took a shuddering breath and let the sensation that Tyler created ride through her. She knew it wouldn't take her long to achieve her ecstasy. His mouth was magnificent as he licked solid strokes and swirled his tongue around her hard nub. "That's it."

She moaned again and thrashed her head from side to side. She was so close. Her grip on him tightened and forced him to stay in the right spot. She thrust her hips repeatedly and watched as he devoured her. As she screamed his name, the climax hit her hard, but before the pulsing vibration of it finished, his pants were down and his cock thrust deep inside her. He was exactly where she needed him to be as they were finally one again.

He gave her a sexy smile and began to pump at a leisurely pace. "You're so beautiful."

"Love me, Tyler," she whispered. "Fuck me. We'll make love later over and over, but right now I need to feel you passionately." She pressed her chest against his and rolled her hips to meet his thrusts at a faster pace. His cock filled her fully and was warm and slick with her juices. It was such a good kind of full.

"Oh, God, Jenna," he moaned. "I can't hold it any longer. I'm gonna come, baby."

She reached between where they were joined to finger her clit. She felt no shame when taking her own pleasure, knowing the sight of it drove Tyler over the edge.

He impaled her all the way to the root of him, shuddering while his release filled her.

Her second climax hit and her eyes rolled back in her head. She kept them closed until her last shudder finally eased, and when she slowly opened them again, it was to get a glimpse of Brady. *What?*

The vision of him startled her, but it also added more excitement. She had them both for an instant. Sweating and breathless, she covered her face as her heart rate slowed. "That was amazing." And that was the complete and utter truth.

Later that night she tried hard not to overthink it. It wasn't cheating. It was just a little imagination, right? Everyone had a highlight reel, and she couldn't wait until the next time to see if it would happen again.

Chapter Thirteen

"Man that was good." Tyler collapsed on the bed beside her. After round three of their lovemaking session, fatigue had begun to overtake them.

"It always has been good, Tyler. What makes it better now, I think, is that we know how it feels to think that we'd lost one another. We have a better understanding of how much love is here, and we appreciate each other that much more."

"I couldn't have said it better." He smiled and caressed the side of her face. "But I'm curious. You said you knew how it felt to think that you'd lost me. You were so sure in the hospital that you even assumed we were all dead when you saw me. It's a scary thought, and I was wondering why. What had you so convinced?"

She didn't know how she could explain herself without sounding crazy. Hell, the whole situation seemed crazy to her. She didn't really want to talk about it, ever, so she just blurted out the first thing that came to mind. "I'm not sure I can explain it to you properly. The mind can be a pretty powerful force sometimes."

Okay, that was stupid, but she never did that great while under pressure. "I honestly don't know, Tyler. When I woke up to see my mother waiting beside me, it was like a déjà vu, like I'd lived it before. The first time I thought I woke up, she told me about the accident and said that you didn't make it." She looked up to see his reaction. "Don't you see? I was convinced you were dead, convinced I'd lived miserably for over a year afterward, but then I woke up in a hospital room with my mother, and a man I thought was dead walked in. It was a cruel illusion, a dream, and I'm not sure why I had it. Am I making any sense? Because, if I am, you might want to explain it to me, please? I'm still so confused."

He laughed, as though he was trying to make light of her explanation. Hugging her tighter, he said, "You're a smart woman, Jenna, so I've never had any doubt that you have a powerful mind, but I don't think I could explain it for you. It'd be nice to have an explanation, though. No matter how confusing it may be."

He was obviously trying to make her feel better by saying that, although she knew none of it made any sense. There were so many unanswered questions, building her curiosity, especially concerning Brady. Tyler was alive, so she should just let all thoughts of Brady go, but she felt she still had some kind of unexplainable connection to him. Yes, Tyler was back, but where the hell had Brady come from? She just couldn't believe she could have made him up. It was almost as if he was out there somewhere; she could feel it. Or thought she did. What frightened her the most was not knowing. If she sought out the answers, discovered Brady was real and found him, what would she do? She was a married woman, and she still loved her husband despite loving Brady as well. Did that make her a bad person?

Tyler was quiet, allowing her time to deal with her private thoughts. Thinking he'd fallen asleep, Jenna got comfortable, hoping sleep would take her along with him now that she was well ravished and fatigued.

"So you lived miserably for over a year, huh?"

She jumped at his unexpected comment. "It's not funny," she mumbled. He was in a teasing mood. She could feel the slight vibration of his quiet laughter.

"You're right, it's not. I'm sorry."

"Good night, Tyler," she whispered lazily, hoping he'd take the hint. "I love you."

She was in a white room, stumbling through a maze. Curiosity consumed her with every step.

At the end, she discovered a large red door. The knob turned by itself and the door opened, but she couldn't see what was on the other side. The image was fuzzy, and the floor beneath her started to move, startling her.

She leaped through the door and found that she was no longer in her pajamas but wearing a formfitting dress and holding a basket full of goodies. She was standing in the main lobby of Tyler's law firm.

Ah, one of our special lunches, *she thought. She liked where this was headed. They never did get around to eating very much, unless it was something on their bodies, and they did make good use out of Tyler's desk. She loved his private quarters at work.*

The main office was empty. She looked at the calendar where a Saturday was circled boldly in red. It would explain the emptiness. Slowly making her way into his private office, she found he wasn't alone.

"Jenna?" he called out in shock. Pulling away from his desk, he rushed to her side.

Ignoring him, she looked across the room and concentrated on his friend instead.

Sitting on the edge of his desk was a beautiful woman with long legs and flowing blonde hair.

Who was she?

Narrowing her eyes, Jenna looked at Tyler. "Did I come at a bad time?"

"Don't be silly, Jenna," Tyler said, raking a hand through his hair. He stepped in front of her to block her view.

The woman approached and placed one hand on his shoulder. Pressing herself against him, she said, "I hope you don't mind sharing him."

Jenna's mouth dropped open, and then she became angry. If this woman knew what was good for her, she'd better get out of Jenna's sight. Jenna was ready to punch the smug look off her pretty little face.

Deep, throaty, feminine laughter filled the room as the leggy blonde escorted Tyler back toward his desk. Jenna lunged forward in anger, but she was blocked by something that felt like a thick sheet of glass. What the hell? *On top of her anger, she had to be subjected to cruelty now as well? A clear barrier stood between them, and Jenna couldn't get through it. It was a sick, twisted joke at her expense. Trapped in a transparent box, she couldn't move.*

Standing there like an angry idiot, she watched as her husband had sex with someone else on top of his desk. That was their desk, damn it. How could he do this to her?

They zoomed away all of a sudden, and she was back in the white room, but this time it wasn't a maze. It was just clear and bright.

"I'm sorry ye had to see that, love," Brady whispered, taking her hand.

She gasped upon hearing the familiar voice and started to cry, realizing how much she'd longed to be near him again. "What are you doing here?"

Brady laughed and kissed the top of her head. "I always will be with ye, love, as long as ye let me."

"But why is this happening? Am I going crazy?"

Brady laughed again and brushed a strand of hair out of her face. After gazing deeply into her eyes, he pulled her closer to him. "No, Jenna, ye'r not goin' crazy, love. This is just a glimpse of what's meant to be."

She sat up in bed, still feeling angry and betrayed, but most of all even more confused. Her heart raced rapidly and mild panic set in.

Brady had come back, but it was just a dream. Maybe she really was crazy? Good God.

It was just a dream, she quietly recited as her heart rate slowed. She was alone, the bed empty beside her, and she plopped back down to her pillows with a thump while trying to will herself to calm down.

Tyler wasn't dumb enough to cheat on her, was he?

***

"Good morning, sleepyhead." Sitting at the kitchen table, Tyler was way too chipper. "Have you been up long?"

"Not really." Coffee was all she needed. Maybe if she had a good fix of caffeine, her uneasiness would go away. The crazy, stupid dream had her all worked up.

"Good, you looked so comfortable I wanted to let you sleep in."

That shocked her a little. "Really? I looked comfortable to you?"

"Weren't you?"

And just like that, Jenna went from being surprised to touched. "Thanks, Tyler, it was sweet of you to think of me." She leaned forward to give him a quick peck. "I just had a bad dream, that's all. It's not a big deal."

"I hope it wasn't about me again," he said as he stood.

"It was, actually." Jenna was on the defensive despite her best efforts, and her anger couldn't help but come out as she thought about him with that other woman. *See? It's crazy, right?*

Tyler wrapped his arms around her and kissed the top of her head while he whispered an apology. "You don't have to talk about it, Jenna. I just hope I wasn't dead this time."

She stiffened and pulled away. Narrowing her eyes, she called him a smartass before going to join Jayden to watch his morning cartoons.

"It's nice to have you back." Tyler chuckled. "I missed that temper of yours and all."

***

That afternoon they sat in the park, watching Jayden play from a short distance away. While he was busy on the playset, Jenna and Tyler enjoyed a leisurely afternoon hand in hand.

"So I'm assuming that you're probably going back to work shortly." Although she loved having him home, she could tell Tyler itched to get back into the swing of things. She was curious as to how much time she would have left with him. Tyler's job was demanding, her days were lonely, and he was exhausted at night after working long hours during the day.

"I see my going back to work isn't a happy subject."

"It's not like that. It's just with the long hours I miss this, the quality time. I understand they're a part of the job. I just wish it wasn't so often. I miss you."

"I know, I feel the same way, but I'll be with you for the rest of this week, and on Monday I'll see what I can do about not working so late. It might be

145

hard to do, depending on how much I need to catch up on, but I'll still try. Who knows? Everything considered, maybe they'll all take it easy on me and I'll be able to start coming home for dinner every now and again."

"Says the man that works way too hard and loves it." She laughed, having the suspicion that more often than not, Tyler worked the late hours voluntarily. He loved being a lawyer and got swept up in paperwork, going through files, putting together case after case, and whatever else lawyers did in their offices and the courtroom.

"But here's to wishful thinking." He raised his hand and mocked a cheer in her direction.

She sighed before smiling. "It never hurts to dream, does it? What can I say? I love you, and I married a man who is passionate about what he does."

"I love you too."

After the three of them shared a picnic lunch, Jayden was off to play again. There were constant interruptions from friends with well-wishes for her recovery, to Tyler's obvious surprise.

"Wow, I never realized how many people you knew," he said.

"I do have a good social circle, don't I? Most of them are from Jayden's playgroup and the park; some are neighbors. He's fabulous at making friends."

"Really?" He feigned shock.

"Oh, shut up." She laughed, really enjoying these moments with him, but it also made her think about how much she missed this too. Their time together would be very different when he returned to work, and she dreaded spending the next week without him.

Her dream came to mind then, a replay of Brady's last words *"This is just a glimpse of what's meant to be."* An image of Tyler and the leggy blonde came back to her, making her grimace. She just couldn't let it go for some reason.

"Are you all right?" He looked worried.

"I'm fine."

He gave her a skeptical look. "Okay, I think we've had enough for today. I'll get Jayden, and we'll go home."

"Wait, let's just give him a couple more minutes." He looked at her with disapproval, clearly ready to argue. "I'm fine, Tyler, and a few more minutes isn't going to hurt anyone. Just look at him. He's having so much fun. Do you really want to pull him away? It's been hard on him too, so let's let him enjoy his time here a little while longer."

He sighed in defeat.

"I'm fine," she repeated, then changed the subject to the question that had been bothering her. "Speaking of work, do you happen to know of any gorgeous young lawyers with great legs and beautiful, long, blonde hair?" She tried to act casual while reminding herself it had been no more than a silly dream.

"What?"

"You heard me; now can I get an answer? Young, blonde, great legs," she repeated, going through the basics. She might have some competition out there she never knew about.

"Should I? No, Jenna, I don't believe there are any lawyers at work that fit that description. Why?"

"Clients?" She felt nauseous.

"Nope, but now you have me curious. If it makes you feel better, I could ask around."

She swatted at him playfully, and they both laughed. The whole thing was ridiculous, really, and it felt good to laugh at what an idiot she was being. She felt better already.

"Should I ask why there is a sudden interest in gorgeous blondes?"

She felt like a dummy for bringing it up. *Stupid dream.* Shaking her head, she could feel her cheeks heat in embarrassment, especially after finding out that no one at Tyler's office matched the woman's description.

Tyler laughed again. "You know, now that I think about it, I do know of one blonde. I'm not sure how long her hair is, though. She's always got it tied up tightly. She's pretty, but I wouldn't say gorgeous. She wears thick glasses that aren't very attractive."

He shrugged indifferently while Jenna narrowed her eyes. The flush in her face burned now, her blood pressure rose, and her pulse throbbed. He was watching Jayden and didn't notice her reaction as she asked, "Who?"

With a smile he looked her way. "Alex, why?"

Okay, it was more than nausea in the pit of her stomach. *Alex, oh my God.* Tyler had gotten so worked up when she'd teased him about her in the hospital, but Jenna had let that go. Could something have been going on between them, or was she jumping to the wrong conclusion over a silly dream?

"Jenna, are you okay?"

Oh God, it was definitely more than nausea. She got up as fast as she could and ran straight for the garbage can. She barely made it there before she lost her lunch.

Chapter Fourteen

Jayden really didn't want to leave, but Tyler wasn't taking no for an answer. He seemed determined to get Jenna home, and between Jayden's tantrum and Tyler's frustration, people were staring.

"That's enough." Embarrassed, Jenna had to raise her voice to be heard. She took a deep breath and turned to address Jayden first. "Mom's not feeling very well, so I need to go home and lie down. Is that okay with you?"

"But I don't want to leave."

"This is ridiculous, Jenna. We need to take you home." She could tell Tyler's frustration was mounting because he was afraid that she might have been physically overwhelmed. He was determined to have her rest, but she wasn't going to abide by his "this is how it's going to be" attitude, either.

"Tyler, I understand your concern. Jayden, go on and play for now." She placed her hand over Tyler's mouth to keep him quiet while Jayden ran toward the play structure again. "Now, this is what I

150

suggest. I'm going to go home, but before I do, I'm going to walk over there and give Jayden a timeline. That way he won't give you any trouble when it actually is time for him to leave."

"Jenna," Tyler whined, and it made her laugh.

"You know, you and Jayden sound so much alike." She mocked them both whining to prove her point. "Honestly, I'm okay. I really just need to go home now and brush my teeth. That's all. I'll try to rest if it makes you feel better, and if you want to keep an eye on me that badly, I could be back in five minutes." Considering their home was only a few blocks away from the park it was doable.

"You have to be the most stubborn woman alive. Won't you ever let me take care of you?"

"You do every day," she said. "That's why you put in all those long hours at work."

"That's not what I mean, Jenna, and you know it."

She laughed. "I'm a big girl, and I'd like you to start believing me when I tell you that I'm okay, because I am."

He rolled his eyes and pulled her into his arms. "I'd kiss you, but the idea is not very appealing right now."

She smiled. "So should I tell him another hour?"

"Fine, he has another hour but not a minute longer."

* * *

Nothing was more disgusting than the aftertaste of vomit in your mouth, and being minty-fresh again felt good. Tyler expected her to relax, but she didn't feel like it. Her alone time gave her the opportunity to think about things, such as how worked up she'd become. So what if Alex was blonde? Tyler wouldn't cheat. He just wasn't that type of guy. They'd been together since college, and she'd known him years before that. Not to mention that she wasn't that type of woman, either, the one who always worried about stupid things she had no way of controlling. She wasn't insecure and certainly had never been one to second-guess herself—or Tyler, for that matter—and she didn't want to start now.

She thought about the dream over and over and came to realize that what bothered her most was not the dream itself but what Brady had said in the dream. If she believed it, either Tyler would end up dead or with someone else. They were doomed to fail either way, which was crazy.

She had to get Brady out of her head for her own good. The decision was final. Being in love with someone she had no sane reason to believe even existed couldn't be good for anyone. Brady was not good for her anymore. The choice was obvious. Tyler was real and in front of her, a part of her life. She could touch him and love him. Most importantly, he was safe and what she knew to be real. Maybe she'd gone temporarily insane.

***

"Hmm, something smells good." Tyler stood behind her and inhaled deeply.

She smiled with him being so near. "Where's Jayden?"

"Bathroom," he whispered by her ear and stuck out his tongue to draw her lobe to his mouth, then nibbled. "I told him to wash up before dinner."

"That's good. We have a couple of minutes, then." She hopped on the counter, pulled him by the shirt into her embrace, and glided her hands down his arms to his waist and then to his finely muscled behind. Her kiss was an eager tongue lashing against his.

She could see Jayden coming down the stairs and regretfully pulled away from the embrace. "Later," she whispered, and Tyler groaned.

Dinner and quality time with Jayden flew by. After the nightly routine of bath and then story time, Jayden was out like a light, which made their "later" come quick enough.

"He's sleeping," she announced proudly as she sauntered into the living room again.

"Wow, that was fast."

"Yeah, well, going to the park has its perks. The little guy was exhausted." Not only was she able to put Jayden to bed, she was also able to change into something more appealing.

He eyed her robe curiously. "Are you tired tonight? It's only eight thirty."

"Not really." She smiled. "But it is *later*, and I was hoping you'd come to bed."

"Bed at eight thirty?" He smiled with her, and it grew wider when she discarded her robe. She'd chosen to delight his senses with a red lace garter and stockings. The heels she'd selected gave her a good four-inch height difference, and the fact that she wasn't wearing a bra or panties only heightened the excitement.

Tyler swept her off her feet and into the bedroom, where he placed her gently on the bed, then walked to the nightstand. He turned on the CD player, and she giggled as he swayed to the beat of Marvin Gaye's "Let's Get It On." Once clothes were out of the way, he grabbed her thighs to pull her closer. He leaned forward and placed his lips on her stomach, then trailed soft kisses downward. Jenna moaned, unashamed with want. She thrust her hips upward and groaned with his teasing movements.

"I want you to tell me," he whispered. "Tell me what you want me to do to you."

She bit her bottom lip. He hadn't asked her to be so bold in quite a while, and it reminded her of the time Brady had asked her to do the same.

"Tell me what ye want me to do to ye, love. Let me hear what ye need." She could hear him as if he were right beside her.

"You, I need to have you inside of me." She was *desperate and aching for him.*

He smiled and eagerly rolled the condom on before he lifted her up to be on top. "Ye can control everythin' this way, and I still have easy access to all yer best parts." He cupped her breasts and *watched as she slowly rose up and down to get used to him while he filled her. She wanted to take her time. It felt too good to rush, and he was big. Gradually she picked up her pace, and she was finally able to take him to the root. He moaned, looking strained, as though he was fighting hard to hold back. He let go of one breast and trailed his hand down her stomach to where they were joined. She was so hot and wet, and incredible greedy for anything he was willing to share with her, so she leaned back a little to give him better access.*

"Come for me, Jenna. I'm so close, darlin'. Come for me."

She hissed an appreciative sound and moaned, riding him harder.

"Stop teasing me." She grabbed Tyler's head and placed him between her legs, exactly where she wanted him to be. "I want your face between my thighs while your talented, wet tongue does its magic on me. I don't want you to stop until I scream your name with my release. Now get busy."

His breath teased her as he chuckled against her heated core, and her groan soon turned into moaning when his tongue began to swirl her into ecstasy.

A few breathless hours later they were finally both sated.

"Wow." Tyler whispered, and Jenna's smile widened because she felt the same way.

She felt so good, she was almost afraid to think about Brady. She had been trying so hard to forget him and to concentrate on her life with Tyler. But, strange things were happening, especially in the dreams that kept coming back to her. Her husband was safe, and the type of connection she'd imagined with Brady only existed in fairy tales. She cuddled up to Tyler and drifted off into a restless night, only to awaken early the next morning. She felt a little more at peace as she watched the sunrise from the front porch with coffee in hand.

"I wondered where you were," Tyler said as he joined her. "What are you doing out here?"

"I watched the sunrise." She stretched before getting up from the porch swing. "I'd better go make Jayden some breakfast."

"Already taken care of. The cereal is in his bowl, and he's settled into watching his morning shows."

"I am really going to miss having you home." She smiled and wished they had more time before it really got hectic.

"So what's on the agenda for today?"

"School started a few days ago, and we need get Jayden registered." She pouted. "You won't be the only one leaving me on Monday."

Tyler chuckled all the way back into the house, but first he held her hand and led the way back in. Just as he'd said, Jayden was sitting comfortably in front of the television, eating his cereal. They stood at the entry admiring him for a few minutes.

"Kindergarten already. Where did the time go?" Tyler murmured.

"Well, we could always have more."

They'd never really discussed having another child before. Deep down Jenna knew Tyler had been afraid to because of what had happened with Jayden's fast home delivery. Speechless, he looked at her in shock.

"Well, we don't have to decide right this second," she assured him. "It's just an option we could think about sometime in the future, unless you've already decided you're satisfied with only Jayden." She examined his expression closely and hated to think that his mind was closed to the idea.

"I've never really thought about it before," he admitted. "Why don't we wait and see? If it happens, it happens, and if it doesn't"—He shrugged.—"then at least we'll have fun trying."

***

Their week together had flown by. On Sunday night Jayden was sleeping, and Jenna had just finished appreciating Tyler some more. She'd enjoyed their time together, and it was drawing to a close now that he was scheduled to be back at work in the morning. They were lying in bed now, and she moved to close the distance between them, cuddling close.

"So what are you going to do with yourself while we're both gone?" he asked.

"I honestly don't have a clue, but I'm sure I'll figure something out. Maybe I can get a part-time job." Now that was a scary thought; she hadn't worked since she'd become pregnant with Jayden. "Are you still opposed to the office lunches we used to have?" She raised a brow, challenging him to answer her boldness.

The truth was she'd loved their wilder days, and his desk at work did create exciting memories. Just the thought of being caught had sent her adrenaline blazing.

"I'm not sure. I'll figure out how hectic things

are going to be, and I'll definitely get back to you."
He lowered his head to give her a quick peck. She
smiled sleepily and had to at least give him points
for his honesty. Tyler had put a stop to their lunches
a couple years earlier. He claimed he'd gotten
busier and expressed his concern about
appropriateness. What Jenna thought was exciting,
Tyler seemed to think too risky, and she'd let it go.

The next morning Tyler was gone before Jayden
woke her up. Jenna found a note by the
coffeemaker.

Jenna,

I'm thinking about you already, so
don't make any plans. It's my first day
back, but I've already decided not to
overdo things today.

I love you,

XOXO

Tyler

The note had been the highlight of her day. Later
that morning Jayden was officially a student at
Oakdale Academy. Dropping him off at school had
been emotional. She sobbed the whole way back.
Her baby was growing up, and it was hard to come
to terms with. She hadn't had free time in so long
that she didn't know what she was going to do with
herself. But the prospect of another child was
something to look forward to.

Twenty minutes later the doorbell sounded, and

she was pleasantly surprised to see Tyler standing there through the window.

"Hello, beautiful."

Her jaw dropped as he lifted her in his arms. "What are you doing here? It's your first day back."

"I left you a note to expect me, didn't I? I talked them into taking it easy on me this week." He laughed. "I actually lied a little, telling them I was still worried about you. I've made arrangements to go to work in the morning and have my afternoons with you."

"Wow." She was shocked speechless. Tyler loved his job; he didn't often surprise her like that. He just wasn't a spur-of-the-moment type of guy.

"No, Jenna, not yet." He moved toward the stairs. Once secure in the confines of their bedroom, he said, "'Wow' usually comes after we do this."

His kiss was passionate as he kicked the door shut. That afternoon was not about taking his time with her. It was filled with hardness, lust, and a whole lot of raw pleasure and need.

Chapter Fifteen

The honeymoon phase didn't last very long. As Jenna had suspected, Tyler became absorbed in his work. Soon, it was back to the "barely ever seeing him again" routine that really sucked. Jayden adored school, and she absorbed as much time with him as possible while he was home to fill the void.

She'd just dropped Jayden off when Sam knocked. "Hey, stranger, how about that much-needed talk?" she said when Jenna opened the door.

Jenna hadn't seen Sam since the day she'd come home from the hospital. The truth was, she was almost afraid to after her strange questions, knowing Sam would want an explanation of the conversation they'd had that day. Jenna didn't think she could give one that wouldn't make Sam think she was crazy. God knew she wasn't too sure she wasn't. Jenna nodded reluctantly and followed Sam into her living room.

"I've been waiting to speak with you," Sam said as she joined her on the couch. "Now, do you mind telling me why you're giving me the cold shoulder?"

"I'm sorry."

"Well, did I do something wrong? First you ask me all of these weird questions, while making me promise to keep them to myself, and now you're avoiding me like I have an incurable and contagious disease. So enlighten me, please, and tell me what the hell is up with you?"

She started to cry. "You're going to think I'm crazy. Those questions I asked are the reason I've been so horrible." Jenna had truly thought she'd gone insane for a while and was terrified someone else would too, especially the people she cared about. But now Sam was here, she might as well get it over with. "I've been having some really strange dreams since the accident, and they're scaring me a little."

"Dreams?" She laughed. "And here I thought you were avoiding me because I did something wrong. This is actually about nothing more than some weird dreams that are freaking you out?"

"I know, Sam. I told you it was crazy. They started when I was in a coma, but the weird thing is that they seem so real. In the hospital I was convinced Tyler was dead, because I could swear I'd lived over a year without him. After I'd struggled to cope with his loss, you forced me to go on this trip to Ireland with you to find myself again. You just wouldn't give up pushing me to move on. When we were there we met people." She took a deep breath. "Caleb and Brady, and long story short, I fell in love again. He was amazing. It was like gravity didn't exist when I was with him. This unknown magnetic force seemed to pull the two of us together, and I had no control. When he touched me, or looked at me, or when we made love, a spark ignited, and I've never had that before. We were perfect for each other."

She laughed at herself. "Honestly, he wasn't the type of guy I'd ever thought of falling for. He was gorgeous, of course, but also quite experienced with women, never settling down with one for too long. Normally that would be a major turnoff, but there was just something about him that made me feel like we were meant to be together. It's hard to explain it properly."

Sam finally smiled. "Incredible. So are you trying to tell me that you're in love with this man you've dreamed about since the accident?"

Jenna nodded and felt foolish. She worried Sam might suggest having her committed. "I asked you those questions because I was trying to make sense of it all. I needed to find some reason for what I dreamed. I swear it was so real to me that when Tyler walked into the hospital room when I woke up, I freaked out. I was so convinced he was dead that I thought I'd died too. Poor Jayden was devastated. It took me a while to convince him I was going to be okay after that. To think I actually put my child through that kind of anguish tears me up inside. It was so horrible that he now has a fear of losing me."

"Jenna, I'm not sure what to say to make you feel better, but I'm here for you. Have you talked to anyone else about this?"

"Like I said earlier, they'd probably think I've

gone loco," she whispered. "It's been a couple weeks since I've had one of those dreams. All of them seem to doom Tyler and me, no matter what. I love Tyler and hate to think I'm going to lose him, Sam. He's my husband, the father of my child, and I can't picture life without him in it."

"Was he dead again?"

"No." Jenna grimaced to suppress a groan. Tyler had immediately asked her the same thing as soon as she mentioned her unpleasant dream. "He cheated on me with some gorgeous blonde at his office. I stood there and watched while it happened. The weirdest part was that Brady came back to me afterward. He said that I was seeing these things because they were meant to be. They feel so real too, and it scares me because if they are, that means Tyler either ends up dead or with someone else. I'm so confused, and I can't understand what's going on." She tried to smile with false bravado. "I'll say it again. I think I've gone bat-shit crazy over here. I have a great husband whom I love and adore, who's been one of my best friends for as long as I can remember, and here I am also in love with this other person I've only seen in my dreams. Someone I'm not even sure exists."

"So now we just have to figure things out," Sam said. "Maybe they're not just dreams. Think about it. Maybe they're possible futures, like a second sight."

"What? No way."

Sam seemed to be excited by the possibility while the thought gave Jenna the willies.

"Come on, Jenna, have you ever had dreams

before that came true? I knew someone who had premonitions once. It was absolutely amazing. Are there any strange coincidences in the dreams you're having?"

She nodded. "Brady is in all of them." Thinking about it, she added, "And Tyler does work with this one pretty blonde. In fact, he seems to get defensive whenever I ask about her, like he's hiding something." But how could she test this theory? A lightbulb in her mind clicked on. "Maybe I'm just overreacting, but I think I may be able to test your idea. You were a big part of my dream, if it actually was what you think. We went to Ireland together, after all."

Jenna smiled with eagerness. Sam's guess was all she had to go by at the moment, and it was worth a shot. "Tell me something. Does the name Antonio mean anything to you?"

Sam went still, and all of the color faded from her face.

"In my dream you told me about a man named Antonio. He was your husband, and you met in Italy. Your visa expired, and long story short, he came here to be with you, but he got really sick and died not long after you married him."

Sam started to cry. "Close," she whispered, "but not quite. I've never been married, but he was my first love, and he did leave me."

"I'm sorry. It must still be hard for you."

"Not so much anymore," she admitted and wiped her face. "What's freaking me out is that you knew his name. I haven't talked about him in years, and I'm pretty sure I've never mentioned him to you before."

Jenna smiled. "Do you think—" Sam nodded in agreement before she could even finish. "Oh, great," Jenna cried. "So now I have an uncertain future that guarantees, love, loss, and unpredictability. Only I can see these things before they actually happen."

"Premonitions are forewarnings of something that may happen before it actually does, without having any concrete evidence to back it up. The future is not set in stone, Jenna, and the possibilities could easily change at any time. Try not to panic and we'll see how it all plays out."

***

At ten o'clock, Jenna was bored out of her mind, and Tyler still wasn't home. He'd called earlier and told her he was still swamped at work and not to wait up. She sighed heavily and grabbed a book before getting comfortable for the night.

She was standing in an open space she didn't recognize and turned around in a circle to figure out where she was. She could see a small cottage ahead and went to investigate.

She opened the wooden door and sensed someone was close by. It was a cozy little place with only one bedroom and a lit fireplace in the center of the far wall. Freshly cut flowers filled little vases set around the whole place and left an enchanting aroma. She was barefoot and moved her toes on the soft surface beneath them. A tiny trail of rose petals led to the small room ahead of her.

"Hello?" she called out, but there was no answer. Moving forward, she followed the trail and opened the door to what she assumed was the bedroom. "Hello?"

The door shut behind her, and she startled when she heard him chuckle. His arms wrapped around her, and he moved her hair from her nape so that she could feel his lips marking her there.

"I missed ye, Jenna. Ye'r fighting it, love, and I really wish ye wouldn't."

She started to cry and turned around to face him. "Then what do you suggest? I'm a married woman, Brady, and I'm not even sure you're real anymore."

He laughed quietly and pulled her forward so they were breast to chest. "I am real," he said and took her hand. "And we will eventually meet."

Before she could respond, he kissed her eagerly. Her heartbeat picked up, and the butterflies returned to her stomach and wanted to jump up to her throat while he moved her toward the bed. She gave in to his every need. Because damn it, it felt so right and she missed him like crazy.

When they'd finished making love, her eyes widened as the sheet over her stomach swelled into a large bump. "What's happening?" she asked, freaking out while he just looked at her with a smile.

"Oh my God!" Jenna squeaked and jumped out of bed to take a closer look in the mirror.

Brady followed and placed his hands on her huge belly.

"Ye'r pregnant, me love." He continued to rub

at the huge bump that hadn't been there a minute ago.

"Impossible," she mumbled in astonishment, but then she laughed in joy while putting her hands on top of his.

"I know how much ye wanted this."

"Ah," Jenna cried in agony and hunched over. Sharp and unbelievably painful cramps twisted through her. "What's going on?" she cried. "Ah, please make it stop!"

"I'm sorry love, I had no idea." Brady said in sorrow.

A lot of blood gushed out from between her legs, and she continued to cry out in agony while Brady held her close. "I'm so sorry," he whispered again, and she felt herself weaken before the blackness took her away.

Jenna sat up quickly in a cold sweat and began to cry.

"Sorry, I didn't mean to scare you."

Tyler was finally home, and she leaped into the safety of his arms.

"Are you all right?"

She nodded. "I guess I just missed you." She trembled in his arms, but Tyler didn't push her to reveal more. The dreams were so bittersweet, and she still wasn't sure what to make of them.

The remainder of the night was long. She'd been restless and afraid to fall back asleep. So she settled on watching Tyler sleep peacefully instead and slipped out before he woke up.

"Good morning." Her husband reached across

her for the coffeepot when he joined her in the kitchen. "You look tired. Maybe you should try to get a little more sleep before Jayden wakes up."

She rolled her eyes. "Thanks," she whispered sarcastically. "I just love when people say that. Telling someone they look tired is just a polite way of telling them that they look like shit."

Tyler made a funny face and they both laughed. Okay, she would've been the first to admit she was testy after the sleep she'd had, or lack thereof.

"Don't be silly. You look beautiful," he whispered next to her ear. He placed a kiss on her cheek and sighed before stepping away.

"Sure, I do." She rolled her eyes. "But I love you that much more for saying so."

A few hours later, Jenna had just returned from dropping Jayden off at school when she saw Sam walking toward the house. Giving up on the idea of a nap, she smiled and waved. It was nice talking to Sam again and an even bigger relief to talk to someone about the weirdness that her life had become.

"Hey, neighbor. Okay, what's the matter? You look horrible."

Jenna laughed as she led her inside. Leave it to Sam to tell it like it is. "I didn't get much sleep. I had another dream, and I was afraid they'd keep coming. But it's nothing a lot of coffee won't cure."

"Or more sleep," Sam grumbled. "You need to take care of yourself better than this."

Jenna smiled and plopped heavily onto the couch. "Yes, Mom."

Sam walked away with a roll of her eyes before

calling back, "I'll get the coffee. You need to get comfortable."

Jenna must have been more tired than she suspected because that was the last thing she remembered of that visit. It felt like minutes, instead of hours, before she woke just in time to get Jayden from school.

Chapter Sixteen

"Hello, Ms. Baker, what can I do for you today?" her doctor asked.

She'd just arrived at the clinic because she'd been feeling under the weather for the last couple days and couldn't take it any longer. "I'm nauseated and throwing up. I also have heartburn all the time and terrible headaches. So I was wondering if you could maybe prescribe something, anything at all, to make this go away, please."

"I'll see what I can do for you." After a quick examination, the doctor told her, "Well, Ms. Baker, unfortunately all that I can do at this point is recommend some rest, maybe a bottle of Tums, or better yet some Pepto-Bismol and plenty of fluids."

"Pepto? Are you serious? Good God," she whined. "I feel terrible."

"They sound like common flu symptoms, but there could be other possibilities. Let me run a few tests and come back and see me next week for the results. Hopefully, by then you'll feel better. If not, we'll have a few more answers, all right?"

After patting her thigh, the doctor stood, and dismissed Jenna, who didn't feel a bit better. Within ten minutes she was out of the office and on her way to Jayden's school. Two months had passed since Tyler had returned to work full time. Christmas was getting closer, and Jenna had decided to volunteer in her son's class to fill her time. She was getting pretty lonely around the house, and she needed the distraction. The last thing she needed, however, was to get sick. She tried to think of happier things, like the new camcorder she'd bought for Jayden's Christmas recital.

Begging for Tyler's attention had become a daily ritual, as had pleading with him not to neglect important events in their son's life. Tyler's hours at work only seemed to become longer, to the point where he wasn't home by the time she fell asleep at night and was gone before she woke up. Some mornings she could have sworn he hadn't bothered to come home at all. The worst thing was she couldn't understand why. What could have possibly gotten so bad at work that he couldn't get home for dinner?

That night when he called to tell her he'd be late again, they had a familiar conversation.

"Jayden's recital is on the seventeenth at seven p.m.," she said.

"Geez, Jenna, give it a rest. I'll be there, okay?"

"Right," she snorted. "Like when you're home for dinner or before I go to bed. Like when you make it to your son's hockey tournament or to even just spend time with him. I mean it, Tyler, this recital is important to Jayden, and you'd better be there."

She hung up on him because she was too angry to continue. Truthfully, the camcorder was her backup, so Jayden would know his father would be able to see him perform should Tyler not be able to come. It was the only thing she could do for Jayden. There had been too many disappointments lately, and she was beginning to doubt Tyler's word. Still, she'd kept her fingers crossed, for Jayden's sake. Her heart was breaking for them both.

***

Her nausea was back, and she had a horrible headache, so she'd been sent home early from volunteering. "Oh my God!" She clutched her chest and waited for her heart rate to slow down. "It is you. I couldn't believe it when I saw your car as I pulled in." She took off her coat and hung it up.

Tyler only gave her a quick glance and became absorbed in reading the file in front of him.

"Hi," she whispered and moved to sit beside him. "Although it's unexpected, it's nice to actually see you here. Have you decided to take a day off?"

"I guess you could call it that. I've got an extra workload ahead of me for the next few weeks. There are people going on vacation, a couple new cases, and a lot of extra paperwork. I thought I'd give myself a change of scenery. So I took some work home."

She rolled her eyes and tried to stifle her anger. He worked all the damn time. "Vacation, huh? Must be nice." He had some vacation days accumulated—quite a few, actually—and she was still bitter that he hadn't taken any.

"Jenna, don't start."

"Hey, Tyler," a voice called. "I hope you don't mind, but I helped myself to a beverage. Beer?"

Tyler stood to grab the drink held out to him while Jenna eyed the blonde beauty in the thick glasses who'd walked out of her kitchen. *What the hell?* Clearing her throat, Jenna also stood and stretched out her hand. "I didn't realize Tyler had brought some company home. I'm Jenna, and you are?"

"Alex Reid. It's a pleasure to meet you."

Jenna could tell the pleasantries were not sincere. Alex had given Jenna an icy look from the tips of her toes to the top of her head. Oh yeah, this woman was definitely hot for Tyler. The question was, did Tyler reciprocate those feelings? His late-night office hours, his avoidance, and the dream…But except for the dreams, those things had been there before the crash as well. Dream aside, Tyler was a workaholic and always had been. Did she really have enough evidence to assume?

Tyler cleared his throat. "Yes, well, Alex and I are working together again, but we were just about to wrap up early today."

"Yep, right after this drink, I'll be heading off." Alex scooted past Jenna toward the sofa and sat in the same spot Jenna had been in only moments before. "I'm afraid there'll be a few more late nights coming up. I hope you don't mind sharing him?"

She laughed as Jenna narrowed her eyes, looking first at Tyler and then at Alex. *I hope you don't mind sharing him.* She wanted to puke. Was Alex the bimbo from the dream? One thing was for sure, Jenna didn't like her. *Snarky, stuck-up bitch. Just who does she think she is?*

Tyler smiled as he cleared away his paperwork. It didn't last.

"Yes, well, sharing him would imply that I have him to begin with. He's at work all the time, but I'm sure you knew that, don't you? A few more late nights, what's the difference? It doesn't change anything. Does it, Tyler?" He was shocked speechless. "Just don't miss the night of the seventeenth, please?"

Alex seemed to have been affected the same way, except her shock shortly turned into complete satisfaction. "Yes, well." She reached for Tyler's hand. "I guess I'd better get going, then."

Tyler stood and immediately pulled away from her. "Right, I'll see you around."

"What was that?" he demanded when the coast was clear. "God, Jenna, I have to work with her. The least you can do is show her some respect."

"Respect? Are you kidding me? That woman is rude and, I might add, has the hots for you. I'm only speaking the truth, and I'm sorry, but I refuse to respect a woman that was clearly trying to bait me into a confrontation with you. Looks like she's succeeded, huh?"

"Jenna," he groaned.

"Oh don't you fucking dare. Just save it, Tyler." She sat down, staring blankly ahead. It had been weeks since he'd touched her. Could Tyler have been dumb enough to cheat on her, and could she forgive him if he had? She was starting to believe Sam's theory more and more, secretly wishing the problems would all just go away. She didn't need this shit. In fact, she would have preferred not knowing at all.

"Why are you crying?"

Was she?

She didn't answer and drilled into him again. "Tell me something. Is there anything going on with Alex? Because if you're as smart as I think you are, you'd tell me right now if you are sleeping with her."

"I can't believe you're asking me this. Have I given you reason to doubt me?" He traced the bottom of her jaw and lifted her chin with his index finger and thumb so they were looking into each other's eyes.

"That's not an answer," she yelled. "I hate thinking this way. I love you, Tyler, but I can't help but notice how awkward it was having her here. You work a lot of late hours, and she happens to work with you. Were you even going to mention to me that you were working together again? We don't have sex anymore, and we argue all the time. Half of the time, it doesn't make sense why you stay away like you do, and it makes me wonder. When I was in the hospital and you brought her up, you became defensive. I could tell that you were keeping something from me, but I let it go. This time I want an answer."

"Of course not, Jenna. There, you have my answer. Now about me not touching you…" He sat on the couch and pulled her onto his lap to straddle him. His lips moved across her throat, and his voice beside her ear became hoarse. "Well, I am now."

His hand traveled to her nape to draw her closer, and his tongue stroked in and out of her mouth while swirling against hers. Before she knew it, her shirt was off and her bra unhooked. Tyler was a pro at undressing, both her and himself. As soon as they were naked, he wasted no time and slid right inside her in one smooth stroke.

The anger seemed to drive her, and her actions were more aggressive than usual as she thrust to meet his demands. Disappointingly, his climax came immediately. He pumped slowly after his seed had spilled into her heated core and began to stroke her. "Come for me," he whispered. "I want to feel you pulse."

She arched her hips forward, clasping his broad shoulders. "Yes," she moaned as she rushed through her own release. "Yesss."

***

"Mrs. Baker is my mother-in-law. Please, call me Jenna, I insist."

"All right, Jenna. Well, the good news is that I know exactly what's wrong. Or maybe what's right, depending on how you look at it. I'm afraid your earlier symptoms may stay with you for a while. How are you feeling today?"

"What are you implying?" Jenna was getting frustrated with her physician. This was her health, not some silly game, and she didn't appreciate being left in the dark any longer. "Is there something wrong?"

"I hope not." He took a deep breath. "Congratulations are in order Mrs.—Jenna. You're expecting."

Out of instinct, Jenna wrapped her arms around her midsection. "Pregnant," she whispered in shock. "Seriously?"

Although they'd discussed, briefly, having another child months before, she wasn't sure how Tyler would react to the news now that he was back to ignoring her again. They'd made love a week ago, if you could call it that. He came too fast, and she was left disappointed and wishing it could have lasted longer.

Alone with her thoughts, she sighed loudly and prayed they would make it through everything okay.

***

It was the night of Jayden's recital and time had run out. Her parents paced the living room while Jenna watched the minute hand inch closer to the deadline.

"Should we assume that Tyler will meet us there?" her dad asked sympathetically. He knew how important this night was to Jayden and could probably see the heartbreak in her eyes.

Jenna nodded and knelt down to Jayden's level. She placed her hands on his shoulders and tried to comfort him. "Don't worry, Jayden. I'm sure Dad will be there. He said he would, and it's still not too late."

Jayden silently nodded, and his disappointment

was evident when ran to hug his grandfather's legs and hid his face.

She'd tried Tyler's office and cell several times after they'd arrived. Jayden's class was one of the last to perform, but Tyler still wasn't there. The empty chair beside her was distracting, and her mother kept looking at her in sympathy. She tried to smile and hated feeling as though they pitied her.

When the time came for Jayden's class to perform, her son was priceless, while Jenna was too emotional. She laughed so hard that she cried as Jayden's voice carried through the whole gymnasium. Was he singing or yelling? He was so cute.

"You were amazing, Jayden, and we have it all on tape," she told him after with a hug. "We'll show Dad later, and I'm sure he's sorry that he missed out, baby."

Later at home she replayed the recital over and over again. Her parents retired to the guest room shortly after Jayden drifted off to sleep while she waited for Tyler to return. It had been an emotional night. An hour or so later, Jenna paused the DVD player and rubbed her eyes, feeling tired herself.

She walked out of the doctor's office with a smile and rubbed her visibly pregnant stomach. She had the strangest craving for ice cream and pickles. As she got into the car, a bag appeared right out of thin air with exactly what she wanted inside. Before driving off, she stuck her hand in the jar to grab a pickle and dipped it in the tub of chocolate ice cream with satisfaction.

In an instant, she was home and could see Tyler's car in the driveway. She smiled at the surprise of having him home during the middle of the day.

The house seemed empty, so she started walking around to look for him. Just as she was about to call out his name, she heard noises upstairs and went to investigate.

The door to their bedroom was open a crack and she couldn't see clearly through it, so she pushed it open, only to find him with Alex again.

God, she was so stupid. Her instincts had told her something was going on. He'd lied and she was too angry this time to cry. "Get out!"

Alex just smirked at her as she shouted.

"Jenna, I can explain." Tyler rushed forward and grabbed for her, but she pushed him away and walked out of the room as fast as she could. It was either that or knock someone out, and she couldn't risk the harm to her unborn child.

She ran down the stairs but tripped over her feet when he caught up to her and landed face-first on the bottom step.

Tyler rushed to her aid as she cried out in pain, but she kept pushing him away, disgusted with herself and him. She made it outside only to collapse on the front lawn. She couldn't walk anymore.

Alex watched from a window upstairs. Her face lit up with a smile as she looked down at Jenna and Tyler. Then Tyler's worried face hovered over her as he whispered, "I am so sorry."

She woke up with a gasp and bolted upright to caress her stomach.

"Looks like I missed an amazing recital." Tyler was sitting at the end of the couch and looked away from the TV toward her.

"You did."

He moved closer, but she inched away. "Jenna, I had every intention of being there. It's just—"

"I'm not in the mood to argue tonight. My parents are in the spare room, and I'm tired of it." She sighed before covering her face. She was exhausted from all of the stress, period. "You picked your priorities, Tyler, and now we all have to deal with the consequences."

He picked up flowers from the coffee table and tried to hand them to her, but she didn't want them. If that was his apology, he could keep it. She wasn't joking when she'd said she was tired. He literally drained her sometimes, making her numb to his advances, and it only got worse the longer it carried on.

"I am so sorry," he whispered, and she shivered as she thought about her recent dream. "I screwed up. What else do you want me to say?"

"What else?" She looked away to wipe away a tear and didn't bother to answer the stupid question. "I agree. You are sorry, Tyler, but there's a little boy upstairs who needs that apology more than I do. He was so disappointed."

He nodded and stood. "Can I make this up to you?" He moved his face closer to kiss her, but she backed away from his advances and turned her head away.

"You could start by getting your priorities straight from now on," she said and caressed her stomach again. "There's a pillow and a blanket down here for you. If there isn't anything else, I'm going to bed."

He stared after her in shock when she walked away. This was the first time she'd ever refused his advances and definitely his first time sleeping on the couch. Jenna usually talked things through when she was upset, but she hoped he realized how much he'd screwed up this time. She knew exactly what he meant when he asked if he could make things up to her. He wanted sex, and for the first time, she really wasn't in the mood. The thought of him touching her after being with Alex gave her the chills.

No time like the present, she thought as she stopped at the stairs and turned around to give him the news. "I went to the doctor today, by the way," she started, admiring his shocked expression. He knew nothing about it. He didn't know anything that went on in his own home anymore, and it was sad as hell.

"Are you all right?" He actually looked concerned and took a step toward her.

"Yes, Tyler, but it looks like I'll be going on a regular basis again for the next few months. It turns out I'm pregnant. Congratulations, Daddy." It should have been much happier news than it felt like at the moment. She wasn't even excited yet and felt so alone for the first time in her marriage. It was unsettling.

"What?"

"You heard me." She walked upstairs and didn't bother to look back.

Their situation needed to change, and it was up to him to figure out exactly what he wanted before it was too late.

Chapter Seventeen

Brady was back. They sat on a porch swing, and he held her close while quietly listening as she unburdened herself from all of her worries.

"I'm sorry, love." His sexy accent was so soothing.

"Why are you apologizing?" she asked, startled because he'd done nothing but give her his support. He was damn near perfect, her dream man.

"Because ye'r hurtin', love, and I can't stand it." He cradled her head against his chest, and she listened to the steady beat of his heart.

"Wow," she whispered in awe. "Are you sure you're for real? That you actually exist?"

His answer started with a kiss, and the butterflies stirred crazily in her stomach while moisture flowed in the area even lower as his tongue stroked in and out, making love to her mouth. "Believe me, love, ye'll soon find out."

The dream was so good that being pulled away from it felt like fingernails on a chalkboard or like a record being scratched to bits.

"Mommy, Mommy," Jayden cheered while he jumped up and down beside her on the bed. "Wake up, sleepyhead."

"Good morning to you too." She pulled him down with a groan and tickled him until he screeched for mercy.

"Grandma has breakfast ready. Come on." He wiggled away, hopped off the bed, and raced out in no time.

"Hey, Mom, are you and Dad still okay to watch Jayden for a little while today?" She called out as she followed her son into the kitchen. Breakfast smelled delicious as she sat down at the table, but with her nauseous state she stuck with toast and grimaced as she pushed her eggs away. "He'll have to be dropped off by 12:45 and then picked up from school at 3:15."

"What appointment might this be?"

"Very subtle, Mom." Jenna laughed. "It's just another doctor's appointment." She shrugged. Her overprotective mother's concern was endearing.

"Of course I'll watch Jayden, dear. Is there anything wrong?"

"No, I'm fine, really. I wasn't feeling very well, and they ran some tests." Before she could finish talking, her mother was checking her head for a temperature. "Not there." She grabbed her mother's hands and placed them on her stomach. "Here. I'm pregnant again. Congratulations, Grandma."

Her mother let out a big whoop of excitement that made her father run in from the other room looking concerned.

"Hey, Dad," Jenna said, laughing.

"She's pregnant!"

"Congratulations, honey." And they laughed again while her mother did a happy dance in the middle of a kitchen while clapping her hands joyfully.

Jenna took a quick peek at Jayden while he stood there wide-eyed and scared. Probably because of the way her mother was reacting. She called him over and lifted him in her arms. "It's okay, honey. Grandma's just crazy sometimes."

"Grandma, you're crazy," Jayden repeated, and they all laughed in unison.

Her appointment that morning was for a sonogram, and with Jayden taken care of she could make a much-needed stop afterward, one she had to make alone. She had to see Tyler, and she wasn't about to wait until he came home again. It was time she paid him a visit at work.

***

With a heart rate of 130 beats per minute, this tiny person inside her actually looked like a baby already. The doctor estimated the gestational age to be about eleven weeks.

Jenna became emotional yet again upon seeing the baby moving around on the screen. She couldn't stop smiling. She could see all the fingers and toes and a cute little button nose. She was still awestruck when they handed her the very first picture of her baby afterward, but it soon turned to worry about what she was about to do.

She arrived at Tyler's law office feeling nervous. It'd been a while since she'd visited, and the last time she'd pictured it wasn't a very pleasant memory.

"Can I help you?" asked the plump redheaded receptionist, interrupting her thoughts.

"No, thank you. I'm here to visit my husband, and I can find my own way."

She proceeded past the desk and stopped abruptly just before she reached his office. A flashback came to mind of a calendar with the twenty-first circled boldly in red when she saw the notice for the staff Christmas party.

"Get it together, Jenna," she mumbled, willing her hands to stop shaking. She needed as much courage as she could get right now. God only knew what Tyler was thinking when it came to her and the pregnancy. Lord, what she wouldn't give to be able to turn back time right now. These dreams, premonitions, or whatever you wanted to call them were frightening enough. The similarities between them and reality scared the living daylights out of her. The added stress of Tyler's avoidance was torture and hurtful on top of everything else. There just wasn't much more she could take.

Peeking through his partially closed door, she saw that Alex was with him again. She was sitting on the corner of his desk laughing and leaned close to him as he mumbled something.

They didn't notice when she walked in, so she cleared her throat. "Did I come at a bad time?" The first thing she noticed was Alex's hand on his. Flashbacks from her dreams hit her in quick glimpses, temporarily blinding her.

When she could see again, Tyler ripped his hand away from underneath Alex's and moved away. "Of course not, honey, we were just about to take a break anyway."

Clearly disappointed, Alex hopped off his desk and straightened her skirt "Hello, Jenna."

"You've got to be kidding me. Nothing's going on, all right," Jenna snapped, looking between the two of them. Why wouldn't they just fess up and lay it all out there? If Tyler wanted Alex, Jenna certainly wasn't about to stick around.

"Jenna, don't be silly. Alex is just a coworker, nothing more."

With a gasp and a dirty look, Alex quickly walked out, leaving the two of them to speak alone.

"Right, Tyler, and in case you're wondering, I'm being sarcastic. Figure out what it is that you want and then let me know. I'm tired of not knowing, and if it's not me, then just say it and stop this torture."

"Come on, Jenna, this is just silly."

"Silly?" She couldn't believe it. "I'm being silly. Okay, I'll play along. Do you actually think I'm that stupid? There's something going on with the two of you. Now the question that has me curious is just how far you've gone." The stress was too much. She hadn't originally planned to confront him about Alex. She'd only stopped by to show him the sonogram picture and talk about the pregnancy.

Jenna held in a groan when she felt a sharp cramp. "I think I need to sit down." The words came out breathless. What she needed was to calm down.

"Why, what's wrong?" Tyler kneeled in front of her, but his concern did nothing to comfort her.

"It's just a cramp. I'll be fine."

"The baby?" He went wide-eyed as if he'd forgotten and forced Jenna's hands away from her stomach. He put his in their place and began to rub.

She concentrated on her breathing. Closing her eyes, she tried to shut everything out as much as possible, especially Tyler's touch.

"I'm so sorry, Jenna." It was Brady's voice. Her heart rate sped up as she glimpsed an image of herself with a huge belly. Jenna smiled, placing her hands on top of his. With flashes of herself on the floor, she envisioned blood gushing from between her legs.

She gasped, and reality came back to her. She pushed Tyler's hands aside in anger. There was no way she could lose this baby. She had to be more careful, anything to change that possible future.

"Should you see a doctor?" Tyler looked helpless, and she tried not to laugh despite her anger at him.

"I can take care of myself. Now stop touching me. I'm mad at you."

"I could never do that," he teased and had the nerve to smile as she glared at him. She pushed him away again. What she needed was to have him out of her sight for a minute to pull herself together. "I could use some water, Tyler, if you don't mind?"

She leaned back in the chair to get comfortable, her head back as far as it would go. Pinching the bridge of her nose, she began to take deep, soothing breaths. *Happy thoughts, think happy thoughts.* Okay, there was Jayden. She thought about his singing/yelling in the auditorium at his school. That certainly was a precious moment, and she couldn't help but smile as she remembered it. Then there was the baby growing inside of her, the fingers and toes, the cute little button nose.

She rubbed at her stomach. "You know I love you already, baby. It'll be okay. I'll do everything I possibly can to love and protect you."

"That doesn't surprise me."

Jenna jumped as Tyler reentered the room. "You always were very loving. Especially when it came to Jayden, and now we have this one to look forward to."

She narrowed her eyes at him, not sure she was ready to forgive him just yet. Her suspicions were not proven, but his absence and lack of reliability still hurt.

"Water?" he said innocently. Closing the door behind him, he handed her the bottle as though it was a peace offering.

"Thanks." She eyed him warily. "I'm not sure that you care anymore, but I originally stopped by to show you our first picture." She slapped it against his chest.

"Of course I care, Jenna," he said as he looked at it. "This is amazing, and wow, it's so clear." Looking awestruck, he pulled her up and into his embrace. She stiffened but then melted into him as he whispered sweet sentiments in her ear. "You're amazing, and I love you. There are things I'd like to do to you now." His voice turned husky as he backed her toward his desk. "I've missed you, Jenna." He lifted her and placed her on the edge, then stepped in between her legs and began caressing her thighs.

"Tyler, I don't think…" His hand was at her nape, fingers tangled in her hair. He leaned down and cut off her protest with a kiss. She shook her head. "Tyler, stop." She was breathless already and couldn't get herself sucked in any further.

With a groan, he pulled away. "Am I hurting you? Are you still in pain?" He dropped to his knees and massaged her lower back while placing light kisses along her navel. Between the massage and his hot breath headed to her lower regions, she moaned, giving in. Sex was certainly one way to blow off steam, and he just felt too damn good to think about anything else, and damn it, she loved him despite the heartbreak he caused her.

Tyler stood again and took advantage of her surrender with another kiss. He tilted her head to the side and plunged his tongue between her parted lips to silkily slide against hers.

"I don't mean to interrupt." Alex stood stiffly in the doorway with her arms folded across her chest. She cleared her throat. "But I think we should be getting back to work."

"Why don't you just come out and say it." Jenna rolled her eyes. Alex had given her a cold glare, and it was obvious she didn't like what she'd walked in on. "Come on, Alex, what you'd really like to say is, 'Jenna, I'd like you to leave so that I can have your husband all to myself.' Isn't that right? You do have a thing for my husband, don't you?"

Her reply came with a smile. "Jenna," she said, holding the door open wider, "I'd like you to leave so that your husband and I can get back to our work. We've got a lot to cover, and you'd just be in the way. Unless you'd prefer to wait around and watch?" She smiled deviously.

Tyler stood there gaping like an idiot. Jenna couldn't believe him. It was yet another disappointment because he didn't have the balls to stick up for her. It was a wake-up call that made her wonder what the hell she was still doing there. Why had she even bothered?

"Right, well, maybe I'll see you later." She shook her head, wondering if any of this was worth it anymore, and then looked at Alex. "Then again, maybe not."

Alex's smile faltered with her short-lived victory. As Jenna slid by Tyler to grab her purse, he grabbed her arm to hold her in place. "Jenna, wait a minute, I'm not ready for you to leave just yet." He brushed his lips against hers and then looked at Alex. "My wife is visiting, and I don't appreciate your disrespectful tone. A family emergency has come up, so I'm taking a week off to get things resolved. I'll do as much as I can from home, and I trust you can handle the rest without me for a few days. And another thing, just so we're clear. In the future, when Jenna decides to visit, I expect a little more respect from my coworkers when they address her. She is my wife, and she deserves that."

What was that about? It was Jenna's turn to stand there with her jaw slack, and the look on

Alex's face was priceless as she stormed off, fighting back tears.

"A family emergency?"

"I'm listening to my wife." Tyler smiled. "And it's about time that I get my priorities straightened out. The holidays are here, and I've missed out on too much already."

"Well, that has to be a first. Since when do you ever listen to what I tell you to do?" Jenna asked, still in surprise.

***

Their house was surprisingly busy. Her parents were still visiting and Sam was there. Jayden was hyper with all of the attention, and Jenna felt joyous watching them all.

"Congratulations!" Sam cried as she approached and gave Jenna and Tyler a hug and a big, sloppy kiss on the cheek.

"You're amazing." Tyler laughed "Does everyone already know?"

"Well, you were the first. Then my mother dragged it out of me this morning, and I guess word got out from there."

"What about Jayden?"

"He heard a bit this morning with Mom, but I'm not sure he understands—other than calling my mother crazy, that is." They laughed together.

After grabbing the sonogram picture from his pocket, Tyler pulled Jenna with him into the living room to find their son. They sat on the couch and everyone joined them. Her mother and Sam cooed over the image while Jenna sat Jayden on her lap.

"Do you know what this is?" she asked.

"No." He glanced from one adult to the other with a perplexed expression.

Jenna smiled. "It's all right, Jayden. This is a baby that is inside Mommy's belly right now. If you squint your eyes, you may be able to make out the head, and these are the fingers." She pointed out all the visible features, trying to help him understand.

When he was done looking, his gaze went from her face to her stomach and then back again.

"Would you like a brother or a sister, Jayden? It'll give you another person to play with eventually."

"Cool." He nodded enthusiastically and the whole room burst out in laughter.

Tyler had insisted they see a doctor before going home. She'd agreed even though she'd just come from there. The cramping hadn't come back, but the doctor insisted she rest for the next few days, just in case. Hearing a strong heartbeat had been a relief to Jenna and an excitement for Tyler. The pregnancy seemed to have become more of a reality for him after he'd seen the picture and heard the evidence. Having Jayden onboard was just the icing on the cake.

***

Having Tyler home was just like old times, or rather like when she'd just gotten out of the hospital. He was attentive and caring and devoted as much time to his family as possible. They skipped his Christmas party, the date she'd seen circled on the calendar, and to her knowledge he actually avoided anything work-related. As they made up for lost time in the last few days together, she decided to enjoy having him around while it lasted.

On Christmas Eve, the gifts were stuffed under the tree, Santa had a feast of homemade cookies left out for him, and the bird was greased and stuffed for the oven in the morning. Their parents were due to arrive early the next day, and of course Jayden would probably be up shortly after dawn with excitement. Jenna crawled into to bed, already tired to the bone just thinking about the busy day to come.

"Jenna." Tyler cuddled closer. "Are you sleeping?"

"No." She giggled as he unintentionally tickled her from behind.

"I miss you."

"Do you? Even though you won't admit to it, I just can't get the image of you and her out of my head."

He groaned and rolled over on his back in frustration. "Just tell me how I can make this right. You wanted more time, and I'm trying to give you that. Alex is nothing to me."

"I need the truth. We've been together for years. Hell, we even spent part of our childhood together. I know when you're hiding something from me. Why won't you just come clean and tell me the truth?"

"The truth," he repeated. "The truth is that I love my wife, Jenna. I love Jayden." He smiled and tenderly kissed her stomach. "And I love the baby we've created. I miss you, and I'm sorry for not being around like I should. The truth is that I want you right now." He continued to kiss her body seductively. "Forgive me? Let me make it up to you. Let me show you how much you mean to me."

Her breath hitched, and she started to breathe heavier, making him smirk. She missed him too and hated that she could never stay mad at him for too long. Jenna gave in to her growing need for him. She still had no concrete proof of his infidelity, nothing other than her instincts and a few eerily coincidental dreams. Her mind had been working overtime, and in order to prevent her from thinking about Tyler with Alex, she thought about a safe haven. Something that would always be precious to her. She thought about Brady.

***

This had to have been the hottest sight imaginable. Pure and simple, she was in a fantasy...two gorgeous men wrapped in nothing but white cotton sheets, ready and waiting—for her.

Tyler looked at Brady, and they both smiled.

"It's about damn time," Tyler said.

"Yes, love, join us." Brady beckoned.

Poof! *She was naked and eagerly crawling toward them. Sandwiched between two gorgeous men, her chest rubbed against Brady's while Tyler's erection nudged her from behind.*

Tyler turned her face toward him and licked then sucked at Jenna's bottom lip while Brady lowered his head to taste her erect nipples. She was wild with need and thrust her tongue to meet Tyler's. In and out, they made love to each other's mouths, eagerly.

She moaned, rocking her hips as she palmed both erections and stroked them. "Please," she begged, a wanton woman now with a need to come. Tyler chuckled while Brady worked her harder with his tongue. They eyed each other, smiling as though they were able to communicate without words.

"All right, Jenna, I want you to ride me backward. I want to see your sweet ass bounce while you fuck me."

She was slick with anticipation as she leaned over to get into position just like Tyler had asked. She reached for Brady.

"Don't worry, love. I'm right here with ye."

Brady tweaked her nipples as she started to roll her hips, then moved his hand down her slender body. When his fingers found her nub, he rubbed her there and spread her lips wider as he leaned down to replace his fingers with his tongue.

Damn, this was so fucking good. Impaled on Tyler, she watched as Brady's mouth brought her into ecstasy. She rode out the final wave, taking Tyler over the edge with her while she pulsed and shouted out to the heavens. His possessive roar echoed as he pumped himself inside her.

Tyler pulled out and sat up so that she was upright against his chest. Brady watched him tweaking her nipples between his thumb and forefinger, stimulating them to stay erect for him.

"Brady," she moaned breathlessly as she took his cock in her hand. It throbbed against her

fingers. With the smell of sex in the air and her breathless pleas for him to join her, Brady grasped her hips. He pulled her forward a little, spreading her wide while the head of his cock sat at her opening. She lifted her hips impatiently and plunged herself upon him. It was his turn to moan. Watching as he stroked himself in and out, covered in her warm, delicious juices, Jenna took matters into her own hands. She braced her feet on the bed, lifted her hips, and moved them to match Brady's thrusts. She slid one hand down to her sensitive nub and applied pressure. Tyler chuckled as Brady's grip on Jenna's hips tightened. Circling the sensitive area, she cried out another release and saw stars as her two men brought her a little piece of heaven.

"Christ, love," Brady swore while increasing his thrusts around her pulsing pussy. With a roar of his own and a scream of her name, Brady came, his cum mixing with Tyler's and her own, marking her.

She woke up breathless, stirring Tyler from his blissful slumber. She was supposed to relax and be careful, but man, with hot dreams like that, who wouldn't wake up wet, wanting, and worked up?

"Is everything all right?" Groggily Tyler stretched and smiled, looking at the time. "And here I expected Jayden to be the first one up."

"I'm fine." She smiled. It was still early, and after that dream, well…maybe they had some time.

Her hormones were clamoring for some loving. She moved closer to Tyler and placed her leg over his hip so the wetness of her sex was in direct line of his semihard erection. "Merry Christmas," she whispered before nipping his bottom lip.

Tyler growled appreciatively, and she squealed as he flipped her over and pinned her beneath him. "A man can get used to an awakening like this anytime, Jenna, anytime." And then he took eager possession of her mouth.

***

"Happy Holidays! It's time for our annual after-Christmas shopping spree to catch all the good sales. Are you feeling up to it?"

"You know it." Jenna chuckled. There was no way she was missing some shopping with Sam. "I feel great, actually, and it might be nice to have some girl time again."

"Good. I think some quality girl time would be nice too. I missed you. We don't get to hang out like we used to. Bring the rug rat. I've missed him too."

After no more than a few hours into it, Jenna had to sit down. The mall was crazy, busy, filled to the max with people, and she was beginning to get hot. Knowing she was cutting their day short, she asked, "Are you ready for some lunch?"

Once they were seated at the food court with food in front of them, Sam asked, "So how are you feeling?"

Jenna had barely touched anything while Jayden sat quietly, devouring his cheeseburger and fries. She shrugged, knowing Sam wasn't only talking about her health even though Jenna had called an early end to the shopping. "My dreams are continuing."

Although the one she'd had the night before last had been unusual, it had been a fantasy, definitely something that would never be reality. She'd been stressed out over so many things lately. Mainly Tyler, but the dreams had her worried as well. They'd felt so real, but at the same time they felt powerful and occurred more often. It was hard to explain.

"And my special ability seems to be getting stronger. I'm getting frequent flashes of images now when I'm awake, and the outcome isn't any better."

Sam frowned, giving her hand a reassuring squeeze. "Well, I'm here if you need me. Vent if you feel you have to. I know it's hard to talk about, but just know that you have someone around for you."

Looking over at Jayden, Jenna smiled. "Thanks, Sam." Her eyes widened and hands flew to her belly. "Wow."

"What? What's the matter?"

"First of all, I don't think lunch is agreeing with me." She grimaced and pushed her tray aside. "And I know it's kind of early, but I swear I just felt the baby move."

Sam moved over and placed her hand near Jenna's to see if she could feel anything.

But nothing more happened until they were in the parking lot. Only inches away from Sam's car, the pain started. Unlike her one scare with cramps, this time the pain was in her head, a bright flash, hurting her as she squinted to clear her vision. She groaned and quickly grabbed for the hood to stabilize her balance.

"What is it?"

"I'm fine. It's just a little headache." She eyed Jayden and then Sam, hoping Sam would go along with it. Jayden had been through enough. The last thing she wanted was to stir up his fear of losing her. She knew it probably wouldn't take much.

As she secured Jayden in his booster seat, she gave him a wink and forced a smile, hoping to reassure him. Sam buckled him safely into his car seat, and once the door was closed, she looked white with panic. "You sure?"

"It's another image. A car actually, but I'm not sure what it means." Jenna nodded and took a much-needed deep breath. "When the images appear, there is also a light, my head aches, and it's hard to take sometimes. But I think I'm going to be fine, Sam, really."

Sam nodded as some of her color returned.

On the ride home, Jenna tried not to show her discomfort. The image kept coming back to her stronger each time.

"Another one?" Sam broke the silence, and Jenna shushed her. "Relax, Jenna, the little guy is passed out."

Relieved for at least that, Jenna had another one of her strange feelings in the pit of her stomach, and it made her sick. "I can't explain it right now, but could you take Jayden to your house? I feel the need to see Tyler alone for some reason."

"S-sure, Jenna."

An awkward silence followed for the rest of their trip home. Having dreams was bad enough, but now a vision had crept up, and she was determined to get to the bottom of things.

At Sam's, Jayden barely stirred as Jenna laid him on top of the couch. "I won't be long," she said.

"Hey, wait a minute." Sam pulled her back as she started for the house. "Tell me what's got you so freaked out first. Do you want me to go with you?"

"I'm sure it's nothing. I keep getting the image of a car we passed about a block from here. I don't understand it, but seeing it as we drove by freaked me out a little. It has some tie to Tyler, and I'm going to figure out what it is. I need someone to stay with Jayden. Please, Sam."

"What car?"

Jenna sighed, getting frustrated. Sam had good intentions, but she just wanted to go. "The red BMW M6 we passed."

"I figured as much. We live in a middle-class neighborhood, and it isn't an everyday occurrence to see that type of car parked on the street. It's too nice." She turned to Jayden. "Take your time. The rug rat is welcome to stay as long as you need him to. Gotta love the little guy."

After thanking Sam, Jenna was out the door. They obviously had company, and she was about to find out who it was. When she reached their house, she got out of the car and walked around to the back door, rummaging through her purse for her keys. Her gut instincts told her that she needed to enter undetected.

As she quietly made her way through the back door and into the kitchen, the house seemed empty.

Tyler, come out come out wherever you are.

He was definitely home. His car was parked in the driveway, and he never left home without it. As she approached the hallway, she could hear the television on at a low volume in the living room, and then someone giggled and exhaled loudly. It became quiet for a moment, followed by more heavy breathing. It was definitely not coming from her. Jenna had begun to see spots before realizing she was holding her breath.

Jenna's entire face burned with anger at what greeted her. Tyler had been a dumbass all right. He actually was that stupid, and in that very moment he threw everything they had away as though it was trash.

Alex saw Jenna coming and played it to her advantage. Her shirt had been ripped open, leaving her bra visible, and her skirt was hiked up to her waist. Grinding her hips, she rode him harder at the sight of Jenna and kissed him aggressively to prove a point. *"Game over, bitch,"* she was saying, *"Tyler is mine now."* The message was displayed loud and clear.

Tyler's pants were down to his ankles, and his hands were wrapped around the other woman's waist. With his face in Alex's chest, he moved with her as she rode him up and down, setting the pace.

Jenna stood there feeling like an absolute fool.

Tyler had been a busy boy all right, and he didn't notice her entrance until she dropped her keys and purse on the floor in disgust.

Chapter Eighteen

Alex smiled as Tyler looked up and panicked. "Jenna…I…"

"You son of a bitch. On my couch, Tyler? In our house? Get out! Get out now!" She'd known all along that something was going on. She was just shocked that he disrespected her enough to do this in their home.

"Jenna, it's not what it looks like. It doesn't mean anything to me." He got up and shoved Alex to the floor.

Jenna laughed humorlessly at the disgusting image he displayed before her. His pants were at his ankles, and his semierect cock was in full view, covered in Alex's juices. Jenna's throat felt thick, and her eyes burned with building tears, but she refused to let him see her cry.

"Not what it looks like?" She couldn't believe his lame explanation. "It sure looks like something to me. You know what? I don't want to hear it. You disgust me, and while you're at it, be respectful enough to at least pull up your pants."

Seeing as how they ignored her demand to get out, she decided it was time for her to leave before she did something she may later regret.

Alex was definitely enjoying the drama unfolding in the living room. Getting up off the floor and dusting herself off, she said, "Tyler, it's about time that Jenna finds out, don't you think? And it was definitely what it looked like."

She chuckled, the evil bitch, and Jenna had the urge to strangle her.

"Shut up!" he yelled and pushed Alex away again. "She's my wife; she's my whole life. What was I thinking?" He covered his face with his hands and moaned, "I've ruined everything."

A traitorous tear slipped down Jenna's cheek, but she wasn't about to give either of them the satisfaction of seeing it. She'd heard enough, and it was time to ask Sam for another favor—a place to stay for a while. She made it safely out the back door before Tyler caught up with her.

"Jenna, please don't go," he pleaded and grabbed her by the arm, clearly hoping to stop her.

"I'm done, Tyler." She pulled away. "Just leave me alone." She should have done something when she'd first suspected his affair, but love had blinded her, and she was angry at everyone in that moment, especially herself.

The neighbors watched the scene being played out on their front lawn. It was humiliating, and she could only imagine what they were thinking. Jenna was almost at a run trying to get away while crying, and Tyler kept reaching for her to stop and pleading with her while wearing nothing but his pants.

"Stop following me," she hissed. "Everybody's starring."

"I don't care."

"I can see that," she snapped. "Now let go of me." A wave of nausea hit her. "Tyler, I need to calm down, and I can't do that with you here right now." She held her belly out of habit, but Tyler took it the wrong way.

"The baby? Is there something wrong?"

She snorted. Of course there was, just not in the way he thought. "The baby is fine, Tyler. You can go back to her now, and I'll make arrangements to get my things another time."

It pained her to see Sam and Jayden watching as a part of the crowd. She slowed down a little and tried to calm herself and wipe her face dry before going to Jayden. He looked confused and scared from the commotion.

What she hadn't expected was Tyler's next move when she went to go to their son.

"Jenna, wait!" Tyler yelled, but she ignored him. Jayden was watching, and she had to get to him. Tyler leaped forward and wrapped his arms around her legs to beg her to stay with him, but it backfired.

"Tyler, nooo," she cried.

The ground was heading straight for her face, and it was as if everything was in slow motion. Her visions overlapped and came back in a flash.

Standing with Brady, their hands overlapping as they caressed her visibly pregnant belly in front of the mirror. The cramps and a glimpse of herself crying out in agony. Tyler running after her down the stairs. Blood gushing from between her legs.

That was the last thing Jenna remembered before her eyes rolled back and she gave in to the blackness.

***

"Sam?" Groggy, Jenna tried to sit up, feeling as though she'd been run down by a truck, and it took a minute before everything came flooding back. "Oh my God!"

"I'm so sorry, Jenna. They couldn't save it, honey. The baby didn't make it."

"No," she moaned, in a state of shock and too disoriented to absorb the news.

Sam hugged her as Jenna tried to gather her bearings, to remember what had happened, and why she was in the hospital again, and then it all came rushing back. *Baby, cramps, trying to get to Jayden, Tyler!*

"No," she screamed as she pushed her friend away and rolled herself into a ball with her knees up to her chest and hands hugging them tight. It was just one nightmare after another. *Why?*

Her parents came into the room with cups of coffee in their hands. "Oh, Jenna, honey." Her mother rushed to her side. Pushing Jenna's hair from her face, she kissed her forehead.

As if right on cue, Tyler walked in the hospital room looking remorseful, but seeing him brought a spark back into her. "I need everyone to leave. Tyler, you stay." It was time to confront him.

"All right, Jenna, we'll be close by." Sam glared at Tyler with an "if looks could kill" stare before leaving.

"Could somebody please tell me what the hell is going on?" Her mother looked between Jenna and Tyler, obviously confused by her daughter's hostility.

"Mom, please."

Persuading her parents to leave wasn't easy. When she and Tyler were finally alone, it was too quiet, as though he was afraid to speak and was waiting for her to start. There was too much to say, and it was hard to think about, let alone voice. She'd spent a good part of her existence with this man, and he'd ruined it in an instant.

"Where's Jayden?" she asked.

"With my parents."

"How is he?" she whispered. God, even talking hurt.

Tyler sighed heavily and combed his fingers through his hair. "He took it hard. He's scared again that he's going to lose you because you're back in the hospital."

"Oh, God," she cried. Her nerves were shot, and she couldn't stop shaking. She couldn't take it and wondered what horrible thing she could have done to deserve this anguish. One of her babies was dead and the other terrified. Rolling onto her back, she covered her face and sobbed.

"What do you want, Jenna?" He sat on the bed beside her. "I'll do anything to make this right. Please."

"Why?" she demanded. Hurt turned to anger

again, and she wanted to be done with feeling sorry for herself, because right then everything was all his fault. "What I want is to know why you threw everything away. Are you happy now that you've accomplished that goal? I feel like a piece of garbage that you've discarded. I gave you several opportunities to tell me the truth. You knew I suspected. Hell, I even asked on several occasions, and you lied right to my face, *every single time*. How long have you been doing this? Have there been others? God, Tyler, just give me the truth this time."

He wouldn't look at her as she finished speaking. He seemed as though he was concentrating hard to think of the proper thing to say, but nothing he said could make the situation any worse. "You don't really want to know. Trust me."

"Trust you," she repeated, sending him a murderous glare. "I don't think so. Now tell me, damn it."

"When you were in the hospital after the accident, it was hard on me. I blamed myself, Jenna. Don't you understand? You'd taken a turn for the worse when the infection developed. I wasn't eating or sleeping. I just sat there talking to myself, holding your hand, hoping you'd pull through and come back to me." A mix of emotions played across his face as he spoke, hurt and then hope that his explanation would suffice. "I hadn't showered or changed clothes in days, and your mother got fed up, insisting that I take a few hours to myself. I was a mess. I went home to clean up, and then I wasn't sure what to do with myself. I needed a distraction, so I went to the office.

"When I got there, everyone could see the condition I was in and insisted I go home. But I just couldn't. I needed something to help me escape. Alex walked in my office and said if I wanted a distraction, she was swamped and could use the extra help, even if it was only for a couple hours. Before I knew it, the time flew and we were alone. We worked through dinner and ordered some takeout. She reached her hand out in comfort and told me she was there for me if I needed it. She gave me a hug, and then I honestly don't know how it all happened. One minute we were hugging, and the next…"

He swallowed loudly as his glossy eyes turned widely innocent. His expression was a lot like Jayden's just before a good cry.

She tried to hold back the bile in her throat. But that all-too-clear image had already burned itself into her head, thanks to her first dream of them together. "I knew it," she whispered. "I could tell you were keeping something from me as soon as you mentioned her the first time, and then I saw it— twice."

"What?"

"I've been having visions since the accident, Tyler, and they keep coming true. Premonitions of the future, and I don't care if you think I'm crazy, because I know I'm not. I saw you having sex with her on your desk at work. That's where it happened that first time, isn't it? Why do you think I asked you about her when we were at the park? I know, Tyler, because I saw it, and let me guess, you did it again the day of Jayden's recital. She was the reason you let us down and stood us up, and you probably would have again the day I showed you our baby's first ultrasound picture. My baby," she clarified, wrapping her arms around herself. She looked away from him. "I had a vision at the mall of her car and knew something was up. That's why I left Jayden at Sam's and walked in alone. Thank God I walked in alone." She shivered. "So how far off am I?"

"I'm sorry, Jenna." He had a pleading look on his face, as if he hoped for mercy. "My biggest regret by far, is doing what I did. Please, just give me a chance to prove to you that I will never make that mistake twice. Give me the rest of my life to prove this to you, please."

"Not making the same mistake twice? Are you kidding me?" She couldn't believe his nerve. "From my count, you've made that mistake more than twice. You did every time you slept with her and God knows who else. The trust is gone, and if you don't have that, you have nothing. Satisfied?

"Dear God, Jayden is at home terrified that he's going to lose me, because here I am in the hospital, yet again. It wasn't your fault the first time, Tyler, but it is your fault this time. Your little stunt murdered our baby. You killed our baby, and you've destroyed me. I hope it was worth it."

"Jenna, no." He began to sob. "Please, Jenna. I'm so sorry, please."

She cried harder, refusing to acknowledge her shock at seeing his tears, and his begging made her heart shattered even more. Loving Tyler hurt too much. She hadn't stopped despite it all, but she was too tired to fight. There was nothing left for them, and she knew then exactly what she wanted. This was one betrayal she couldn't get past and would never be able to forgive.

"I love you, Tyler," she said softly, too emotional to raise her voice. "And I probably always will despite everything. You're Jaden's father, and we've had a lot of years together, but I know what I want now, what I have to do."

She pulled him closer, kissed him fully on the mouth, and cried out in anguish when she pushed him away.

"Anything, Jenna."

She looked into his eyes and saw a flicker of hope inside them. The sight made her wince, so she finally came out with what she had to say. "I want a divorce."

She could think of no other option. His infidelity had ruined everything, taking away half of her life in the process. She owed it to herself to move forward, and although doing it would be hard, she had to if she ever wanted a chance at happiness again.

"No, anything but that, Jenna, please, just not that."

It was pointless arguing over it, her mind was made up. He was in denial and refused to believe what she was telling him. With constant pleading, he joined her on the bed, cuddling close while he cried. In a few minutes, her parents and Sam returned and gasped at the sight of them. She'd assumed they'd never seen Tyler so emotional, and, in truth, neither had she.

"What's going on here?" Sam asked.

"She's leaving me," Tyler whispered. "She wants a divorce."

The sight of him and the sounds of his pleas were making Jenna nauseous. "Dad, I need Tyler to leave," she said. "Could you please help me out with that?"

"Come on, son," her father said as he took Tyler's arm. "Let's give Jenna some time."

Tyler reluctantly followed him out. "Jenna, please," he pleaded one last time before her father escorted him out of sight. "I'll do anything. I'm begging you."

Her mother and Sam rushed to comfort her. Tired of talking, she leaped forward as soon as her mother was close enough to reach, feeling as if she were five again. Hugging her close, Jenna sobbed, trying to let it all out.

What a nightmare that day had been.

Chapter Nineteen

When Jenna was released first thing the next morning, the staff almost looked relieved to see her go. The previous night's drama had caused headaches for more than just her, she guessed.

Her parents had picked up Jayden and brought him to Sam's house. He ran for her soon as he saw her and landed straight in Jenna's open arms, sobbing his little heart out.

"I'll never leave you again," she vowed. "I promise you."

Sam offered to let Jayden and Jenna stay as long as they wanted, and that got her mother going, of course. "That's not necessary, but thanks anyway," she said. "Jenna and Jayden will be coming back with us."

That shocked Jenna. She hadn't expected her mother to argue or be rude. "No, Mom. I love you, but I'm not going anywhere. I refuse to run away. Jayden's got school now, and I can't just pull him out like that. I'm staying, and I have enough to deal with, so please just understand."

"Okay then, if that's what you want. Just know the offer is there if you ever change your mind, honey."

***

A week after that horrible day, it was time to stop sulking and start living, time for Jayden to try living like a normal child. He'd been traumatized yet again and had developed separation anxiety, yet another thing she could thank Tyler for.

Right then her biggest problem was retrieving her car. It was still parked in front of the house. She was afraid to go after it and chance seeing Tyler, afraid to start a scene, afraid she might change her mind, that he'd be able to persuade her to do so. She was vulnerable, emotional, and drained. So she held Jayden close when she had no other choice and tried hard to keep her emotions in check on the short walk over. As she buckled him into his car seat as quickly and safely as possible, she felt Tyler's eyes on her. The hairs on the back of her neck stood up when they made eye contact, and she quickly rounded the car to get in before he could stop her.

As she backed away quickly, she glanced up and saw Tyler still standing in the doorway. His eyes were pleading and his expression was pained, and her heart tore just a little more. She'd known Tyler half of her life, had been with him almost the same amount of time, and, damn it, she still loved him despite what he'd done. Even though she couldn't forgive him.

Pathetic, she thought, but she was determined to

stay strong and forced herself to turn her back on him to leave. After dropping Jayden off at school, she looked for a good divorce lawyer to get things going before she lost her backbone. When the attorney asked the reason she wanted to leave, she was only able to come up with one word, *betrayal*. Others came to mind afterward, but most were inappropriate to use in a courtroom. She cried the whole way back to pick up Jayden. Her actions that afternoon had made everything final, but instead of feeling relieved, she hurt more. The pain just didn't seem to end. How could one person claim to love you so much and do what Tyler had? What was it with men? Did they all take some secret class called Manipulation 101? She could have sworn sometimes that they were born with a special gene because they sure had a good way of making you feel bad when you hadn't done anything wrong, or maybe that was just Tyler. Sighing heavily, she pushed these thoughts away. It was time to reevaluate her life and figure out her next steps, without Tyler. She hadn't worked in over four years, letting go of her job before Jayden was born. Her options were limited, but she needed an income and had to figure out how she could make a living while still being able to be at home with Jayden.

Two weeks later, Jenna decided to take a leap by going home again while Jayden was at school. With pulse pounding, heart racing, and hands shaking, she was finally able to breathe again seeing that Tyler's car was nowhere in sight. She knew she couldn't avoid him forever, but right now, "out of sight, out of mind" was the best she could manage.

As she walked in, she felt as though she was having a panic attack. Heat spread to her face, she started sweating, her hands shook, and her heart felt as if it were ready to leap from her chest.

"Hello," she called out to ensure she was alone.

No answer.

Trying to steady her breathing, Jenna stopped at the stairs and turned toward the scene of the nightmare from a few weeks ago. Now empty, the living room still looked like it had on that day. Magazines from the coffee table were scattered on the floor. Alex had knocked them over when Tyler had thrown her off him the first time. She closed her eyes as they began to water. A sudden burst of anger mixed with a pure rush of adrenaline consumed her then, and she charged for the kitchen. She grabbed the largest knife she could find and went back to the living room.

"In my house!" she screamed. "On my fucking couch!"

She stabbed and shredded it while shrieking and crying, finally able to release some of the rage. Jenna backed up, admiring her temporary lapse in sanity. Boy, it felt good. She loathed that bitch for what she'd done but was disgusted with herself for not being able to hate Tyler just as much.

She screamed again, letting the knife drop from her hands, and realized she needed the couch out of her sight. It represented Tyler's betrayal and all of the loss she'd endured. Charging forward, she lifted it easily and was able to pull it to the curb to be taken away with the rest of the trash. Thank God for the effects of an adrenaline rush, she thought. She felt too good to worry about the stares she'd received from the neighbors or how sore she would be later. The new renovation was good, and she smiled when reentering the house. As she imagined Tyler's expression at seeing the destroyed couch on the curb, her smile turned into a humorless laugh. So much for him not knowing she'd stopped by.

She went upstairs to pack another suitcase and realized how tiring it all was, and missed being at home. Jenna sat on the bed and admired the picture on the nightstand—the three of them from a happier time. She picked it up and ran her fingers lovingly over the image. They were on the beach, and Jayden sat in front of them with a shovel and pail. He was about two at the time, and Jenna was laughing while wrapped inside Tyler's arms. Tyler's face was partially covered because he was kissing her throat. He was smirking and looked like a man absolutely infatuated. Looking at it only made her wonder more about what had gone wrong. Had Tyler strayed because something was lacking in her?

Sighing, she threw the picture in the suitcase. That one was a keeper, and she told herself she'd pull it out every time she felt the urge to strangle Tyler.

She only noticed the faded picture on Tyler's pillow as she zipped up the suitcase, and she gasped as soon as she realized what it was of. Fingers and toes and the cute little button nose. She held it close and sobbed again.

Good God, she was tired of crying.

"I have the same reaction. I look at it every night. It's a constant reminder of what I've done to you, and I'll never forgive myself for it."

Tyler moved through the doorway and didn't stop until he sat beside her on the bed. "Jenna, I'm so sorry," he whispered, reaching up to touch her, but he pulled back before he did.

She was too emotional to voice it, but she actually believed he was sorry now that she saw him again. He loved Jayden so much, and she knew he would never have intentionally hurt him, at least. She leaned forward for comfort, needing to be held and hating that she needed him right then. Wrapping her arms around him tight, she sobbed her grief into his shoulder. Out of everything, the loss of their child had been the hardest to cope with. Accident or not, she'd held him responsible for everything and couldn't let that go.

"I know what I've done is inexcusable. I understand that," he whispered. "You were right to blame me for the baby and everything else. I just wish I could take it all back. I'd do anything to fix this." He kissed the top of her head. "Hell, this was my first attempt at going back to work, and I couldn't even make it through the day." He held up a large envelope in one of his hands. "They just served me with the divorce papers."

Her eyes widened as she glanced at the envelope and then saw for the first time that he had tears rolling down his cheeks too. "Not only am I losing my wife, I feel like I'm losing my best friend too. You've been that to me for years. I need you to know that, and I also need to know if you can ever find it in your heart to forgive me."

"Tyler, I…" It was so hard to answer. Was it

possible to love someone and hate them at the same time? Because that's how she felt.

"It's okay. I'm not entirely sure I actually want an answer to that right now." He tried unsuccessfully to smile. "If this is what you want, it's the least I can give you." He took the papers out of the envelope and placed them on the night table, then signed them in front of her. "You can have whatever you want. I'll be moving out. You can come back home so that Jayden can have his room again. The house is yours and so is your car. I'll still make sure you're taken care of. Ugh, I miss you guys so much already. Please know I don't want this at all. I'm just making the first step to try and make amends." Taking her face gently into his hands, he said, "I love you, Jenna."

She let him kiss her one last time. Then he turned and walked out the door without looking back, giving her the privacy he knew she needed. She hated how he knew her so well, but at the same time having space was good. She felt a sudden impulse to stop him and bit her tongue to fight it. It was time to be strong and pray that her suffering would soon come to an end.

Jenna left the room without taking anything she'd packed because the time had come to stop hiding and mooching off supportive friends. It was time to start living again, or to at least try.

She still wasn't sure what to do with herself, and although it was nice of Tyler to give her the house, she hated having to take anything from him, period. She was still bitter and angry. Then a flood of memories came back, and it gave her the urge to go through some old photos. There had been more good times in that relationship than bad, and she wanted a reminder of them. Laughing and crying as she looked through them, she eventually began to feel guilty and realized that although she hadn't had sex with anyone else, she still wasn't innocent, either.

She'd depended on her visions of Brady, lusted for him and loved him, thought of him while being intimate with Tyler, and dreamed of him regularly. So was she any better?

After starting to second-guess herself, she began to wonder if she should have given Tyler another chance. Maybe she could learn what she'd done wrong to drive him away. It might at least rid her of some of the heartache. Starting over felt terrifying right then. She felt so alone.

***

That afternoon while Jayden napped, Jenna paced the hallway, too nervous to stay put as she waited for Tyler to arrive so they could talk. He didn't know she was back in the house officially, and she wondered how he'd react if she brought up counseling and a willingness to start over.

She finally settled at the bottom of the stairs and was looking through old photos again when his car drove up, but her smile faltered immediately at seeing his expression.

"Jenna? You decided to come home?" His last words came out in a whisper, making her smile again before she answered.

"I did a lot of thinking today and a lot of reminiscing." She looked down at the album beside her. "Tyler, I…"

She was about to tell him that she wasn't sure about her decision anymore, that she wanted to give it a try again, but she was distracted as Tyler adjusted his position to block her view of the open front door. With eyes glossy and wide, he looked guilty, yet apologetic.

"Tyler?" Jenna whispered. She felt hot with embarrassment and sick to her stomach as the situation she'd put herself into dawned on her.

"I didn't think you were going to forgive me." He stepped forward. "You served me with the divorce papers, and I—"

"Sorry it took so me so long, but it's hard to find good parking around here." Alex's smile faltered when she noticed Jenna on the stairs. Narrowing her eyes, she moved closer to Tyler, and Jenna couldn't help but think, *Congratulations, he's all yours now.*

She tried hard to hold on to her emotions, not wanting to give Alex any satisfaction. Alex's game was obvious, but Jenna wasn't playing anymore.

"Hello, Alex," she said stiffly, trying to look stronger than she actually felt. "I apologize for the intrusion. I hadn't realized that Tyler was bringing company into my home again. The couch is gone now, so were you planning to soil our bed as well?"

Tyler pushed Alex out of his way, and Jenna laughed at her insulted expression and especially at the sight of her storming off in anger. Tyler hadn't noticed.

"Jenna, I need to know what you were about to

say. Are you willing to give me a chance?"

She could see the hope in his expression. She didn't speak as she examined him closely and realized how much he could read right through her. It was as though he expected to be able to do anything he wanted while she looked the other way, grateful just to be with him regardless. Damn him for that. She wasn't as stupid as he clearly thought.

He took advantage of her vulnerability and the opportunity and pulled her forward. She closed her eyes, allowing him to kiss her, and let a little bit of anger come out in how aggressively she responded, because it really was good-bye. There was no way to turn back now. Tyler lifted her into his arms and carried her upstairs before she snapped out of it. As the door to the bedroom shut, she quickly pulled away.

"Oh my God, what am I doing? What are you doing to me?" She was out of her mind. He'd literally driven her insane.

"Jenna, I might not have known it before tonight, but having you here, seeing you when I walked in, the albums—you still love me, just as much as I love you. I know you were about to tell me you wanted to be together, to stay together." He grabbed her hands, held them, and waited for her to answer.

"You're right, Tyler, but you're also very wrong. I missed being at home, and so did Jayden. Then I started to think about things after I got here and reminisced through the memories and began to second-guess myself." She wanted to explain herself clearly to him so she wouldn't have to repeat what she was about to say next. "I was delusional for a brief time. I wanted to work things out with you, and yes, that's what I was about to say when you walked in, but then you gave me a reminder that you're not going to change. Alex is your addiction, apparently, and you aren't going to stop. I can see that so clearly now. So we can't be together like this anymore. It's over."

He stood there silent, looking crushed, and she smiled, because the admission made her feel so free. "Tyler, you have been my best friend since I can remember. One of the best parts about our relationship was how easily we got along together. But clearly this is not meant to be. I'm not sure what happened between us to change things, but you have to admit that you could see it too, or you wouldn't have looked elsewhere. Something's missing, and I was blinded until now. Can't you understand? If I let this continue, I'm going to end up hating you, and I don't want that. We need to move on. I need some space so I can get through all of this anger and hurt, because I don't want to lose you for good. I want my good friend back one day, and Jayden needs his dad."

She'd finally realized she'd been holding on to what they once had, not what was still there. She'd been unhappy for a while, and it was time to move on. The hard part would be learning how to forgive, because Lord knows she'd never forget what had happened.

Chapter Twenty

Tyler moved out that night. She helped him pack and didn't want to know where he was headed, whether to a motel or Alex's place. She preferred not knowing for certain; it probably would have made her angry again because she suspected it would be the latter.

A fine line really did exist between love and hate. She loved the friend she used to have, the father of her child, and the many good years they'd had together. But she also hated him for all of the lies, for causing her to miscarry, for throwing away everything they had between them, and for the ultimate betrayal of sleeping with Alex. Still, although she hated to admit it, this had been a far better outcome than her original vision. At least he was still alive, and that mattered.

The next part was the hardest. They had to tell Jayden, and she'd asked Tyler to join her a few days later so they could tell him together.

She'd just finished making him his snack, and they were both nervous when they approached him.

They sat on the couch together, and Jenna held Tyler's hand as she called Jayden over.

While Jayden looked up with curiosity, Tyler looked at her with a sudden panic, the coward.

"Thanks," she whispered sarcastically, knowing he was leaving her to start off the conversation. After taking a deep breath, she wasn't sure where to begin and needed a minute to collect her thoughts. "We wanted to talk to you about some changes," she told Jayden and was surprised by his expression. While sitting on the floor in front of the coffee table he looked at Tyler, sighed loudly, and then put his head down as he played with his fingers. She knew then that her little boy understood more than she gave him credit for.

"Jayden, Dad and I are separating, so you need to know that he's not going to be living with us anymore."

Honestly, how were you supposed to explain this type of situation to a four-year-old without getting a negative reaction? She didn't know what else to do but come right out with it while trying to be as sensitive as possible in the process.

Jayden silently let her words register and then leaped into Jenna's arms to cry. She wasn't too far behind him, shedding some of her own tears.

"It doesn't change how much we both love you," she assured him, and Tyler finally stepped in.

"I'll still be here whenever you need me to be, and you can come stay with me sometimes too, if you want."

Jenna sucked in a shocked breath, knowing instantly that she shouldn't have that reaction. She hadn't thought about not having Jayden in the house all the time. That was an adjustment she'd definitely have to make.

Jayden pulled away and hopped off Jenna's lap. "First Mommy and now me. Why are you hurting us?" he yelled, then ran up to his room and slammed the door shut.

Stunned into silence, neither one of them knew what to do next. Obviously, she wasn't the only one who'd built up some anger over all that had happened.

"Maybe I should go," Tyler suggested.

"You're not going anywhere. Did you expect any other reaction out of him? Just give him a few minutes and we'll talk this through. The least you can do is stay for that."

Tyler agreed and stuck around through dinner. Jayden sulked at first, but she played the mediator and eventually got him to open up to his father.

***

"Okay, you're driving me absolutely nuts," Sam told her. "What's wrong now?"

It was a beautiful summer day, and they were at the park with Jayden. Almost six months had passed since all hell broke loose, money was tight, and she still felt useless. Jenna had managed to get a part-time position at Jayden's school after months of volunteering and hated that she still had to rely on Tyler's child support. She had to figure out what she could do to achieve financial independence and still be able to be home for Jayden. She fantasized about the day she could actually tell Tyler to take his money and shove it. Okay, not really, just as long as it wasn't a means of supporting her. Maybe one day she'd be financially comfortable while still being a loving mom for her child and Tyler's money could go toward Jayden's college fund instead of food.

"I just feel so useless, like I haven't accomplished anything in my life. I'm a twenty-eight-year-old divorced woman, and I still have no clue what I should be when I grow up." She sighed, knowing she'd been off in her own world trying to figure things out. It didn't help that Tyler had started to take Jayden around Alex lately—more stress she didn't need. He'd jumped into that relationship immediately after she'd let him go, moving in with Alex that same night.

"I've failed at everything."

"Not everything." Sam laughed, pointing toward Jayden, and she couldn't help but smile and agree. "When it comes to that, you're the luckiest person I know."

"How did you do it?" Jenna asked.

"How did I do what?"

"Become established enough to stand on your own two feet without anyone else."

She laughed. "Anyone can do it. Your life is what you make of it. All it takes is a little hard work and determination to be successful if you want something badly enough. You just have to figure out what it is that you love and work from there."

Jenna groaned. "It's easier said than done."

Sam laughed. "It's not that hard, Jenna, think

about it. What is it that you love the most?"

"Jayden," she blurted out without a need to think about it. "I love being able to be there for him, sitting here in the park, helping out at his school, and telling him his favorite bedtime stories at night. I love being a mom, but unfortunately it's not a job that pays you in money. It pays you in rewards."

"Well, then, there's your answer," Sam said. "Sounds to me like you've come up with two options. You either continue what you're doing and keep the small job at school so you can be there for him always and maybe build it into more, or you can go into business for yourself and be there for him always. You love telling him his bedtime stories, Jenna, and I've heard some of them. They're not bad. Have you ever thought about trying to write some of them down, maybe try a career creating children's books to share with others who also enjoy a good bedtime story or two?"

"Children's books?" The more she thought about it, the more appealing the idea became. Maybe that was something she could work on with Jayden. It definitely wouldn't hurt to try, and she laughed at the thought. When she pitched idea to Jayden later that night, he seemed just as excited as she was.

Jenna got to work right away and got what she wrote down "Jayden approved" before she would even consider attempting to get it published. She wrote three children's picture books within the first couple months, sent them out, and eagerly awaited a reply.

The first few rejections were the toughest, but her patience was rewarded when she got her first acceptance. By the time she was slowly on her way to becoming established, another six months had passed.

Just before Christmas, Jenna had more great news. Her publisher had signed her for three more books. She was getting ready to go to dinner with Sam, Jayden, and her parents to celebrate when Tyler stopped by unannounced.

"Did I come at a bad time?" He asked after she let him in.

"We're going out to dinner." She extended an invitation for him to join them but could instantly tell something was up by how uncomfortable he looked.

He shook his head. "I'd come back later, but I really need to talk to you. Do you think you could stay?"

"Are you sure that's such a good idea, Jenna?" Sam asked and went to stand beside her. She folded her arms and began to tap her foot with impatience. Good ol' Sam, her protector.

Her parents cleared their throats and decided to take Jayden outside. "We'll just go and wait in the car until you or Sam let us know what the plan is," her mother said.

"It's fine, Sam. You all go ahead to dinner and I'll fill you in later, okay?"

The only reason she agreed, other than her insane curiosity, was because he genuinely looked upset. She sent the others on without her, promising they'd all go together another time.

"Okay," she said once they were alone. "I'd say we have a good hour or two before they're back, so let's talk." She directed him to the dining room table and took a seat, gesturing for him to do the same.

"I still miss you," he whispered.

She already didn't like where he was heading. "Tyler, please don't start with this. I'm only beginning to get my life back on track, and I can't afford to take a step backward."

"Fine, it's Alex. I actually came over here to talk to you about her, hoping you could be there for Jayden or at least to help me out if he gets upset. Most of all, I'm hoping you don't hate me even more after this."

"I'll definitely be here for you, whenever I can. You know that, and you also know that when it comes to Jayden, my answer is clearly the same and then some." Smiling, she added, "And about hating you more, I'm not sure if that's humanly possible."

Teasing him seemed to cheer him up for a brief moment, and he smiled with her.

"So what, have you decided to marry her or something?" she asked, and he laughed, shaking his head.

"Hell no, although she isn't opposed to the idea."

"I'm not a mind reader. You came here to tell me something, so tell me."

"Jenna, this is harder for me to say because it's such bad timing, but you have the right to know. I thought it was fair that you find out first." He looked away again, as though he was ashamed. "Alex is pregnant."

Jenna sat there frozen, trying to collect her thoughts. In that second, she couldn't stop thinking about herself. Just about a year ago to the day, she'd been pregnant with his child, and his news brought back all the loss she'd suffered. Now he was sharing the experience of a new life with someone else, and all of it came to the surface again. Of all the things he could possibly have said...

She quickly moved her hands away from his, needing a minute to absorb what he'd said. She could feel the lump in her throat, and her vision blurred, but she wouldn't let him see her cry. "I just need a minute," she whispered and walked upstairs for some privacy.

This was her first breakdown since he'd walked out the door the last time, her one weak moment just as she was beginning to feel strong again, the one and only thing that would get to her. *Bad timing? This is horrible.* As if it wasn't hard enough with the anniversary of her loss approaching, he had to follow her up the stairs to witness her hurting.

"Tyler, please," she begged. She needed some time to pull herself together. Not listening, he pulled her into his arms. She hadn't cried that hard in months.

"I'm sorry," Jenna managed after a few minutes. "You're having a baby, and all I can think about is the baby we were supposed to have. It's not fair," she cried. "It's just not fair."

She pulled away but he only tightened his arms around her.

"I could always trip her," he said. He'd always had a twisted sense of humor.

"That's not funny. I wouldn't wish that experience on anybody, not even Alex."

"It's nice to hear that not everyone is that mean." He smiled, and she knew exactly what he was talking about. Unlike her, Alex had actually been pleased when she'd lost the baby. It was one less obstacle toward her goal of winning Tyler.

"Yeah, but you're the one that chose her," Jenna answered and actually laughed a little. "She is mean, but mean is what you wanted. Life is what you make of it, and you have to live with the consequences of your actions." She repeated what Sam had told her, adding a little more to the wisdom.

He sighed heavily and gave her another squeeze before letting her go. "I did, but it's like I told you before, losing you is my biggest regret. I'm always going to love you, and no one could ever replace that. I just screwed it up beyond repair, and you're right. Now I'll have to live with those consequences. The toughest part is going to be when you actually meet someone you want to be with," he admitted. "I have no doubt it's going to happen, and I'll be the first to tell you I'm not going to like it." He sighed before continuing. "And one day you'll have more children, and I don't think I'll be handling it as well as you have."

The last part made her smile. "Are you trying to make me feel better?" she whispered, leaning into him as they sat on the bed.

He sighed again. "If it's working, I'll take it. But honestly, Jenna, I'm just telling you the truth. You're much stronger at handling this kind of stuff than I am."

"It's working," she teased, and this time he

laughed.

They hadn't had a decent conversation with each other in so long. Her one weak moment with him led to more. One minute they were laughing and on somewhat good terms, and the next, he brought his face closer to hers and tried to kiss her.

She backed up in disgust to fend him off. "No, Tyler, this can't happen. You and I are over. Don't make me into the other woman, because it won't happen." She laughed then at the thought. "How is it that I would become the other woman? It's just too weird." She shook her head when he didn't answer. "I think you should get back to your pregnant girlfriend."

She hoped not to get caught being in such an intimate place with Tyler. It would have been a mistake if she'd allowed anything to go further between them. She was making progress with her new life, and the last thing she needed was to take a step back. Or worse, that she would get Jayden's hopes up, because a reconciliation was out of the question. There was no going back. She wasn't like Alex, and she certainly wasn't into cheating like her ex-husband apparently was.

"As far as I'm concerned, you're the only woman who matters," he said, looking hurt by her rejection, but she couldn't allow herself to feel sorry enough for him to take him back.

"I'll still be here for you whenever you need me to be—to talk, that is." She wanted to clarify that fact. "And I'll back you up when you decide to speak to Jayden about the baby, although I don't think he'll get as upset as I did." Then she smiled shyly. "Sorry about that. Next time I won't be so self-absorbed." She held open the bedroom door and gestured him to follow her out.

They were standing by the front door now, and he squeezed her hand. "No, not self-absorbed," he said. "You are far from that, and you also have a right to be upset, considering what I threw away."

She could see that he was hurt by the loss of what their relationship had been; she'd always known that, but it still wasn't enough for what he wanted.

"Thanks for understanding, Tyler."

She was grateful when the arrival of her parents and Jayden interrupted them at that point. She felt as though they were about to have another moment, and she didn't want to have to repeat her protest. Things would have only gotten worse if they'd become intimate, especially for her.

He stayed a little longer to spend time with Jayden and looked reluctant to leave as the evening wore on. She smiled, then exhaled loudly, seeing his expression as Jayden dragged her with him to walk Tyler to the door. The situation made her feel like this was another good-bye to what once was, and Jenna actually felt bad for him.

Bad choices turned into entrapment, and she could see why he wasn't exactly ecstatic at the idea of having a child with Alex. He didn't love her, and he never looked as happy as he used to, but she also couldn't help but smile knowing it.

He'd chosen his path and now he had to live with it.

Chapter Twenty-One

She was in the empty white room again when Sam appeared. She was shocked, secretly hoping she would see someone else. Brady hadn't been around for the last couple of weeks.

"Here," Sam said with a grin. "An early birthday present, or call it a late one, whatever makes you happy."

She held out an envelope, and Jenna took it, regarding her skeptically. "What are you up to? My birthday is not for another five months."

Two blank strips of paper were inside. Sam laughed at her confusion. "It's a surprise, silly, and I can't go ruining it for you yet. But you'll find out soon enough, and I can't wait to see your real reaction. I will tell you that it's something you've always wanted, though."

Jenna was started to get annoyed.

They were in Jenna's kitchen suddenly and everyone was over. Tyler entered and looked behind him impatiently. "Are you coming, Jenna?" he asked, and like magic Jenna had a cake in her *hands for Jayden's birthday.*

As she walked into the other room, she made a shocking discovery. Alex stood beside her son with her hand on his shoulder. Tyler didn't usually bring her to these types of events, and Jenna tried hard to compose herself for Jayden's sake. Alex being included was bound to happen sooner or later.

Alex's belly was huge, and she was flaunting in front of Jenna as much as possible. Taking a deep breath, she decided to be the bigger person as she approached.

"Alex, I wanted to extend my congratulations to you personally."

Alex smiled and looked smug. "We're having a girl," she'd said proudly. "Did Tyler tell you?"

Jenna nodded even though he hadn't. "A girl, that's amazing." She tried to sound enthusiastic.

Sam stepped up beside her for support and started a conversation with Alex to relieve Jenna of her duty of playing the nice hostess. "Have you thought of any names?" she asked.

Without hesitating Alex answered, "Skyler, because it's similar to her father's, and I know they're going to be close."

Alex was rubbing it in, and Jenna couldn't take anymore. Rolling her eyes, she watched herself walk away.

She woke up feeling weird, wondering what all that was about. The room was pitch-black, and she tried hard to fall back to sleep but couldn't. *Dreams*, she thought, *weird dreams*. Then Brady came to mind. Why wasn't he in them anymore? It was silly, but she missed him desperately.

She turned on the lamp and got up to get a book to read. Nothing was more relaxing than a book, she decided as she turned on the lamp. She laughed after picking up the one she'd supposedly read when she thought she was in Ireland. It was a weird coincidence after thinking about Brady only a minute ago. She smiled and wondered if maybe this might bring him back to her somehow. With the lack of romance in her life, reading about it couldn't hurt any. She missed the intimacy of having someone to go to bed with, to cuddle up to, and even just to talk to.

Sighing heavily, she crawled back into bed and moved what used to be Tyler's pillow to her side as she got comfortable. Holding it made her wonder when she was going to find love again. She read the first five chapters and sighed when the good parts were coming. It was beginning to feel depressing reading through the romantic parts. Suddenly feeling as though she'd read enough, she lay back down and cuddled against the pillow beside her. She eventually drifted back to sleep, but there was still no sign of Brady.

In the morning, Sam stopped by for coffee. "So I had another dream last night," Jenna began. "It looks like Tyler's going to have a girl this time." She laughed. "Alex likes the name Skyler."

Sam rolled her eyes and called Tyler a dick. She'd been more upset than Jenna had been initially when Jenna told her Alex was pregnant. It was pretty comical, but Sam always knew how to make her laugh without trying.

With a smile, Jenna continued, "By the way, you were quite annoying last night, I'd prefer to wait until you're actually ready to give me my gift instead of handing me an envelope filled with blank paper."

"What are you talking about?"

"I'm not sure, actually. In the dream, you said 'Happy Birthday' and handed me an envelope with blank paper in it. Only it was Jayden's birthday, not mine, and then you said you didn't want to ruin the surprise right away but looked forward to my reaction and that it was something I've always wanted. It was all kinda frustrating." She shrugged and watched Sam's reaction closely.

"So where was Brady?" she asked, taking the subject off herself.

"I don't know," Jenna admitted with disappointment. "He hasn't come to me in months, which only proves that I'm insane for holding on to some kind of hope that he's real and we share this incredible connection."

Sam gave her a wide smile. "Well, one of these days you're just going to have to find out. You didn't meet him here, Jenna."

"True, but I also doubt I'm going to ever get out of this place. I'd hate to think of poor Jayden stuck with Alex for a few weeks." Jenna shuddered at the thought. "The poor baby." But the thought of taking a vacation sounded appealing. She hadn't had one in ages, but the prospect seemed highly unlikely any time in the near future.

***

The anniversary of Jenna's loss had come and gone, and it was time to tell Jayden the important news about becoming a big brother, no matter how painful it was. Tyler had come by so they could do it together.

"You're not going away again, are you?" Jayden looked as though he was about to hyperventilate.

"No, Jayden. Your dad is having a baby with Alex this time, not me. I'm not going anywhere."

Explaining things to Jayden seemed to calm him a little, but then he looked confused. "You could do that?" he asked Tyler. He'd asked so innocently that they both laughed. Tyler had been pretty quiet up until that point, and he almost fell off the couch he laughed so hard. That was it for Jayden. Shrugging, he rushed off to go play.

"You see, I knew he'd be fine," Jenna said, rubbing it in. Tyler had been overly stressed out about breaking the news to Jayden, but it was all in vain. Their little man was a trooper. Jenna sighed. She seemed to have been the only one who took the news hard at first. She needed a subject change. "By the way, I had another vision, and it was about your baby."

"The visions, right." He laughed, looking at her as though she was a nut.

"Test me, then, if you're in such disbelief," she challenged.

He sighed, getting comfortable on the sofa. "All right, Jenna, I'll humor you. Let's have it. You've had a vision..." He paused, waiting for her to continue.

She smiled, excited from the anticipation of

freaking him out and knowing that she'd prove herself. "It's a girl this time. And Alex likes the name Skyler because it's similar to yours."

He laughed at her, but Jenna shrugged it off, not really caring whether he believed her or not. He'd soon find out, and then she'd be the one laughing.

***

Three months later she stood in her kitchen. Tyler and Alex had just arrived, and the rest of the family and a few of Jayden's friends were due at any minute. Tyler didn't usually like having Jenna and Alex in the same room, so it was a shock to see her in the living room again. Alex was sporting a little baby bulge, and Jenna needed some air. She had to get over it. She knew she did. But seeing a pregnant Alex was something she hadn't mentally prepared herself for. It brought back all the betrayal, and visualizing Alex naked again certainly wasn't a highlight of her day. She escaped to the kitchen.

"Get a grip," she muttered to herself. This was her son's birthday. If anything, she could pull it together for him. "Might as well get used to it. Whether you like it or not, Alex is going to be a part of the family." She shook her head to clear away her thoughts and busied herself with preparing food and refreshments instead.

Sam walked in looking worried. "Are you okay?"

Jenna nodded. "Yep, just finishing up before the house is packed with family and friends."

"So that's why you're hiding in here. I thought

maybe it was because of Ms. She-Devil in there. You know, I used to think she was a bitch, among other things, but now I'm thinking she's more like a cow. Let's hope she gets huge stretch marks, spider veins, and a long and painful labor and delivery." Sam wiggled her hands as if she were casting some sort of spell, making Jenna laugh.

"You're a wicked woman, Sam. Remind me to stay on your good side. Now behave and help me take this stuff into the living room."

Jenna had bowls of chips and cheesies, nachos, pizza, mini subs, and a veggie platter with dip. She'd expected a good turnout and overplanning was better than coming up short on anything. "Let's hope everyone is hungry."

"Wait," Sam said. "Before you mingle, I was hoping we could talk about something first."

Jenna put down the tray of food she held and wondered what couldn't wait until later. "Sure, Sam, what's up?"

"Well, you kind of ruined the surprise a couple months ago, but I want to tell you about it now so you can make the proper arrangements. I also wanted to brighten your day. You could use it." She looked toward the living room. "I've been thinking about you and Brady, and it's time you finally moved on, so here." She reached out and placed a white envelope in Jenna's palm. "'Happy Birthday' is what I apparently say, right? It's a little early but…" She shrugged.

Jenna smirked while remembering the dream. "Let me guess. Is it empty? Or…I know, it must be blank paper."

"Just open it."

So she did anxiously. "What's this?" Taking a closer look, Jenna felt as though she was going to tear up right then and there. It was that or faint. "A travel brochure, Sam? To Ireland? Are you kidding me?"

"I've made arrangements to go this summer, so there is plenty of time to make arrangements for Jayden. He goes to your parents around that time every year, and I thought it'd be perfect timing." Sam gave her a hug, looking anxious yet excited at the same time.

Smiling wide, Jenna was still in disbelief and actually had the butterflies-in-the-stomach type of excitement at the possibility.

Sam seemed to interpret her silence as hesitation and began her argument. "Jenna, I've already made all the arrangements, so I'm not letting you back out. You have to find him, so you'll know for sure. He's the man you love, and you know this was meant to be. Your visions have said so several times. Take a chance, please."

"I'm quiet because I'm touched, not because I don't want to go. I'm a little nervous, I'll admit. I mean, what if I'm wrong about him, or we can't find him, or even worse, he's just a figment of my imagination? What then? But mostly I'm excited."

Sam screeched in delight while Jenna giggled at her enthusiasm. "Finding Brady," she said when the initial shock that the trip was actually going to happen wore off. "Wow." She'd always wanted to travel, and Sam had just given her the opportunity. The worst that could happen was that she would prove herself wrong and not find him, but regardless it was going to be an experience of a lifetime.

"I wondered what was keeping you." Tyler cleared his throat as he stood in the doorway and would not take his eyes off Jenna. "Need any help?"

Jenna eyed Sam and wondered how much Tyler had heard. She quickly put the brochure into the cupboard and grabbed a few trays to carry out. "Sure, you can help with these." She nodded in the direction of the remaining things and headed into the living room. "Sounds like everyone is finally here. You coming?"

She left feeling Tyler's eyes still on her, and she wasn't sure why she was nervous about him overhearing their conversation. Knowing Tyler, he wouldn't like it, though. Traveling, mysterious men, and possibly moving on were not subjects of conversation anyone wanted to have with their ex.

His eyes stayed on her for most of the afternoon. Almost every time she turned around, he was there, watching. Something was definitely bothering him, and she knew she'd eventually find out how much he'd heard. Lost in thought and the surrounding commotion, Jenna hadn't noticed Alex's approach.

"It's a girl. Did Tyler tell you?"

"Um, congratulations, and no, I haven't had much of an opportunity to speak with Tyler today. A girl, that's just amazing," Jenna repeated, trying not to laugh. "Do you have any names picked out?"

"I was thinking either Alexis or Skyler, since they're both similar to Tyler and mine."

"Skyler is a very beautiful name. I mean, they

both are." She began to giggle, unable to contain it any longer. Oh, she had to see Tyler now that her vision had been confirmed, because it was time for an "I told you so." This was going to be good. "If you'll excuse me."

Tyler was across the room, talking with Jenna's parents. Jenna approached them with a smile plastered on her face. Nothing was going to get in the way of her upcoming gloating session.

"Tyler, can I see you for a minute?" Before he could answer, she tugged him away. "It won't take long."

The house was packed, so she led him to the basement, thinking that nobody would look for them there. When they were finally alone, she grabbed his hand and laughed again. "So I've heard the good news. Are you freaked out because I've finally made you believe in my visions?"

"Jenna, who's Brady?"

Jenna sat down on the couch with a thump "A man I've been seeing for a while," she whispered. He had heard, but it was hard to explain. She couldn't look at him while she did. "A person I'm not even sure exists. I've only seen him in my visions." She felt stupid telling him, knowing how crazy it sounded, and she waited for him to say something.

He sighed heavily and joined her on the couch. "And you and Sam are planning to go find him because you love him."

Jenna nodded. "Stupid, right?"

"I was afraid of this. I told you that one day you'd move on and I wouldn't like it, but what scares me more now is that you'll probably find him."

She sat silently, staring at him, wondering how he was so sure.

"Jenna, when you came out of your coma after the accident, you called out his name often while you slept. I was always curious about who he was, but was afraid to ask. When things happened with Alex, and you first told me your visions, they were correct, but I was in denial, thinking it was kind of crazy." He chuckled quietly. "Then when I tested you, you told me I was having a daughter, going far enough as to tell me her name, and you were right again. I believe you, and that's what scares me. Having visions of this Brady guy convinces me more than ever that you're going to find him, and I'm heartbroken."

"Join the club," she snapped. If anyone knew heartbreak, she did, and Tyler was the source of it.

"I deserved that," he whispered, trying to smile again. "I know this is something you probably don't want to hear, but I have to get it off my chest before it's too late. I still love you unconditionally, and I need you to know that no one else will ever be what you are to me. I screwed up royally and have been paying for it ever since. If there was one chance that I could be with you again, I swear I would spend the rest of my life making things up to you. I know you know this, because I've tried telling you so many times before. I guess I just hoped that one day you would change your mind and we'd be together again. We did have several good years together. Try to remember them."

Jenna couldn't believe what she was hearing. She'd been certain that she'd made things clear before, but obviously she'd been mistaken. She knew she had to think carefully before speaking, because she was just about to blow up at him. He was trying to take advantage of her vulnerability again. But before she could say anything, he leaned forward and pressed himself against her. He nipped at her bottom lip and forced his tongue inside her mouth as he slowly tried to topple her.

"Tyler, stop," she yelled and shoved him to the floor. "I can't believe you. You want to talk about hurting, how about we talk about the countless times you slept with another woman while we were married? The countless times you lied to my face? The times you ditched your son and me to be with her? Then maybe we could bring up the times you disrespected me enough to do those things in my house? How about the baby I lost as a result of that, or the fact that you moved in with her the first chance you got, or the fact that she's pregnant with your child right now, and the list goes on." She looked at him in disgust. "It's never going to work, and I just can't do it anymore, so I need you to stop trying. I mean, my God, I hope now more than ever that you're right. I hope I find him, or someone else, who knows, and then maybe you can get just a glimpse of the pain I suffered because of your actions. You have no idea, do you?"

"You're right," he whispered, looking hurt. He took a step in her direction, and she just couldn't do it anymore.

She moved farther away from him "I can't,

Tyler. I just can't love you that way anymore. It hurts too much," she whispered and had to get away before she began to cry. She made a dash for the stairs, leaving him there. Tyler was fine when he'd thought she was alone. As soon as he thought she might want someone else, he turned on the head games. It wasn't fair, and she was sick of it. She hoped she'd finally made things clear once and for all.

She sighed after reaching the party again. Holding back her anger, she tried her best to be happy and sociable as though nothing had happened.

Tyler wasn't such a good sport. Within the hour he apologized and gave the poor excuse that he wasn't feeling well. Thankfully, Jayden barely noticed them leave.

Chapter Twenty-Two

Life was so unfair sometimes. Jenna had to excuse herself for a minute. Tyler had looked like a wounded dog in the brief time before his departure, and it upset her. She needed a distraction, so she hid in the kitchen, trying not to be too obvious about her distress.

Sam followed. "What happened?"

Busying herself with the dishes, Jenna decided to give her the short version. "Tyler overheard us. Long story short, he didn't like it."

Sam laughed.

"It's not funny. He got really upset, almost panicked for once, and he wanted me to take him back, practically begged me to, again." She sighed. "He said he'd counted on me changing my mind one day and hoped I'd reconcile with him. I just get so angry, because he makes me feel horrible, and I shouldn't have to feel that way anymore. It's like I'm being tortured over and over because he decided I wasn't enough for him. It sucks!"

"I always thought you and Tyler were meant for

each other," Sam said. "I was obviously delusional. You deserve better, Jenna. Don't forget that."

"I'm sorry." Jenna sniffed. "I thought the same thing once. Obviously, we were both delusional. I'm trying to let go, but it's so hard to just turn off the love I had for him all of those years. I wish I could just snap my fingers and *poof,* it would be gone. I guess that's what makes this all so hard." She made an unsuccessful attempt at smiling. "Damn Tyler. Just when I finally think things are getting better, he does something like this and sucks me back in."

"He's such an ass. So what did you tell him?" Sam asked, curious.

"I yelled at him and pushed him to the ground after he tried to kiss me. Then I reminded him of all the hurtful things he did to me and to Jayden. Finally, I told him I hoped I did meet someone else so he could taste a little of the pain I had to endure, and that I couldn't love him like I used to anymore because it hurt too much."

After giving Jenna a hug, Sam leaned back to look at her again. "I'm proud of you."

"Hurry up, summer." Jenna laughed while wiping her tears away. "Thanks, Sam."

"That a girl." Sam smiled. "By the way, one of these days you're going to have to dish the details on this Caleb guy. He's the one I end up with, right?"

"Yes, Sam." Jenna giggled. "And we have until the summer to get you educated on the subject."

"Tell me what he looks like again. What does he do for a living? Describe his voice for me. God, I just love a man with an accent."

"Whoa, there." Jenna laughed. "We'll get to it, but first I want to say thanks for the distraction."

It was Sam's turn to laugh. "Anytime, Jenna." She put an arm around her shoulders, and they walked out of the kitchen to join the others.

Jayden's birthday party was filled with so many emotions that Jenna was completely drained by the end of the day. He was absolutely spoiled rotten, and she agreed to let him sleep in her bed that night. He requested to watch a movie after she'd told him his bedtime story, and she couldn't deny him on his birthday.

Time had flown by, and her baby was already six. Sighing as she closed the door to her bedroom, she went downstairs to spend some time with her parents.

They were on the couch watching some boring nature show when out of the blue her mother spoke. "I hope you know that we're proud of you."

"For what?"

"Well, for everything. Despite it all, you've really made something of yourself. There was the car accident, the way you handled the Tyler situation, then there's taking care of Jayden as well as you do, and for the new career choice, making it on your own, and we're proud of how you managed yourself today. Having Alex here and her being pregnant on top of it, well you handled it all really well, and I just wanted you to know that we're proud."

"Thanks, I'm really trying."

Thinking about Tyler and especially about

Alex's pregnancy was depressing, and although it was a little premature, she decided to tell them about Sam's gift earlier. "So Sam had a surprise for me today. It turns out that she's going to Ireland this summer, and I'm thinking of going with her. Since Jayden usually has his yearly visit around that time with you guys, I was wondering if he could stay with you a week or two longer."

"Is Tyler okay with that?" her father asked, and it really irritated her.

"It isn't up to him," she snapped, but it only made her father smile.

"What I meant was that Tyler might want some time with him too. You know how much I love having Jayden around. I just don't want to cause any trouble."

"Tyler knows about the trip, actually, and I guess I'll figure that out closer to the time. Alex will have had the baby by then. But Jayden really doesn't like staying at Tyler's house, and I guess I just wanted to make sure I had an alternative, just in case I can't depend on Tyler."

"Of course, honey, he can stay as long as you need him to," her mother assured her.

***

Her suitcase was packed, her parents had just picked up Jayden, and Sam stood at her bedroom door waiting.

"Come on, Jenna. The taxi's outside, and if you take any longer we'll miss our flight."

Jenna laughed at her and found it really hard to

contain the excitement as she rolled her suitcase along behind her. "Okay, I'm finally ready." And she was, in more ways than one.

She smiled the whole way to the airport, anxious to find out if he existed, the point of it all.

"Do you think this is crazy?" she asked nervously, making Sam laugh as they stood in line to check their luggage.

"No, not crazy, Jenna, I'm just excited to see if it will all work out."

Jenna laughed again. "Are you ready to meet Caleb?" she teased, making Sam's smile widen as she pulled Jenna along to their gate.

The scene changed, and Jenna was back in the white room again, suddenly alone but for the sound of footsteps behind her. "Sam?"

Turning around, she found that he was closer than she'd thought, and her face pressed against his chest. She'd missed his smell, missed everything about him. She placed her hands on his waist and looked up, enjoying the moment and taking advantage of the opportunity to feel him against her once more. She could feel his breath as her lips touched his, and she smiled.

"I missed you so much. Where have you been?"

She was afraid of letting him go, in case he might disappear on her. He smiled as if he'd read her mind and looked as happy as she felt in that moment.

"Don't ever leave me again," she whispered and pulled him flush against her. The kiss started off slowly and ended with both of them breathless.

She wanted him, real or not.

"I'm here as long as ye want me to be," he repeated. At least she knew she'd heard those words somewhere before, but she couldn't remember where. "Jenna, ye've been goin' through a lot and kept me away, love. Now I'm the one who should be tellin' ye not to leave me." He quickly kissed her again. "But I'm just happy ye'r here now and that we'll be together soon enough. So hurry up and come get me."

"I'm working on it, and if you're real, I will find you."

The white room vanished, and they were in the airport in Ireland. As she stood with Brady, she watched herself and Sam in the distance while they waited to grab their luggage.

Jenna gasped. "What's going on?" she asked as he smiled lovingly at her.

"I'm showin' ye what's meant to be, darlin'. Be patient."

She watched her distant self looking nervous as she talked to Sam and continued watching as she turned around in the opposite direction only to see Brady standing there, just staring at her.

Jenna gasped. "Oh my God! Speaking of beautiful scenery," she said, repeating what she knew Sam had said.

"What?" Brady laughed beside her.

"It's what Sam said when she noticed you and Caleb standing there, staring," she explained. "We're there; we are actually there together." She was in awe looking at the scene from a third perspective, and then it disappeared, and she was horrified.

"What are you doing? Where did we go?"

"Patience, Jenna. I just wanted to show ye that it's goin' to happen, love, so come get me as soon as ye can." He moved the hair away from her face and looked her deep in the eyes. *"I love ye, darlin'."*

The butterflies in her stomach reached her throat. She loved every time he said those words to her, but then a thought came to her and she panicked. *"Are you going to know who I am?"*

Her visions were pretty close to what always happened if not right on, but what if something happened and screwed everything up?

"Do you have visions of me?" She had to know.

He shrugged. *"Trust me. It'll come together."*

She had more questions, and she knew he could see them coming, making him laugh. *"Jenna, I've got to go for now. So stop yer worryin'; it's goin' to work out, love."*

All she'd heard out of that was that he was going, and it made her want to grip on to him tighter. *"Don't go,"* she pleaded. *"Not when I just got you back."*

He caressed the side of her face lovingly. *"It's time to wake up now, but don't worry, we'll see each other again. Quite often, I'm sure of it."* And then *poof,* he was gone.

"Mommy, Mommy wake up." She could hear Jayden in the distance, his voice getting closer. She opened her eyes and smiled, hugging him tight. "I want breakfast," he whined, and she laughed after hearing his stomach growl.

Good-bye fantasy land, hello reality. It was time to wake up and enjoy her present company. Brady had come back, bringing along the enthusiasm to help her forget about the stresses of the previous day and filling her with excitement about her up-and-coming trip to Ireland. It was going to be a long remaining winter and upcoming spring. Sighing, she said, "All right, Monkey, let's eat."

***

"So what's going on?" Sam eyed her curiously.

Shrugging, Jenna continued to clean the breakfast dishes.

"Okay, Jenna, spill it. You're in an extremely good mood this morning. Not that it's not nice to see, but usually after an argument with Tyler, you're not so chipper, even the next day."

"I have to let go someday, Sam, and I'm tired of letting him get to me. But it also doesn't hurt that Brady's back, and my mood is partly due to the wonderful dream I had and its possibilities."

"He's back." Sam smiled. "And there's possibilities, huh? I like the sound of that. So what happened this time?"

Sam had always had an intense interest in her dreams and believed in them even when Jenna thought she was going crazy. When it came to Brady, Jenna assumed Sam was especially interested because of her curiosity over Caleb, although he didn't appear in very many of Jenna's dreams anymore.

"It was the summer, I guess. You were waiting

for me at the door and were worried that we'd miss our flight. We were both very excited, and you gave me a pep talk about looking forward to seeing how everything turned out. All of a sudden, you were gone, and I was back in the white room. Brady was there, and we talked about me coming to get him. I was worried, and he tried to prove to me that I was going to find him. Then we were back at the airport in Ireland, and I was watching as you and I picked up our luggage. I looked nervous and then you turned me around, and there they were, staring. "

"Who was staring? What?"

"Come on, Sam, keep up with me," she teased. "Brady and Caleb were staring. Like in my original vision, the one I was convinced was real when I woke up in the hospital. It all went away after that anyway, and I woke up shortly after." She shrugged.

Jenna laughed at Sam's disappointed expression. "Man," she mumbled, "I wish there was more to it. I mean, we already know that part."

"Maybe more will come tonight; who knows." And then the reality of the situation came at her. "It's really happening, isn't it?" she asked excitedly. "We're really going?"

"Yes, Jenna, and I think I'm looking forward to it as much as you are. Promise me you'll keep me updated on all of the good stuff, though, okay?"

"I promise."

Sam was a true believer, and for that Jenna was thankful. They were on a countdown, especially now, and it was the longest winter and spring she could ever remember.

The anticipation of going on her trip and her excitement over finding happiness again were interrupted by Tyler's gradual distance. Since his last confession and their confrontation at Jayden's birthday, he seemed to be avoiding them. Unfortunately, it was Jayden who suffered the most from it. Tyler was able to see him three weeks later for a few hours, and then three weeks turned into a couple months without a word.

Jenna had given him enough space, and she wasn't sure what to do. Jayden's hurt eventually turned into anger, and then finally into a numbness, and then he didn't seem to care anymore. She tried her best to remain strong, but Jayden's pain hurt her. She was furious at Tyler and decided it was time he had a wake-up call.

She showed up just as Tyler was about to finish work. Alex was on leave, being due in only a few weeks, and this was the only way she figured she'd be able to get him alone.

"Did I come at a bad time?" she asked after letting herself into his office. Without waiting for him to answer, she closed the door.

She guessed he was having a bad day just by looking at him, but she didn't care whether he wanted this or not, she was confronting him. Jayden deserved better.

"I was wondering how long it was going to take for you to show up." He cleared his throat and looked uncomfortable before he had the nerve to smile.

"This is not a game," she snapped and narrowed her eyes. "This is about our son and why he doesn't seem to matter all of a sudden."

Tyler's expression hardened, and she could instantly tell she'd hit a nerve. "He matters," he snapped back. "Don't ever imply that he doesn't."

She laughed humorlessly. "Then please enlighten me, why don't you? You have seen him all of three times in the last four months, Tyler. How is that sufficient?"

He slammed a book on his desk and leaned forward so they were almost touching and stared at her in silence.

She refused to break eye contact with him. She wanted answers and hated that he always made everything about him. She was leaving to go on her trip soon and hoped to get this all resolved before she did.

"Tyler, I didn't come here to fight with you." Okay, well, that had been her initial intention, but when she was actually face-to-face with him, she just couldn't avoid it. Despite everything he'd done, she still had strong feelings for him and probably always would. Damn, that realization sucked. Tyler had hurt her badly, but this was about Jayden. She forced herself to stay focused.

"Then why did you come?" he asked and looked down at her mouth and back up to her eyes before she took a step away from him.

"I came to see what's going on with you. I came because I wanted to know if you were okay, and most importantly, I came hoping that I could salvage the relationship you have with our son."

She exhaled loudly as if she'd been holding her breath. Man, she'd thought she might lose it a second ago and was pretty sure that if she hadn't taken a step backward, Tyler would have kissed her. Then nothing would have been accomplished. It would have been bad, really, really bad.

He laughed suddenly, hysterically, making Jenna smile. Raking his fingers through his thick head of hair, he finally said, "I'm sorry, Jenna. It's just been work, hectic and as crazy as ever, and Alex is driving me nuts. She complains all the time. We've been getting ready for the baby and all of that fun stuff." He paused for a second. "And I've been selfish, which is not a good enough excuse at all. Last time we made everything so final, and I hadn't believed until then that you were never going to take me back. Since then it's been hard for me to be around you."

Hearing about the baby still hurt, but to learn that it was hard for him to be around her was something else altogether. She was shocked. "So you avoided our son because you couldn't bear the thought of being near me?" She had to be sure she understood this idiocy properly. "Because if that is the case, then you're definitely right, but I could also think of a few other words to call you besides *selfish*."

Her temper was about to get the best of her. He smiled again, putting more fuel on the already ignited flame inside her.

"I'm sure you could," he teased. Typical Tyler, trying to make everything into a joke.

Her hands rolled into fists at her sides. "You're not funny, Tyler," she snapped, "and if you know what's good for you—"

"It's over. I get it now, but I don't have to like

it."

She could feel another argument coming on and sighed heavily, really tired of it all.

"But you're also right," he continued. "My actions have been inexcusable, and I promise to make some more time for him. Maybe one day we could work on you and I being friends again too."

"I think I'd like that," she said and decided that now was a good time to make her exit before he pushed her buttons again. "He'll be around for another couple of weeks, so now is as good a time as any to see him while you can. Then he'll be at my parents' for his annual vacation." She looked back and smiled when she reached the door, hoping her visit had worked.

"Ah, your trip to Ireland," he said.

Jenna decided the best way to answer was with another smile. "Good-bye, Tyler. I really hope to see you around."

She'd done the best she could to talk some sense into him. It was up to him now to make an effort to be part of his son's life. It was time for him to grow up. Just as Jenna began to get herself together, things seemed to get worse for Tyler, but she couldn't feel any pity. All she could think was, *Welcome to my world.* She'd been suffering for almost a year and a half by then, and it was about time that reality hit him. The worst part was that this was the reality he chose to live when he decided to be with Alex, and Jenna was more ready than ever to move on with her life.

Chapter Twenty-Three

Her confrontation with Tyler seemed to work for the first week, and he made the effort he should have all along to be with Jayden. He saw him almost every day, and it was almost like old times. Unfortunately, it didn't lasted very long. The following week Tyler saw him only once and hadn't even bothered to call to say good-bye or wish him well before Jayden went to his grandparents' for the summer.

Jenna later found out that Alex had gone into labor and had the baby. It was Tyler's last distraction from his son, and she understood. It just would have been nice, though, if he'd included Jayden by allowing him to meet his new sister, but she kept that to herself. Her conclusion was that maybe they were better off without him, no matter how harsh that sounded. Tyler had created a new life that carried nothing but hurt and disappointment as far as they were concerned. Although her door would always be open, she just knew that he didn't plan on using it anymore.

It was heartbreaking.

***

She was alone and all packed. Jayden had left for his summer vacation that afternoon. It was an emotional good-bye for Jenna this time, because she had never been away from him for this long—willingly, anyway.

She couldn't sleep that night. Her nerves were getting the best of her, and she figured that sleeping on the plane would make her trip seem shorter, so she sat there fantasizing about Brady and what she would say if she saw him in real life, wondering if she'd be nervous or not. Who was she kidding? Of course she would be. She'd have the urge to touch him, to make sure it wasn't a dream. She smiled thinking about it.

She'd been alone about a year and a half now and had gone without sex for just as long. She missed having someone to cuddle with and be there for her as well, although she had to admit the sex was something to look forward to. Substitutes just weren't the same.

She got comfortable and decided she needed some type of release. She ran her fingers down her body and cupped a breast with one hand. As she rubbed and tweaked the nipple, she slid her other hand inside her shorts to the girly bits that ached the most. She was wet the instant she pictured her Irish dream man and moaned, "Hmm, Brady—"

Jenna lifted her hips and applied pressure. She circled her budding nub while picturing his tongue there, sliding between her folds to eat her, taste her. She would run her hands through his soft, thick, dark hair to hold him in place, and he knew what she liked, hitting just the right spots.

Her breath turned rapid. Release was so close, and her excitement built as the fantasy continued. She moaned again.

"Jenna?"

Holy shit, had someone just called her name? Or was it her overactive imagination? Please, not now.

"Jenna, are you up there?"

"Shit," she groaned, and her playtime came to a crashing halt. *So close, so damn close.* "Yeah, Sam, I'm in my room. I'll be down in a minute." With a sigh she covered her face to try to calm down before she went downstairs. She met Sam in the kitchen a few minutes later and started a pot of coffee.

"I couldn't sleep, and I saw your light on, so I came over. I'm so anxious." Sam rubbed her hands together and sat down.

Jenna smiled. "Me either, I'm just too excited." *Literally and figuratively.* "I feel nervous and excited at the same time, actually, but it also feels so surreal right now, you know? I've waited to go for so long, and I just want to be there already. I need answers."

Sam looked like a kid on Christmas Morning. "I know. *Eeee*, I can't believe it. In just a few short hours, we'll be on the plane and on our way. I haven't been this stoked for a long time."

Jenna laughed and was glad she wasn't the only one feeling that way. Then she sighed. "I seriously have to stop drinking this coffee," she said, pushing her cup aside. "I'll never get to sleep if I don't." She needed to come down from the high for a bit, but it was easier said than done.

"All right, that's my cue to go. We really should get some sleep," Sam advised, looking bug-eyed and ready to climb the walls. "Thanks for the coffee, and I'll see you in the morning."

Hugging Sam, Jenna laughed again. "We'll at least try to sleep, although you look like you've drunk about ten pots already."

"Very funny," Sam mocked. "I'd say the same for you, and I only said that we should get some sleep, not that I was going to." She winked. "I'll see you in a few hours, Jenna. I'm going to go home and try to count some sheep now."

***

In theory, counting sheep didn't sound that bad, but it never worked. Jenna's bags were packed and ready by the door. Her clothes for tomorrow were laid out, and the alarm was set to make sure she wouldn't sleep in the next morning. That is, if she actually was able to fall asleep. Crawling into bed, she forced herself to relax. With her eyes closed, she thought of only happy things and the possibility of them coming true, hoping they would. She was a little embarrassed to admit it, but she needed Brady to be real, wanted him desperately, and didn't know what she would do if he wasn't there. That just couldn't happen. She wouldn't think that way.

His face was picture-perfect in her mind: those piercing blue eyes and that thick, wavy, black hair, his athletic body and full, kissable lips. The visions she'd been having lately were so clear, and most of them were replays of the times she'd already seen. Deep down, she knew it was her way of trying to convince herself she was going to find him. That everything would be okay. Oh, how she hoped it would be. Soon she'd become relaxed enough that he came back to her.

They were in his bed cuddling close, and she reveled in the sense of security being with him gave her.

"Together again shortly," he whispered and she smiled.

"Together for real," she corrected him. She could feel his silent laughter in the vibration of his stomach. His excitement, she could feel against her leg.

"Is it bad that I'm not sure I want to wake up?" Jenna whispered.

He adjusted himself onto his side so he could get a better look at her, then traced her lips with his finger and smiled before he kissed her. "Ye have to wake up, love. Otherwise it'll never happen, and it's goin' te happen."

Her heart fluttered, and the butterflies in her stomach flew to her throat to release her last ounce of fear.

His beautiful eyes studied her, and his attention took her breath away. He examined her and then laughed. "God, I love ye, Jenna."

Knowing she felt the same way and knowing instantly because of all of this, that it was going to be love at first sight the moment she glimpsed him, she replied, "And I love you too, Brady."

She pressed herself against him and decided to take control again as they started to make love. She needed to have him, especially then, in case this was their last time. Imaginary or not, she wanted him always, but then he began to fade away with the annoying beeping sound in the distance, and she struggled to hold on as long as she possibly could.

"No," she groaned and reached out to nothing but the empty spot beside her. Reality came back to her, and she managed to shut off the alarm clock while still half asleep. It felt as though she'd just closed her eyes, and she was at such a good part in the dream.

Closing her eyes in a stubborn attempt to go back to sleep, she finally realized what day it was. *Oh my God, this is it.* She gasped as she sat up with a sudden, overwhelming burst of energy.

She jumped out of bed and headed straight into the shower. After drying off she got herself dressed and did her hair and makeup. She was sure she wouldn't look as good when she finally landed, but if the vision was correct, she would see him for the first time at the airport, so she had to do what she could to at least look decent. Okay, she was more nervous than she had been, ever.

She rolled her luggage downstairs and decided to call Sam. "Just making sure you're up, and I'm making a fresh pot of coffee if you want some before we leave," she told her.

Sam laughed. "Sounds good. Just give me five

minutes and I'll be there."

Her best friend let herself in while Jenna sat at the kitchen table, more anxious than ever to go on their trip.

"Oh my God," Sam said and laughed at her. "How much coffee did you have?"

It was only her first cup. "Very funny," Jenna mocked, giving her a smile. "I'm just a big bundle of nerves over here. That's all."

"But are you ready?" she asked.

"In more ways than one, Sam, in more ways than one."

The cab ride to the airport was refreshing, bringing them that much closer to their destination, but the wait at the airport was excruciating. Having to be there hours before they were actually due to board sucked, but it was either twiddle her thumbs there or at home. But at least she knew they weren't going to be late, and they'd cleared security with no problems.

Then finally after what felt like a lifetime, it came time to board. She received her first international stamp in her passport and couldn't stop staring at it. As pathetic it felt, that just made everything official.

It'd been a long journey to get where she was, and she worked on calming her nerves with alcoholic beverages aboard, so the flight wasn't so bad. The drinks relaxed her, and she slept dreamlessly for the first time in a long time for a good portion of the flight.

***

The first thing she did when they got to the terminal was look around, but she couldn't see him. *Of course, it's just my kind of luck*, she thought with disappointment.

Sam could see it in her transparent expression, and she rubbed her arm sympathetically with a smile. "Patience, Jenna. We have weeks to find them."

Hearing how confident her friend sounded always made her want to laugh. Was she the only one who still doubted herself?

Apparently.

It was more fear than anything else, and it scared her to know that deep down she needed Brady to be there. But he wasn't.

"You're right," she said and took a deep breath. Sam looked just as anxious as she did. Walking arm in arm, they headed toward the baggage claim to retrieve their bags.

"By the way, thanks." Jenna said, trying to stall a little longer. "I wanted to tell you that, in case I forget to do it later. If it hadn't been for your push to get us here, God only knows if it would have ever happened. It's an experience of a lifetime, and I can't wait to see the beautiful scenery up close and in person."

"Anytime, hon." Sam smiled and gave her a hug. "Besides, I love Ireland, so it's no big deal." She looked around the airport, and Jenna did the same. "Now if only we could bag us some dream men." She wiggled her eyebrows.

"If only."

They had their bags in hand, and it was time to

go. Jenna sighed heavily and tried her best to exude confidence despite her lingering doubt.

"Are you ready?" Sam asked, and she reluctantly nodded but took her time to move forward.

"Okay, let's go." After taking one last look around, she picked up the pace to a normal speed, and they were on their way.

As they approached the doors, Sam pulled Jenna to a stop. She cleared her throat before speaking and looked at Jenna with hope evident on her face. "Speaking of beautiful scenery."

Jenna's eyes widened as Sam nodded to the right, but she couldn't stop looking at her because she was too afraid to be disappointed already.

"Sam, don't toy with me," Jenna warned but then became breathless. "Please?"

"Jenna, I'm not toying, just look."

Her friend turned her around with force. Although two men were staring at them, they weren't the right ones. *Damn it!*

"It's not them." Jenna turned around and clutched her chest as that would help calm her heart rate. Her hopes had plummeted, and she was shaking with nerves. "I'm sorry, I really wish it was."

"It's okay, honey." Sam squeezed her hand and then threw an arm around her as they exited. "I saw them looking and had to take a shot. It's too bad too, because they were hot as hell. But nothing is set in stone, and I'm not giving up. Neither are you, okay? We've come too far for that."

And Jenna knew she was talking about more than their traveling. Sam was talking about the big shitstorm Jenna had been through since the accident, because she was one of the people who'd helped her survive it, and it hadn't been pretty.

She nodded. "Thanks, Sam. I love that you believe in me so much. You're totally awesome, babe." With the wrong airport men forgotten, they hailed a cab and headed for their hotel to start their search and enjoy their vacation time.

Indeed, not everything turned out the way it had the first time Jenna was there. It was hard to believe it had been an illusion when it felt as real then as it did now, but that was life, at least hers anyway, since the car accident. One severe hit on the head and a near-death experience, among other things, and she was blessed with the second sight—or cursed, depending on how you looked at it. Lord knew she could use a few more blessings, but then again, so could everyone.

They were staying at a castle hotel and it was extremely elegant. It had a grand circular staircase in the middle of the lobby made of solid oak, which was surrounded by beautiful tapestries on the walls and against the windows, yet the castle had a homey feel. It was a huge red-brick building with white trim from the grand entrance all the way up to the towers high above. And their rooms—Good God, she felt like a princess. They'd grabbed two single suites a few doors down from each other. Hers was pale, with white walls and purple accents, where Sam's had golden tones and flowery wallpaper. In the center of Jenna's room was an enormous king-sized bed with a beautiful purple-and-beige canopy and matching accent pillows and a lush down comforter. To the right of it, a two-seater table overlooked the acres and acres of dreamlike greenery that could be seen through the glass doors that led to a small private terrace. On the other side of the room was her master en suite, where she'd been able to get up close and personal with the claw-foot tub a few times since she'd arrived. There was nothing like dimming the lights after a hard day and soaking in the tub to relieve your everyday stresses. Especially when you didn't have to worry about your child banging on the door whenever he needed something.

Jayden.

Jenna sighed. She missed her baby like crazy, and with every passing day she was beginning to think they'd made the trip for nothing.

All too soon a week had passed, and still there were no sightings of her Irish dream man, or Sam's for that matter. They did the sightseeing thing, went to a few pubs and on a couple of tours, including that amazing helicopter tour she'd once imagined, taken a ride in a horse and buggy, and had shopped galore. So much so that she'd had to buy a new carry-on bag for the souvenirs she'd bought for Jayden and her parents.

This morning, Jenna had just finished getting ready to meet Sam to check out a few more shops and have breakfast. She kept her fingers crossed that perhaps today would be the day something— anything—would happen. She'd been so distracted with finding Brady, if truth be told, that she felt she'd missed the enjoyment of most of their activities. *Breathe easy, Jenna. Take a deep breath and let it go. If it's meant to be it'll happen, and if not you'll know you at least tried to find him. Have some fun, damn it!*

So she forced herself to let go, and did.

"So what would you like to check out next?" Sam asked later that morning. They'd stopped at the Loft for a bite. It was a quaint, cozy little café in the shopping district that had incredibly good food.

"We're on Grafton, so we might as well do some shopping." Jenna took a sip of her coffee to help wash down the muffin she'd been eating and smiled as Sam groaned.

"Jesus, those books of yours must be selling like hot cakes. Aren't you all shopped out yet?"

"I have some savings. Besides, this is a once-in-a-lifetime opportunity, and I guess I just want to bring as much of it back with me as I can. Most of the souvenirs are for Jayden and my family, but they're for me too. I'm making the dream a reality, and I want it to last. Does that make sense?" She chuckled. "Because I tell you, Sam, I want to make the most of this trip from now on. Life is way too short, and I plan to live it to its full potential. I may not find Brady but damn it, I'm done stressing myself out over it. So let's throw caution to the wind and have some fun, shopping by day, and a few drinks at another local pub tonight, whatever you want?"

"Well when you put it that way..." Sam winked, threw some Euros on the table to cover their bill, and reached across the table before Jenna could stand to leave. She squeezed her hand. "So you're stressing, huh?"

"Maybe a little." She bit her lip nervously and looked out the window before she sighed. "I want this so much I…"

"I know."

"I suppose you do, and don't get me wrong, I'm not giving up or anything. I've just vowed to have a good time from now on. This whole week I've been so distracted with my thoughts that it feels like I've let my experiences here so far slip right past me. I'm in love with a man who may or may not exist." Jenna smiled at her friend, knowing how ridiculous that sounded out loud. "And here we are with no sight of him or his friend for you."

"Have a little faith, sweetie. If it's meant to happen, it'll happen." Sam shook her head. "Just enjoy yourself."

"That's the plan, and I'm done second-guessing everything. So are you ready?" Jenna scrapped back her chair and stood as she waited for Sam to lead the way out. It felt like a whole new beginning once again, only this time with much less stress ahead of her.

The sky was a clear blue filled with big, fluffy white clouds and sunshine. The moment they hit the pavement again, Jenna stopped to take a deep breath. *Here goes nothing. With every new day is a brand new beginning. Count your blessings and take advantage of the escape. So buck up, buttercup, this is Ireland. Make the most of it…*

After visiting a few local spots, she decided to get Sam a little something as a thank-you for being so supportive and patient, especially over the last few years. So when Sam became distracted in the bookstore they were currently in, she saw an opportunity to make it happen.

"Hey, I'll meet you back here in ten, okay?"

"What? Why?" Her friend clutched the book she was holding to her chest and looked puzzled.

"Because I already found what I'm looking for in here, and I wanted to check the store across the road." She held up the bag of books she'd already purchased and smiled.

"You want me to come with?"

"It's not a big deal." Jenna shrugged. "Finish up here and meet me over there when you're ready."

"Okay, I'll try not to be too long." Sam grabbed a few more photography books as though she was rushing.

"Take your time." Jenna chuckled as she waved. "I'll see you in a few."

Blarney's was a Celtic gift shop that was filled to the brim with everything from your regular tourist tee down to some unique custom jewelry. She lightly traced her fingers along a necklace that caught her eye and thought it'd be the perfect sentiment. It was a sterling-silver chain with a Tree of Life pendant. *Better grab it before she meets you here. You don't want to spoil the surprise.* It was a symbol of family pride and earthly and celestial energies combining to form a balance between heaven and earth. And, most importantly, the Tree of Life reminded her of love and grace, an end, and most importantly new beginnings. It was perfect.

"Jaysus, 'tis been a donkey's years since I been here. Care to help an ol' bogtrotter out?" The old man winked and Jenna jumped. Her heart beat faster, and she could feel the blood drain from her face as if she were seeing a ghost standing right in front of her. *Holy shit!*

Familiar blue eyes stared back at her with sudden concern as she lost her balance and had to grasp the display table for support. Eyes she'd been dreaming about, only these didn't belong to her dream man but to the next best thing…

"Charles?" Jenna gasped, "Is that really you?" *Brady's dad…could it be?*

"Cian Charles Connelly at yer service." He helped to steady her and gave her a hesitant smile. "Ye look a li'l gobsmacked, child."

"I'm fine, really, thank you." She blushed. "You just looked a little familiar, but I must have been mistaken. I'm sorry."

"Stop the lights, whut for?"

"Why don't we start over?" She held out her hand and stood straighter. "Hello, my name is Jenna Baker. It's a pleasure to meet you, Cian."

"Lovely, Jenna." The old man winked again and softly kissed her hand before releasing her.

She grabbed the necklace for Sam and took a step back. "Now what is it you were asking me to help you out with?"

"I need a gift for me *bhean chiele*, an I was hopin' ye'd be able to help an ol' *bodach* find somethin' grand for her."

Some of the words he spoke escaped her, so she made a guess. "For your wife, then?"

"Aye."

"Okay, how about these?" She pointed to a pretty pair of earrings locked inside the display cabinet and waited for his reaction. They were platinum Celtic knot drop earrings. According to the tag next to them, the unbroken lines of the knot symbolize eternal life and love. Each earring showcased a quartz drusy stone, which dazzled with the tiny crystals covering it. The earrings also had a secret trinity knot in the back. They were breathtaking. "Any woman would love them, trust me."

"Well then—" Cian smiled "—looks like I have whut I'm lookin' for, thank ye." They chatted quietly as they made their purchases, but not until they were outside did she decided to take the risk of asking him at least one question before he left her. It may be her only chance to make progress.

"So Cian, you wouldn't happen to have a son by any chance, would you?" The old man seemed pleased she'd asked, and Jenna realized then that he probably thought she was flirting with him. "I mean…"

"'Tis no worry," he assured her and chuckled. "Me buck is in the USA at the moment. He up and left in a hurry too. Not sure when he'll be back."

"I see." Her shoulders hunched in defeat. *Would fate be that cruel to let me come this close to Brady only to miss him? Fickle bitch.* "Do you need help with anything else?"

"Nay, but I tell you what, I don't normally invite *bures* to the *gaff*, but there's somethin' special about ye, familiar." He scratched his head before shaking it. "Sarah'd call me a muppet if I did'na ask too. Wer havin' a pairti for her tomorrow, and I'd be daft to not offer an invite to such a fine thing like yerself."

"Seriously?"

"Aye, 't'id be grand if ye were there when she got this. Ye know?" He pointed to the bag with the earrings.

"That would be lovely, and I'd love to meet Sarah. Thank you." Just then Sam caught up to her. "I'm not alone, though, so would it be all right if I brought my friend along?"

There was an amused sparkle in his eye when Cian nodded and answered, "Aye." After a wink directed at both women a handshake, he gave them directions to the house, and Jenna watched as he casually walked away.

Chapter Twenty-Four

"Do I look okay?"

"You're gorgeous, now stop fidgeting." Sam smiled and held her steady. Jenna had taken extra care to make herself look nice for the party. Cian had looked so familiar that Jenna still held on to the hope that somehow he and his wife might be the link they were hoping for.

"Okay." Jenna took a deep breath and thought of her conversation with Sam the night before in her hotel room.

"So what's up with the hunky older guy?"

"I think the happily married *older guy might be Brady's father."*

"Oh as if, Jenna. I wasn't trying to imply I was interested." Sam rolled her eyes and threw a pillow at her. *"I didn't mean anything by it."* And then as if she'd just registered the full extent of what Jenna had said, she did a double take and squealed. *"He has a son and you think it's your dream man?"*

"But his son is in the US right now." Her

posture slumped a little at the thought. "I honestly don't know what to think anymore. It's like finding a needle in a haystack, and all I've got in my corner is a little bit of hope and faith I'll one day find him. Maybe I just need to move on."

"But you have been moving on, and you've been doing it for a while now. So stop stressing and live your life. It's not going to be the end of the world. We're giving this a shot, though, okay?"

"You're right." She nodded. "Cian was really nice, and I'm sure his wife is just as lovely. We'll go have some fun and there'll be nothing to it. Have I told you lately that I love you?" Jenna smirked and reached over to give her friend a big hug. "You're the sister I've always wanted, a great friend, you've always been there to listen to me, and you know when to kick me in the ass to keep moving forward." She chuckled. "So…" She got up to search through her bags. "When we split up earlier, I got you a little something to show my appreciation."

"Oh wow." Sam sat up straighter and squealed as Jenna held up the box. "You really didn't have to, but thanks!"

Jenna handed her the box, and Sam gasped when she opened it.

"Oh my God, it's breathtaking. Now help me put it on."

It was back to reality as they now stood in front of a large, newly renovated Victorian house set against the scenic backdrop of the Dublin mountains on its own large piece of land with a driveway and automatic gates. What was even more breathtaking was the view. The house was situated on acres and acres of greenery, with gardens, colorful flower beds, livestock at the other end of the property, and the spectacular ability to look over Dublin from right where she stood. "This place is amazing, don't you think?" Awesruck, she gripped the bottle of wine she'd brought from the Wine Rooms.

"It is." Sam giggled. "But you might want to pick up your jaw up from the floor and wipe your mouth a little bit before we go in."

"Oh, stop teasing." She playfully nudged her friend. "It looks like there are quite a few people here already." Judging by the amount of cars nearby, Cian's home was party central. "You ready?"

The inside of the home was just as spectacular as the outside, even more so, actually. The modern touches mixed in with the character and charm of the older house was impeccable, from the dark hardwood floors with regal-looking rugs, to the thick oak staircase in the center of the foyer that split on each side, to the pale painted walls down to the white wainscoting at the bottom. There were beautiful flowers arranged to and fro, unique-looking landscape paintings, and personal photos she undoubtedly wanted to take a closer look at once she got the chance. Could her Brady be in any of them?

Deciding that being there was exciting, nerve-racking, and an honor, Jenna almost missed Cian welcoming them. "Ah, 'tis grand ye made it. The pairti is just beginnin'. Jenna and…" He looked toward Sam to catch her name, and Jenna cringed a little, remembering that she'd forgotten to introduce them properly the last time.

"It's Sam." Her friend elbowed her in the side to keep her from continually staring awestruck. "Thank you for inviting us today. You have such a beautiful home."

"Aye, well…" Cian blushed before he bellowed a laugh. "Jenna, Sam, I'd like to introduce ye to me auld *segotia,* me *bhean cheile*, Sarah. The reason I breathe, me *gra*, and the reason for today."

The curvy beauty beside him blushed at his words and playfully swatted him. "Thank you. Jenna, Sam it's lovely te meet ch'ya." Sarah extended her hand to shake and drew them toward the crowd after Jenna gave them their gift and accepted their gratitude.

"Jaysus, I love it when she blushes." Cian grinned cheekily and winked when his wife replied with "Oh, would ya shtop?" The love they displayed was endearing, and it was nice to see how playful they were toward each other. It was clear to everyone around them that each complimented the other, and her heart broke as she wondered if she'd ever feel the same way again. She'd thought she found perfection in Tyler, but she'd obviously been wrong and now here she was, divorced, and loveless. The hope was there, though, and she was tough enough to find out if her dream man existed. It just wasn't clicking like she'd hoped, as if the pieces of her future were still scrambled. *Join the club, why don't you? Nobody is supposed to know their future, and it's not set in stone. Remember the positives. You have a beautiful little boy, loving parents, great friends, you're on a fabulous vacation, and it's a once-in-a-lifetime experience. Don't forget, Cian looks so much like Charles, and Sarah is the same name from your visions. Could she be Brady's mom?*

There was only one way to find out, and it was going to take patience before it all fell into place, her life, love—whatever—because nothing worthwhile ever came easily.

After mingling a little, the partygoers drifted outside to the yard, and Jenna leaned against one of the large French doors connected to the house while Sam went to fill her plate with goodies. She took a sip of wine and smiled when their host seated the guest of honor in the middle of the crowd and tapped his glass to gather everyone's attention.

"We're here to celebrate the love of me life. Sarah blessed this ol' heart years ago, and I thank God for her every day. May we drink to celebrate, get drunk to fall asleep, because when we fall we commit no sin, an' when we commit no sin, we go to heaven. But, before we continue on I've got a li'l somethin'…" Cian reached inside his pocket and withdrew the small box with Sarah's gift. She gasped the moment she laid eyes on the delicate pair of earrings and laughed and cried joyously when he put them on her.

Jenna smiled wide and wiped a tear of her own when Cian began his speech again. "May God grant us both many years to go on, for sure he must be knowin' the earth has angels all too few. *Slainte*

chuig na fir, agus go mairfidh na mna go deo. An'
for those who don't know what I be sayin'…" He
held his drink high. "Health to the men, and may the
women live forever! I love ye."

Cheers and whistles erupted, and that might have
been why she hadn't seen him approach until the
last second. "The ol' man sure has a way with
words."

"I think it's beautiful." Jenna smiled and turned
to face the good-looking stranger. "If only we were
all that lucky." She tipped her drink toward the
kissing older couple and then took a sip while she
watched him from above the rim. Whoever he was,
he was tall, slender, and very pleasing to the eye
with his short, tousled dirty-blonde hair and
sparkling green eyes. She instantly liked him.

"Aye, if only," he agreed. "The name's Callum,
and 'tis always a pleasure to meet such a lovely
bird."

"Oh you definitely have to be related to our
hosts. I've never met a bunch of men with such
flirtatious charm. Or maybe it's just the Irish in
general." She giggled, "Whatever it is, it's quite
refreshing."

"Oh, well I'm glad ye think so." He winked.

"Definitely, Callum." She placed her hand in his
to shake, only he had other plans and brought it to
his lips for a kiss. She gulped. "M-my name is
Jenna, Jenna Baker."

"So how long will ye be visitin'?" he asked
curiously. "Ye gotta love a woman who's as
perceptive as she is stunnin'. Family, they are.
They're like me own ma and da up there."

"What?" Jenna did a double take. "Your parents are Cian and Sarah? I thought they said their son was in the USA?"

"Aye, that'd be me cousin. Me ma and da died when I was only a boyo, an' me Aint Sarah and Uncail Cian looked after me after it happened." He shrugged.

Oh wow! "I'm so sorry. I didn't realize—I mean…" She winced and noticed how she kind of sounded like a fool. "What I mean is I'm sorry for your loss, but from the impression I'm getting, those two would be a fabulous substitute. I can't even imagine." She reached forward to touch his arm out of compassion and didn't want to imagine how hard it must have been. "How old were you?"

"Nine. Now enough of that. I'd much rather hear more about ye, and ye never did answer my question about yer visit."

"Oh." She fanned herself to try to hide the flush in her cheeks. "Sam and I will be here for another three weeks." After gesturing toward the table near which her friend was standing, she bit her lip. What was it with these attractive Irishmen and their wayward charm? It was flattering, fascinating, and a little unnerving. She was here trying to find Brady and was suddenly feeling quite guilty at being attracted to the man standing in front of her who could be his cousin. *Gah!*

"Please tell me yer pointin' to the girl and not the guy she's talkin' to." He laughed and gestured toward the portly man her friend was engaged in conversation with.

"Yes, I was, actually."

"So Jenna, I was wonderin' if ye might be free tomorrow for a bit? I can show ye how to play hurling, or we can grab a bite or a pint. Can I buy ye a bag of chips, maybe?"

"She'd love to!" Sam strolled up and nudged her shoulder after answering for her, and Jenna went wide-eyed in disbelief.

"Uh, dinner and a drink, then?" Now that Sam had answered for her, she really had no choice without being rude. "Uh, Callum, this is my very helpful friend Samantha."

"A pleasure." He locked eyes with Jenna as he gave her friend the same courteous greeting as he had Jenna with a kiss on the top of her hand. "A bite sounds great, then. I can pick ye up around seven if ye'll tell me where to do it."

Whether she was ready or not, the date was set for the following night, and she wasn't sure how to feel about that. Callum seemed really nice, and he was definitely nice to look at, but her heart still longed for her dream man. She shook the thought away. The only difference was that one man was real and the other—well, that still remained to be seen.

It's one date. What's the worst that could happen?

***

"So how'dya meet me aint and uncail?"

He'd taken her to the Auld Dubliner for a few drinks and a taste of coddle. It was a delicious, hearty stew made with traditional local sausage, bacon, and potato. It was quite a charming place, and a fabulous spot for tourists to listen to live bands playing traditional Irish music. It was also busy, but they'd managed to get a couple of stools so they could sit and get to know each other while enjoying their surroundings. She was quite charmed, actually, from the moment they'd walked in and loved that he'd taken the touristy route when he chose to bring her here for their date.

"Sam and I were doing some souvenir shopping, and I was fortunate enough to stumble upon Cian as he was searching for his wife's gift. He was as charismatic as can be and asked for my help to pick something out." She bit her lip to hold back a smile and shrugged. "I hope those earrings were a big hit."

"The ol' bugger always had remarkable taste, and I bet he knew exactly what to get her. Seeing ye just provided him a chance to talk to a beautiful bird. He's harmless, really, and loves me aint like crazy." Callum shook his head and chuckled. "Who could blame 'im? And now I get the pleasure of accompanying ye thanks to that friendliness of his, a score for me." He winked and she blushed.

He was gorgeous. Really he was, with his blond hair, striking light eyes, his easy demeanor, slim, athletic frame, and drool-worthy accent. His respectful behavior also made her completely comfortable. Tall, light, and handsome he was, but the spark just wasn't there, and she really wished it could be. Her heart, however, belonged to the clichéd Mr. Tall, Dark, and Handsome from her visions, and that scared her as well, considering they'd never even met before outside of her dreams.

She took a sip of her beer. "It's a score with me as well. The great company, I mean." Jenna smiled fondly. "Your aunt and uncle are wonderful people, and I'm always up for making new friends." She gestured back and forth between them. "I'm having a great time with you, thank you."

"Ugh!" He smiled and grabbed his chest dramatically. "Ye're pulling the friend card on me already. I must be doin' somethin' terribly wrong."

"No, not wrong." She chuckled as he feigned pulling a knife from his heart and acted goofy to lighten the mood, and was grateful he was being such a good sport about it. "You're an incredible guy, and any girl would be crazy lucky to have you. I can tell that about you already. My heart, however, belongs to another. I'm sorry."

"'Tis okay, me lovely Jenna." He winked again. "Or should I say somebody else's lovely Jenna? If anythin', I'm still glad to meet ye. Who doesn't love havin' a beautiful woman on their arm even only for a short time?"

"Thank you." She blew out the breath she'd been holding, and a weight lifted off her shoulders. She'd been reluctant to accept this date because she didn't want to lead him on, but now she was glad for it. Callum was incredible, and she'd love to keep in touch with him even after she went home. *He'd be so good for Sam, actually*, she thought and smiled at the thought of the possibilities for her best friend currently back at the hotel.

"What'dya say we get to know each other anyway? I'd love to learn more about ye and this other man of yers who's lucky enough to have yer heart."

"Well…" She cringed. *Get ready for the crazy, mister, 'cause you asked for it.* "There's not much to tell, really. Okay, I lied. There is. So here is the short version of the long story, if that even makes any sense. I'm from Canada, but I currently live in the States with my incredible little boy. He's my world, and I'm extremely close to my folks. Jayden, my son, is with them as we speak while Sam and I are on this vacation with sort of a good but unusual reason motivating us. My ex and I divorced almost two years ago now.

"You see, I got into a car accident, and it nearly took my life. I was in and out of it for a while, and lost a bit of time, so while I was out of it fighting for my life, Tyler—my husband then—was so overwhelmed with guilt over the accident that he sort of took comfort in the arms of his coworker, and I saw it before actually finding out." She squeezed his hand and took another sip of liquid courage, aka her beer, before getting to the unbelievable part. 'Cause hey, he asked for it, and for some reason she felt as though it was important for Callum to know…everything. She wasn't exactly sure why, but there it was. It was as if it was only the two of them in the room suddenly. The background faded, she tuned out the noise, and he seemed to hang on to every single word she spoke. "So anyway, you're probably going to think I'm a certifiable nut case after this, and I assure you I'm not, but when I got hurt, I hit my head among many other things, and I believe that's when the visions started."

"Visions?" His eyebrow rose in disbelief, but he seemed interested for her to go on, so she did.

"Yep, visions." She let go of his hand and licked her lips nervously. "This is the crazy part. You ready?"

He nodded and sat back to make himself more comfortable.

"Okay, so when I woke up from a coma, I was convinced my ex had died and a year had gone by before I'd moved on and fallen in love with this man named Brady who I met here in Ireland. He was amazing, very caring, and sensitive to my needs—a caretaker. Tough on the outside, but on the inside, he was all teddy bear. You know? Gorgeous really, and everything I could ever want. My dream man figuratively and literally. He was tall and muscular with hair so dark it looked black, and he had these piercing, light blue eyes one could get lost in—a real ladies' man." She shook her head before going on. "Anyway, it turns out it wasn't real, at least physically. Tyler never died, and Brady didn't exist. So I tried to make things work with Tyler. I mean, I loved him. He was my husband, the father of my child. We'd been together for so long. Everything was great too for a while. Tyler took some time off and we spent a lot of time together at first, and I thought we fell in love all over again until I kept seeing him with the other woman in my dreams. It was silly, right? I tried to ignore the sinking feeling he was having an affair, but the visions kept coming to me stronger, so I asked him about it, even going as far as describing the woman he was sleeping with behind my back."

Jenna laughed without humor, and this time it was Callum who held her hand. "It's okay, go on," he said.

"Anyway, he denied it until he was blue in the face, and I got pregnant with our second child in the midst of things. There were complications because of the stress too, but it wasn't until I walked in on the two of them having sex on our couch that everything went to hell between us. Tyler chased me outside, fell on me, and I lost our baby."

"I'm so sorry." He cupped her face and signaled the bartender to bring them another pint. "This is a lot more than I'd hoped to learn. Ye don't have to go on if ye don't want to."

"I appreciate that, but I've already gone this far, and it'll help you understand more about the one I'm in love with. It's a lot to take for our first outing, huh?" She smiled shyly but still had this crazy need to get the whole story out there.

"Go on." He nodded in encouragement.

He probably thinks I'm crazy and is suddenly glad I only want to be friends, but I don't care. "So there I was going through a divorce, trying to get over the loss of losing a child, and trying to keep it all together for my son, and I still kept having dreams of this Brady fellow. He was my shining light in the darkness in my world, and I loved him even more for it. I still do. The problem is, I'm not sure he even exists. Sam thought it'd be great to take this trip since in my dreams-slash-visions, or whatever you want to call them, I'd met him in Dublin, so here we are. You ready to run yet?"

"What?" He looked thoughtful but didn't even crack a smile. His sincerity was a little surprising, actually. "Of course not. I'm actually fascinated by it all, and yer kind of crazy doesn't scare me at all."

"Gee, thanks! I'm glad I could amuse you," she teased, and a smile came back to both of their faces. "The weirdest thing of all is how real he feels, and Sam seems to think he exists. She wouldn't have convinced me to come all the way here otherwise. She's such an amazing friend."

"Good to know yer friend is here to give ye a little push."

"There's that and the fact she's hoping to meet her own dream guy. I forgot to mention that I had visions of her with someone special as well. He was Brady's best friend. Silly, right?"

"Oh, I don't know. Fate works in mysterious ways, Jenna, and ye never do know what she has planned." He smiled and rubbed his hands together as though he had a plan of his own in mind but wasn't ready to share it with her. "So his pal was fated to yer friend? Interestin'."

"I agree. Do you have any insight for me? Does his description sound familiar at all?" she couldn't help but ask and tried not to get her hopes up too much, but they were a little.

"There are a lot of Irishmen with dark hair and light eyes, love. I know many anyway, so I'm not sure how to answer that. I'll check into it for ye, though." His eyes crinkled a little at the sides while he chuckled silently. "Why don't ye tell me a little more about yer friend, and then I'll tell ye more about meself? How's that sound?"

"You know, I was just thinking Sam would be perfect for you." Jenna giggled, and as the night wore on she had a fantastic time. Callum was something special; he just wasn't hers. Sam however, who knew? Only time would tell. They talked, laughed, danced, and drank for a few more hours before they parted ways but not before he made her promise to see him again in three days time with Sam at Cian's again for some afternoon tea.

Intuition told her he had something up his sleeve, but she couldn't pinpoint it. One thing was certain: she already cherished the new people in her life and looked forward to seeing them again.

Chapter Twenty-Five

"What do you mean he's perfect for me?" Sam fidgeted and smoothed her hair down as if to make sure not a strand was out of place.

"Well, we got to talking the other night at the pub, and I had this feeling. You know we decided we were only friends. I told you that the night of our date. Heck, it even feels weird calling it that. Callum is super sweet, and you look beautiful by the way, so stop fidgeting." She smirked.

"Fine." Sam groaned while Jenna rang the bell at Cian and Sarah's. It was an overcast day in Dublin, and she hoped the rain would hold off enough so they'd be able to sit out in the backyard again. The last time they'd been there, the landscape had been so serene, and she couldn't think of a better place to unwind and get to know the fabulous new people in their lives. She took a deep breath of fresh air and tried not to obsess over her own appearance. It was nice to see Sam being the nervous one for once, thanks to Callum's new interest in her, but Jenna wanted to make a good impression as well.

It had been three days since she'd last seen the Connellys, and while she and Sam had made the most of them, yet there was still no sign of you know who, and she was getting discouraged. She shook the thoughts away as the door opened to reveal one very appealing man.

"Jenna." Callum smiled wide and brought her in for a hug. "Thank ye for making it." He stepped aside to let the ladies in, and once the door closed behind them, he once again focused on her friend. "And Sam, 'tis so lovely to see ye. Jenna here has told me so much I feel like I know ye already."

"Oh really?" Sam looked at her skeptically and raised one of her eyebrows in curiosity.

"Mmm," he said and took the liberty of taking her hand in one of his so he could kiss her palm. "All good, I promise."

He winked, Sam looked as if she were about ready to melt, and Jenna laughed.

"Callum O'Donnell at yer service, me lady." He bowed to them, and Jenna's heart felt as though it had stopped beating for a second.

"Wait, what?" Her eyes went wide, and a sudden flash came back to her from before…

Whelan's was just getting busy by the time they arrived.

"I think we need a few drinks," Sam announced, raising her voice to be heard above the band.

Jenna held on to her hand as they made their way to the bar to order. After getting their drinks, they found one of the only free tables and sat down to enjoy their surroundings and each other's company.

"I'm not sure I'd be able to drink this stuff too often, but it's not bad," Jenna said after finishing off her Guinness. The foamy, thick beer went down smooth. "Want another one?"

Just as Sam nodded, more arrived, brought to them by one of the waitresses working the floor.

"Wow, talk about service," she teased.

"They're from a couple of admirers." The older woman gestured toward the bar. Jenna tensed as the woman left.

"Okay, Jenna, don't freak out," Sam warned.

"The same two guys? First the airport and now here? What are the odds? Did you know they were here the whole time?"

Sam nodded. "I noticed about an hour ago. Are you up to this? It'll be kind of rude if we just leave, don't you think? But we will if that's what you need."

Jenna shook her head and took a deep breath. "I'm fine, really. I mean, it's a free drink. Who could be upset with that?"

As a polite gesture, Jenna turned toward the bar, held up her drink, smiled at the same one who had caught her eye the day before, and took a sip. She told herself she was doing this for Sam since Jenna still felt bad about their earlier encounter.

"Wow, Jenna, I'm impressed, but now you've done it." She gestured toward the two men, who were now approaching them.

Jenna laughed. She was surprised at how comfortable she felt, as though her old self was resurfacing. Maybe it was because of the surroundings without the constant reminders of home anywhere near her, or, then again, maybe it was just the drinks. Either way, she'd felt better about herself in that moment than she had in a long time, and she enjoyed the change.

"Hi there," Sam purred, scooting her chair closer to Jenna so the men could sit with them. "My name is Samantha, and this is my lovely friend Jenna. It's a pleasure to meet you both."

Jenna gulped nervously as the one she was attracted to took her hand into his. He didn't take his eyes off her the entire time he spoke. "Lovely, Jenna, Samantha, the pleasure is definitely ours, I assure ye." He lifted her hand and kissed her palm before continuing, "I'm Brady, Brady Connelly, and this is my good friend, Caleb O'Donnell."

"Hey, are you okay?" Sam took a step toward her, but Jenna just held up her hand to keep her put. She didn't answer because there were other things she had to know first.

"Did you just say your name was O'Donnell?"

"Aye, what of it?" The poor guy looked both concerned for her and confused at the same time.

"Do you by chance have a relative named Caleb?"

At the mention of Caleb, her friend gasped as she put two and two together, and Jenna looked at her as if to say, *You see where I'm going with this?*

"Not that I know of. Why ye askin'?"

"Do you remember how I told you my story the other night? The one about my love for this mysterious dream guy, and when I told you I'd envisioned Sam with his best friend?"

He nodded but stayed silent.

"Well, his name was Caleb O'Donnell. Or at least I thought it was. Caleb, Callum…" She looked toward Sam, who was now beaming with hope and excitement. "The names are just way too similar to discredit, right? I mean, oh my God, this is too weird."

"Not necessarily." They all jumped at the sound of Cian's voice as he descended the stairs to join them in the foyer. "Yer feet will always bring ye to were yer heart truly lies. Now…" He clapped his hands together as if he was quite pleased with himself. "Me lovely boyo here tells me quite an interstin' story of undeniable love under the most gone-in-the-head situation."

"Sure looks it." The younger of the two men spoke, but the girls were left stunned speechless for the time being. "It's like hen's teeth, it is."

"Aye," Cian said and held out both arms for each woman to take as he guided them toward the back of the house. "I'm sure me love, Sarah, has already wet the tea. Now what you say we relax with a cup and ye can tell me all about it while these two get to know each other better?" He winked at Sam and guided her over into Callum's capable hands before giving Jenna his undivided attention.

And before she knew it, she was relaying the whole story again while sipping on tea with the older couple. They were just as patient as Callum had been as she bared it all. Here and there, they asked questions before nodding as if they understood.

"Crazy, right?" she finished.

"I don't mean to gawk, dear, but 'tis quite an unusual feat yer telling us here." Sarah scooted her chair closer and steepled her fingers. "Has Cian mentioned our boy to ye?"

"Your son?" She gulped and put the small cup on top of its saucer. "The first time I met Cian, I actually asked if you had a son. Your husband seemed so familiar to me, and—"

"And there was probably a reason for it too." The older woman smiled fondly at him. "We have all sorts of senses: taste, touch, smell, sight, and what we hear around us. But there are the ones we overlook too. Like the ability to connect with the soul. 'Tis our intuition, empathy, and peace that sometimes give us the foresight to look beyond the norm, my girl, and not all of us are as lucky as ye seem to be, to be able to tap into that."

"Jaysus," the old man interrupted. "As beautiful as she is smart, that she is." He leaned over to kiss his wife, and his eyes twinkled mischievously. "Now do ye remember what I told ye about my son?"

Jenna nodded. "He was in the US."

"Aye, but the wonderful part of it is he was there te—"

"I think I've got it from here, Da."

The deeply accented baritone came from behind them, and Jenna felt as if the world had stopped and everything was going in slow motion. Sam and Callum were at the other end of the yard getting to know each other. Sarah and Cian sat quietly on the patio as they watched it all unfold, and Jenna's heart felt as though it was about to burst through her chest. *Because holy crap, can it finally be? Seriously?*

She stood abruptly and held on to the table for support as the man came into view, and she looked him over from head to toe, afraid she would miss something. "Brady?" He was tall, with thick, black hair and a smile that definitely made her heart skip a beat. His blue eyes pierced right through her and straight into her soul. "Please tell me I'm not daydreaming or something."

"'Tis not a dream, Jenna." He moved closer until he stood only a foot away. "I could have sworn Callum was fluthered when he called me a few days back and demanded I return home from abroad. Ye see, there was this beautiful Yank he met right here in me parents' home who had tales of loving this man from Ireland with dark hair and light eyes. Only she'd never officially met him. He talked of the hardships she told him about, of betrayal, heartache, and visions of hope, and I couldn't believe me ears. I had to see for meself before it was too late."

He reached up to wipe away her tears and held on to her shaking hands while he continued. "And I could'na get here fast enough. Ye see, Jenna, whut me da, ma, and Callum forgot to mention was that I left here for the very same reason. For months I thought I might be mad as I dreamed about this woman with such beautiful long brown hair, so soft to the touch, who had the most amazin' green eyes." He cupped the side of her face, and she closed her eyes to lean into his touch. "I had to find her, so I left to start searchin'."

"And I came here," she whispered.

"Aye." He nodded. "So ye did. I don't know how to explain what we've got goin' on, but one thing I know for sure is I have to give it a go. I feel like I've known ye for so long already. What'dya say, me lovely Jenna, my other half. Will ye do me the honor and take some time so we can get to know one another?"

"I thought you'd never ask." It felt like sparks of current leaped out of her and into him wherever they touched, the chemistry was so good. And before she could say any more he crushed his lips against hers. Suddenly it was as if only the two of them existed, and nothing else mattered. He was a real dream come true, and she held on to him for dear life.

After so long, she'd finally become alive, had felt whole for the first time in a long time, and when they broke apart to applause and whistles from his family and Sam, it was a whole new beginning.

"Allow me to introduce meself properly. The name's Braeden Rhys Connelly." He held her flush against him and refused to look away. "I noticed ye the moment ye pulled up, but I had to wait to be sure. Then I heard everythin' come out of that beautiful mouth I could'na wait any longer. This here is my ma and da, and over there is me other family and me best friend Callum O'Donnell."

"It's nice to finally meet you, Braeden. I'm Jenna—Jenna Baker. That woman standing next to Callum is my best friend Sam, and I can't even express in words how happy I am to be here right now."

"Good to hear." He chuckled. "I'm just about wrecked from the travel, but it was completely worth it to have ye in me arms."

His father cleared his throat to remind them of everyone else's presence, and their little bubble where only the two of them existed popped for the time being. Throughout the afternoon they touched constantly, caught up, and had a great time with his family. Sam and Callum hit it off, and sparks seemed to fly all around the three couples. The older couple were madly and deeply in love, the other was testing the waters, and Jenna and her dream man—well, that was love at first sight.

***

"I can't believe we've got to go back already," Sam pouted. "Good-bye fantasy, hello reality."

"What are you talking about?" Jenna laughed and looked at her friend as though she was nuts. "They're coming back with us, Sam."

"I know, but being here just seems like a fairy tale. I guess I'm just afraid that when we get home it might burst the bubble."

"Nonsense." Callum kissed her friend senseless and only pulled away when Brady came back to their booth with another pitcher of beer. They'd finally made it to Whelan's to celebrate an amazing couple of weeks and their last night in Ireland before the big move back.

"What's this about bubbles?" Brady asked and pulled Jenna closer as soon as he got comfortable.

"Silly Sam over here thinks she's in some kinda fantasy land and things might change when we go with them tomorrow."

"Well, I can't speak for ye, my friend, but it only gets better with each passing day between Jenna and me." He wiggled his eyebrows and both men laughed.

"I agree, but are you ready?" She was curious if the thought of meeting Jayden and her parents made him nervous at all. She, however, was looking forward to it.

"I think I am, actually." He seemed so confident as he smiled down at her. "I can't wait to meet Jayden. I just hope he likes me. But I'm mostly lookin' forward to bringin' ye both back here forever after it's all settled over there." His brow creased for just the slightest second with uncertainty. There was still so much to do before she and Jayden could move back here for good. The house needed to be sold, and she needed to work visitation out with Tyler, but she tried not to dwell on that.

"Forever. I like the sound of that, and try not to worry about Jayden. I'm sure he'll come to love you as much as I do."

Forever with Brady…someone needed to pinch her to make sure she wasn't dreaming again. She couldn't wait.

"That little squirt is all kinds of awesome. Don't worry about it, he'll come around," Sam said and raised her glass for a toast. "So I say we drink to Ireland and to our families…"

"To new beginnings, and our happily-everafters..." Jenna chorused and held her glass high as well.

"To taking chances..." Callum cheered.

"And cherishin' the women we love more than anythin'. We've taken a leap, my friends, and I don't regret one minute of it." Brady joined his frosted glass to theirs before taking a sip.

"I love you," she said. "And thank you."

"For what, love?"

She kissed him and then placed her forehead against his while she cradled his face. "For being so understanding." She kissed him again. "For being so supportive, but most of all for loving me back."

"That I do, love. I truly do."

They finished their drinks and said their good-byes to each other. That toast seemed to have brought out an urgency in both couples for a little alone time together, and she couldn't wait to make love some more.

About an hour later they were at Brady's house and he had her spread out and writhing with need before him on a blanket in front of the living room fireplace.

"I need you, Jenna murmured. She giggled as he rolled her over so that he was on top. Stroking her hair away from her face, he gave her a little smile and whispered, "I think that can be arranged."

"Good." She lifted a brow. "Lay it on me, baby."

"Christ, I love ye." He traced her lips with his tongue before slipping it inside of her mouth. The warm wetness of their tongues met with a mutual passion, and he moaned when he pulled away to say, "Yer a witch, I swear it. I've never met a woman I've wanted more." He smiled at her shocked expression. "I've been bewitched from the very start, and I can't live without ye anymore, love. Marry me; let's make this official." He reached over to grab his pants, searched the pocket, and pulled out a small box. "I know 'tis soon and ye can take all the time ye need, just please say ye will."

She gasped and stared between Brady and the platinum one carat diamond ring he held in front of her. "Really?" She nodded before he could say anything more. "Yes, Brady, yes." She threw her arms around his neck and laughed. "This is so wonderful, thank you."

"Jenna." He chuckled. "Yer hangin' on a li'l too tight, love, and I hate to be ruinin' the moment but—" He loosened her grip around his neck. "Ah, much better." He took the ring from the box and placed it on her finger with pride. "Good, 'cause I'm stakin' my claim, and ye've now made it official. I can't wait to make ye me one and only, Mrs. Connelly."

"Mmm, I like the sound of that, Mr. Connelly. Now there's only one thing that could make this perfect." She kissed him.

"What would that be?" He raised a brow, silently challenging her to continue.

"Make love to me. I need you more than ever. I'm aching over here."

His hips flexed, grinding his aroused flesh into her wet panties. "Like this?" he teased and did it again. "Or, maybe like this—" He lowered himself and trailed light kisses down her belly to love her every way he could. After hooking a finger in her underwear, he pushed them aside and flicked his tongue in and out of her opening. She moaned while lifting her hips and enjoyed every single moment. His tongue flicked, licked, pumped, and circled her aroused wetness until she cried out her release.

After wiping his mouth he climbed on top of her, pulled his hips back, and thrust his hips to enter her in one smooth stroke, and she vowed to do everything she possibly could to make him happy. And after whispering sweet sentiments and promises to each other, they took it slow, to enjoy the moment and their undying love.

Epilogue

Sam and Callum caught up to them and married the following summer with Jenna and Brady front and center beside them. Sam made a beautiful bride, and they couldn't be happier.

Speaking of happier endings, Jenna and Brady were blessed further when she gave birth to their daughter. Shelby Sarah Connelly was born happy and healthy on a beautiful spring morning. It was another home birth by Jenna's choice, but their little princess hadn't been in a rush like her big brother had been.

Jayden adored her and loved getting another baby sister but whined once in a while that he wanted a brother because he was severely outnumbered.

Brady didn't need any convincing. "Ye know, love, givin' the children a brother sounds pretty good to me. Ye know how I love tryin'," he told her and smiled wide.

Jenna laughed but agreed. Being a mother was a blessing, her best accomplishment and decision, so having a large family was never in doubt. "Sounds like fun. But we'll be taking precautions for a little while longer." The last thing Jenna needed to think about was the pain of delivery again, and the delay would give them all some time to adjust and enjoy little Shelby first.

The stork hadn't finished his rounds by far, but it was Sam's turn next.

The End

About the Author

Jennifer Labelle resides in Canada with her husband and three beautiful children. After her third child she became a stay at home mom. In her busy household Jennifer likes to spend her down time engrossed in the stories that she creates. She is an active reader of romance, mystery and anything paranormal. With an education in Addictions work she's decided to take a less stressful approach in life and hopes that you enjoy, as she shares some of her imagination and artistic inspiration with all of you.

Facebook:
https://www.facebook.com/pages/Author-Jennifer-Labelle/168414043184292

Twitter:
https://twitter.com/1JenniferLabell

Goodreads:
https://www.goodreads.com/author/show/4649930.Jennifer_Labelle

Website:
http://www.jenniferlabelle.com/

Google+:
https://plus.google.com/u/0/110192794885898998367/posts